The Century of Zara Keff

The
Century of
Zara Keff

A novel

Jeremy Waxman

First published in Great Britain in 2025 by
The Book Guild Ltd
Unit E2 Airfield Business Park,
Harrison Road, Market Harborough,
Leicestershire. LE16 7UL
Tel: 0116 2792299
www.bookguild.co.uk
Email: info@bookguild.co.uk
X: @bookguild

Typeset in 11pt Minion Pro

Printed and bound in Great Britain by 4edge Limited

ISBN 978 1835741 214

British Library Cataloguing in Publication Data.
A catalogue record for this book is available from the British Library.

For Matthew, Nicholas and Katherine

Genesis

Chapter 1

Cambridgeshire, 1940

Zara opens her notebook at a fresh double page and stares at the dog-eared charts on the wall. Her classmates do the same, roughly speaking, each pondering in their individual way the challenge Mr Garver has set. One chews a pencil, a second scrutinises the gas mask by his desk, fellow scholars steal anxious glances or cast their eyes blankly heavenward. Zara flips a plait back over her shoulder and copies the date from the blackboard, recollecting the days when, for exactness, she had been given to add '20th Century Anno Domini'. She smiles and reaches for her wooden measure. Keeping space for the heading, she marks out a long-shafted arrow to stand as a margin, etching a notch by every second line.

Zara starts by printing the year 1900 to the left of the arrow, and notes to the right that her father was born then; she places 1908, for her mother, above the first notch. The dates carved on the local memorial are followed by her own birth in 1930, her sister's arrival, the outbreak of the present conflict, the day she packed her suitcase for the journey from London. She schedules the end of the war three years hence, for it must surely last no longer than the first.

It occurs to Zara that whatever she writes now she can simply make up for herself. She anticipates that children will soon become kinder to each other, forecasts the discoveries that she imagines being made and completes the column by inscribing the impossibly distant '2000' at the foot of the timeline, beside her shaded arrowhead. Mindful of Mr Garver's talk that very morning, Zara predicts next to it, 'People have stopped using words that make trouble in the world'. She hopes that will not be the work of an entire century, but deems it a fitting way to round off the piece.

How much of this would come true, though? It was one thing to picture the future, after all. Hundreds of teachers must have asked thousands of children to do that over the years. Yet here they were. Mr Garver had described this as the most terrible of wars. She will add paragraphs to the page opposite, she decides, and set each alongside the events to which it belongs. That way, she can breathe life into the story, and tell of the part she might play, starting here, right now, in the village she is beginning to call home.

Zara stops, catching sight of the gap she has left at the top. Casting around, her eyes alight on a faded poster, *One Hundred Years of the Railways.* She allows her fingers to tap, tap, tap on the desk. She's laid down a hundred years herself. One hundred years of... She takes in the date, alive to the way she would once have extended it. The title comes to her, and she picks up the pencil again.

Chapter 2

Łódź, 1906

It was by no means the first time that Isaac Kevlov had dropped in on the shop by Bałucki Rynek, the marketplace, to make sure that his father left promptly for home. The smelly shop they called it, Abraham's Polish neighbours, and Isaac had no quarrel with the definition, a description of reality, he thought, rather than personal imputation. A shop full of tripe, herring and all manner of pickled goods was smelly for sure: that was the word for it. The Sabbath was due, and Abraham had stuck out for a third reminder, running close to the deadline after which he was obliged to pay a fine at the synagogue. It was Advent, after all, and trade was brisk.

'Are you here to drag him away? He'd sell more herring if he stayed open.' The customer's walrus moustache was doing its best to disguise a smile.

'He'll be open on your Sabbath – don't you worry,' replied Isaac.

'Pay when you can,' Abraham was telling another, whose crumpled suit and mariner's cap matched those of his compatriot.

'Come,' beckoned the first to the counter. 'We'll land him in trouble again.'

Abraham grinned, catching his son's eye, kneeling to put galoshes over his felt-lined boots. He heaved a beaver coat over the shapeless gabardine he wore and turned up the fur collar.

Isaac shook his head, sure as he was of the rough and ready admiration these locals had for their storekeeper, of the slender profit he'd be content to make on a large turnover, of his willingness to make a deal, or to be easy-going when a debt was due. Children left with five *groszy* and a light pinch of the cheek, on top of the groceries they had been sent for. His customers stuck, the Poles among them; it was rare to turn your back to the shelf and find the place empty.

Isaac hurried Abraham along. He had his father's raw-boned face and angular features, with but the first shoots of grey and a beard trimmed short of the full patriarch's. His gait, more upright than the old man's, with a pronounced knee bend and feet at ten to two, implied something of a swagger. Their route took them up Zgierska, with its bustle of stores and stallholders. As Abraham had, many were bringing the day's trading to a rapid conclusion.

'Last few apples,' cried out one. 'Apples like raspberries. So juicy they're worth a kiss.'

'Take this home to your mother. She can settle up on Sunday,' said a second, dangling a silver-coloured trinket before a puzzled boy.

'Lady, come see me. Ay-yay, how beautiful you have become in this dress.'

'Abraham!' exclaimed an old friend. 'You closed up early this week.'

They continued along Nowomiejska, glimpsing an enterprise through every window, the alacritous trimming of material giving way to the bent concentration and sharp-eyed skill of the seamster. Then on to Piotrkowska, a Tower of Babel, Russian, German, Polish, Czech and Yiddish competing to be heard above the throng; everywhere the fierce cutting of deals by bearded, cap-clad Jews, policed by white batons in the glare of the crossroads and stool-pigeons in the shade of the trees.

Moishe Beigelman, diminutive and wiry, stood at the side of the street in a *shabbat* suit that, but for his years, he might have been growing into. With a hand on the shoulder or the pull of a sleeve, he extended an invitation, summoning folk to the next concert to be held in the family dining room. Moishe's younger son David was reputed to be a prodigy, and tomorrow's debut with the *klezmer* was eagerly anticipated. The audience would likely spill over to the hallway.

'We'll be there,' said Abraham. 'Roza wouldn't miss it.'

From time to time, Abraham threw off the gabardine to patronise the Café Astoria. There you could sip the best tea in the city and rub shoulders with theatre directors of local renown, busy creating their Yiddish versions of operettas and Shakespeare. He took Isaac, too, to the skits the café hosted in the back room, where stubbly, half-crazed collectives doffed their hats to the left, combining digs at the government with the preservation of the language.

'Have you caught up with the news?' Moishe asked, suspending his advertising campaign for a moment. 'The Russians have granted an eleven-and-a-half-hour day. They call that progress.'

Moishe belonged to the *Jewish Labour Bund* and Abraham broadly approved of its socialist stance and opposition to Russia. He scoffed at the notion of their so-called client state, remarking that he'd be out of business if he treated his own clients like that. But Isaac had stood, merely listening, at an impromptu gathering broken up by Cossack guards, and his back carried wheal marks from the curved reverse of the swords wielded to disperse them. He'd been branded a rebel, he said, by a bunch of comedians.

'You should come along, Abraham. We could do with some familiar faces. People think we're an outpost of Wilno.'

'I have to put bread on the table,' Abraham replied. 'The shop doesn't open itself.'

'Hey!' Moishe called out, spotting a fellow malcontent in the half-light of an alleyway. 'Don't we need Kevlov and son in the *Bund?*'

The figure stepped out, cautious, in well-worn factory overalls, clutching a sheaf of papers covered loosely in cloth. He sported a broad moustache like the Polish.

'We need revolution, Beigelman. A Jewish party can only take us so far.'

'Look, we're four of us here,' said Abraham, 'fair game for the Cossacks. Roza doesn't want another week bathing her family's wounds.'

'Łódź must change. You can't shovel thousands of workers together and treat them like dirt for all time.' He pressed them to take a pamphlet. 'Tell him, young man. The tide of history's with us.'

Isaac shrugged and extended his palms to say, it's not that I disagree, you know, but I intend to keep hold of my flesh.

Abraham felt his son's hand ease him away, and bade them *Gut Shabbos*. He had no argument either. Migrating from a village, where life as a weaver had become impossible to sustain, he had met Roza and taken on the shop that her father had run. It has a good name, they said, and he adopted it. Now he saw the city pass half a million strong with no vestige of a water or sewerage system, an almighty cocktail stirred by agitation, even as meetings and political parties were banned, and pogroms fed on the blind eye turned by a dynasty of Czars. Isaac and his wife, Estera, herself a refugee from a rural upbringing, had two young children of their own. He could not foresee much of a future for them. Abraham had friends whose boys had left the city, seeking to make a port, hopeful of reaching England, even America. It nagged at him when news of an emigrant's success arrived, and his family set out to join him.

As for Isaac, each time he caught his back in the mirror, he was reminded how straightforward it was for the authorities to make life difficult. You're scarred for life, he would say to himself, and the city holds nothing for you. And when you've trained as a cabinet maker, but see many good craftsmen around, you're more ready for the talk than your father had dared to hope.

* * *

'Don't forget to practise your Yiddish,' Issac teased Estera. He was set to trek, with a half-dozen like-minded men, some five hundred miles through Poznań, across the Oder, and by the north of Berlin to Hamburg. 'They don't speak Russian in London.'

'Watch out for the sharks,' said Abraham, repeating the tip one of his regulars had passed on. 'Don't fall for the tricks, however hungry you are.'

Word had reached the city of the tactics the 'sharks' used, quartering a newcomer at a boarding house, loaning a few shillings on the surety of his luggage, turning him onto the pavement, possessionless, when that had been exhausted.

'Remember to wait,' Abraham urged, as Isaac gathered up his sack and strapped it on top of his thick cotton clothing. 'Wait for one of our own!'

Isaac took the first step and feigned a sudden pain, grasping his spine and spinning around with a wink. He saw them forged as one, taking his leave at the last from Estera, her eastern peasant skin taupe against those who had endured the city longer, her eyes fixed on him until he broke the tension by shaping a pose fresh from the Astoria's back room.

* * *

Isaac walked the gangplank onto the steamer from Latvia, with its scores of migrants on board. They had left in droves like so many before them, each wave dispossessed in turn by poverty, expulsion, revolution, drawn west by hope – of a second passage, perhaps – or by the reputation the Jews of London's East End had for hospitality. He turned over the roubles his father had saved for him and gave up his name for the manifest. He found a place next to a huddled pair, sisters, whose mother had set them to sail, armed more in hope than expectation with a scribbled list of possible contacts. Isaac had them in stitches one broken night, commanding that the spirits speak through him, issuing a grave warning to keep their eyes peeled on the quayside. They made room, from dock to dock, for those who had trudged to some other boarding point by the North Sea, the ever-contracting space a price to be paid for completing the voyage. The comrades with whom Isaac had walked disembarked in the north of England, and he wished them luck on their journey to the New World.

The Port of London drew near, the bascules of the new Tower Bridge lifted in salute. Isaac descended to a smaller boat and, brought within yards of the shore, had then to wade through mud for the final stretch. Hauling his baggage up a flight of steps to the wharf, he stopped to draw breath. On the quayside, women wrapped in roughly tied headscarves kept half an eye on their offspring, slouched on the boxes alongside them, while men stood with the conviction they could muster beneath the resewn flaps of their baggy caps. Isaac heard three blasts of the steamer's whistle and watched it edge its way back down the Thames. He was surrounded by a panoply of trunks, parcels and sacks, chaos, and was struck by the sheer magnitude of his position, atop the Irongate Stairs, on the brink of a possible life, alone and unprepared.

A snapshot came to him: a girl with a heavy bag, traipsing her way down a cobblestoned street, humming a lullaby, *'Rozhinkes mit Mandlen'*, a song about raisins, almonds and honey, and the promise of a sweet life. That was the picture his wife had painted, of her days in a village, a few *złotys* sequestered in an outsized pinafore pocket, sufficient for treats for a task well executed. They had always a place to look back to, wherever the times had taken them.

Isaac was soon holding a rudimentary form he could not decipher, courtesy of the makeshift immigration service. He noticed the hustlers Abraham had spoken of, salivating at the prospect, preying on tiredness. Then welcome passed by in a familiar tongue, and Isaac held out his arms to say, 'well, what d'you know'. Pointed to the Poor Jews Temporary Shelter in Leman Street, he found himself thinking of the sacrifices his father had made, carving out a life in an unforgiving conurbation, unafraid to send his son off to the unknown. When Isaac tendered his document, he was addressed as 'Mr Keff'. He replied, 'No, no, Kevlov,' and was told, 'It's Keff now – it's Keff for your whole life now.' He'd been about to argue, but thought: Keff? That's not so bad, you know, and what's in a name?

The Professor I

Camden, 1999

The emeritus professor took brunch on England's Lane, a habit acquired since his formal retirement. He made for the table by the French doors at the rear, where the view, being of the back of a pleasantly bricked building, was not spectacular, but where the light was natural. Spreading his notes on the empty place opposite, he unfolded his newspaper: a great wheel, he was amused to read, was making steady progress toward the upright. He put the broadsheet aside when the eggs Florentine were served and ate them ravenously while scanning the opening of his lecture. He could rely on a capacity crowd for this evening's landmark event. The bus from the end of the road took him straight to Bloomsbury.

Though the freshers were first in, they were soon joined by a smattering of the more seasoned, and by keen postgrads too, and finally by the professor's colleagues, content to stand in the aisle. When he breezed in, notes and texts in a disorganised bundle under his arm, it was, for new undergraduates, their first sight of him in the flesh, this grizzled, lopsided historian, in a much-travelled suit and thick black spectacles, whose accent carried echoes of a distant time. They had seen him on television, of course, often invited as a counterweight to liberal economists; on late-night panels, he was demonstrably expert in books and jazz. An overhead projector stood on the right of the dais, useful in recent years for the summary of detail, and for the odd map, but the professor did not require it for the broad sweep of the matter at stake today.

He ran his eyes over the audience. A new headteacher, proud to be in the vanguard of a government devotion to education so staunch they had named it three times over, had invited him to present the prizes at her school in the Borough of Camden, close to where he lived. He had found himself, to his delight, engaged by her energy and had lingered a while in her office, encouraged by the retrieval from the cabinet of a fifteen-year-old single malt. She had prompted a certain thought about the lecture, he had invited her along, and he was eager to see if she had come.

It had taken some writing, this one, and it had taken some thinking. His wont, when it came to the course's inaugural address, which had been entrusted to him for the past dozen years, was to synopsize the twentieth century with a slant that varied from year to year. He might surprise even his colleagues by devoting the entire hour to a component of economic history – grain production, for example, or industrialisation – and tag the politics onto it. He might surprise them less by focussing on film or music and the impact upon culture of the forms of government that had characterised the period. You could go a long way with that. He would always surprise those fresh from 'A' level who rarely imagined that an introduction to the course would toy with their intellects in the way that the professor often did.

He was known for his naming of centuries. The last he had styled 'the long nineteenth', tracing its dominion from the French Revolution to start of the First World War. Its broad playbook had brought the incongruity of the Dreyfus case and the election of Disraeli, the gold rush and voyages to the world's end, the first manned flight and the iceberg that sank the Titanic. It had permitted the work of the Curies while experimenting with the concentration camp, modernism and the glories of industrial architecture alongside the deadliness of factory work. It had stared into the atom, while conceiving a *War of the Worlds*. The current century he had dubbed 'the short twentieth', bookended by the assassination of Archduke Ferdinand and the collapse of the Iron Curtain.

He tossed a blue whiteboard pen into the air, gathering his thoughts. The plastic did not fall as naturally to his palm as the chalk had once done, but he was no opponent of progress and would take up the red or the green to emphasise a phrase with a flourish.

'In history,' he began, without undue ceremony, 'there is much talk of ages and epochs: we do relish our subdivisions.' He held up his newspaper. 'I note that our plans for the end of the year are teetering on the brink.'

The packed hall welcomed an immediate chance for laughter.

He glanced to the sides. 'My advice to you fellows? Don't buy a ticket for the Dome. Its doom is historically inevitable.'

Further enjoyment at the disarming earnestness of the remark.

He looked directly at the audience. 'We like to squeeze the past into patterns, but it's not that simple, you know. You can't take a digit and three zeros and ascribe a significance they fail to warrant. You'll be among the first undergraduates of the third millennium. But marvel at that too long and you'll wind up in a cul-de-sac. For you'd be nine years too late.'

He paused: perplexed looks now.

'The twentieth century may have wound up early, but boy had it done its work.'

Some recognition. He put an index finger to the air and stepped off the rostrum toward a young woman in the front row. Her glossy file, obtained, he imagined, during an excited visit with friends to WH Smith, was furnished already with the tabs that would punctuate the course. He held it aloft.

'These dividers can be of help, so long as we are flexible. Our Century, after all, had spent its formative years in the shadow of a predecessor which had lived, by its own account, to be one hundred and twenty-five, that rare thing, born ahead of its time, surviving to cause tumult in the adolescence of its successor.'

He made to weigh the folder in his hands, a *tabula rasa* scoped out to receive the essence of things long cast, but capable still, he hoped, of interpretation. He returned it with a nod of approval, regained the platform and, turning a page for the first time, dwelled for an instant on the tiniest splash of yolk.

'You see, it's important to choose your starting point.'

He wrote three words on the board and underlined them as he spoke.

'It had everything – the long nineteenth – or so it thought, and for good measure bequeathed a chain of antagonisms, dragging great alliances to war – and to stalemate. Recruits were expendable, farthings thrown onto a card table that dealt no aces. Exhaustion brought the madness to an end.

'Yet our Century planted seeds of hope. Troops played the enemy on Christmas Day. Women transfused the life blood of the economy. Poets, backs turned on the haunting flares, flourished in the turmoil, anthemic for doomed youth. Poppies poked up in Flanders fields, brandishing a torchlight amid contagion.'

There she was. The headteacher: a few rows back and off to the side, leaning on her elbow, her lips partly open. The peaty trace of a companionly Ardbeg wafted across his memory of their first meeting. It was she who had set him thinking not merely of the darkness, the beginning of which he had seen himself, trailing home with a satchel on the very day when it seized power, but of the optimism that might be invested in a century.

'After four years of war our Century came of age and allowed those seeds to germinate. Britain built homes fit for heroes. New republics emerged. Leaders worked in league to preserve peace. The Century reached its twenties with the jazz age; it flew the Atlantic; it brought surrealism, the Odessa Steps, talking movies and Lady Chatterley.

'So, may we conceive that a century has personality as I have been playfully suggesting?'

The slightest lowering of the glasses and a survey of the audience.

'And if an age has a tendency, toward revolution or empire or the extreme, does that engulf us all? Or does the individual prevail?

'Take an itinerant boy, schooled in Berlin, forced to ply his trade elsewhere, suitcase eternally at the ready, or a child sent from the metropolis as the catastrophe drew near, oblivious to the forces that had brought her to an unfamiliar village. Or an occupant of a great city hemmed in by the gathering gloom, trapped in a friendly attic. Could they shape the Century, or can only the great bend the arc of the age to that of their own lives? Could they, could anyone, famous or no, now that it threatened to bring a reckoning of its own: could they, could anyone, give the Century the fight of its life?'

The headteacher smiled at the mention of the child dispatched from the city and dared think she might, in fact, have met the boy from Berlin. The professor was shuffling his first few pages to one side, and she fancied that she caught his eye. Surely that had not been a sly wink.

He extended his arms to embrace the auditorium. 'Let's step into the maelstrom.'

Exodus

1927–1943

Autumn sunlight streams through the classroom window, and swirls of chalk-dust tumble and fall before Zara's grey-green eyes. Her timeline complete to the year 2000, she glances at the clock, then at the blank facing page. Eight of its twenty printed lines correspond to the time that has elapsed since the beginning of the Century. She has lived for only a quarter of that period herself, but is reluctant to leave the vast space unfilled. Mr Garver would regard that as something of a waste of paper in their days of rationing, after all. Zara places a protective arm around her work. *I am nearly ten years old,* she starts to write, opposite the first notch on the arrow so that she might fit things in, *and this is my Century. I used to live in Stoke Newington, where I loved to go to the library. I helped with the shopping and looked after my sister, who can be ever so trying sometimes. I did my very best to keep away from one boy at my school. You see, he kept on calling me names.*

Chapter 3

Puss Coe caught the train three stops up the line and climbed the steps to the front of the big terrace. Estera answered the door, as she had the previous time, her white hair pulled back, kind hazel eyes given full rein to absolve her apron and headscarf of the weariness they might otherwise have signalled.

'Welcome, my dear.' Her words were slow and warm, and she led Puss through.

Isaac was sitting at the head of a walnut dining table. 'Take off your coat,' he said, 'and come, sit down.'

Estera offered them tea, while Isaac raised an eyebrow and turned to the sideboard. 'Unless you fancy a little tot?'

'I think I could fancy that, Mr Keff.'

He waited for the door to close. 'Now, do the honours, please,' he said, adding in a theatrical whisper, 'neat – and not so little if you don't mind.' He watched her deft handling of the decanter.

Puss brought a couple of tumblers over, Isaac's own measure amply fulfilling his order.

'Your good health, sir.'

'*L'chaim,*' returned Isaac. 'To Life.' He took a gulp and

shook his head with an expulsion of satisfaction. 'Now tell me: your sister wants to become part of our family?'

'Oh, she does, Mr Keff. There's no doubt about it. She can't stop talking about Sol.'

'There's more to marriage than a rush to the head, Mrs Coe. Or hadn't you noticed?'

'It's a beginning, though, isn't it? I didn't imagine in my wildest dreams…'

'So this was in your dreams if you could imagine it?'

'Oh sir, for Mops – I mean for Mary – to be settled, to have prospects: that is my dream, Mr Keff.'

'You are a Tottenham family though, I think. And we are different, and quite new to this place.'

'We don't hold much with the church, sir. We're happy to adapt.'

'That will not be easy, my dear. It may take her two years. There's much to learn.'

'She is ready for that.'

'Tell me then, tell me something of your family.'

Something of the family, Isaac mused. It was the invitation his first employer had extended, all those years ago, before he loaned him an attic on Bacon Street. Isaac remembered asking the small-time timber merchant whether people were religious thereabouts. 'They are Jewish,' came the reply, 'if that's any help.' Now the Century had brought him northward, to Stamford Hill, and a house by the railway, plied by the steam-pulled trains departing Liverpool Street for Hackney and the outer suburbs. And what of those East End years, of a single cold scullery tap and drunken escapades on the landing below? The long days he worked to be able to send for his family. The workshop he established in the backyard and the see-saws made by his boys with the half-rotten planks they rescued. Time had made them tales to be recounted, of the days before Isaac became a timber merchant himself, inched by the grit of the migrant to a modest prosperity.

Puss sipped at her whisky. Christened Elizabeth, the eldest of the seven children of Michael Dodd, a master printer from Cork, and his wife Violet, she had been raised at a large end terrace off the High Road, where Mary had been the last to arrive. Their father broke the strike during the great dispute of 1911 and never worked again. When their mother left, she raised the family herself. She managed to relay most of that to Isaac.

'That's some history, Puss. I may call you that?'

She laughed. 'None of us use our given names. Quite how I became Puss I'm afraid I've rather forgotten.'

'You speak so well, *sheyne meydel.*'

Puss smiled, accommodating the phrase. As the years went by, it was true, she had urged her sisters to become conversant in the King's English, that being helpful, she emphasised, to the capture of a good husband. Puss had looked, too, for the chance to broaden her family's horizons. Her attention caught by a card in their newsagent's window, seeking a maid for a household on West Bank, she presented Mary, at eighteen, with her unruly brown hair and nickname to match. One of the sons of the house had conducted the interview.

'That small advertisement of ours – you didn't mind that we were Yiddish?'

'No, sir. Not at all. That's to say, sir, we don't have religion. That went the way of our father: his life didn't give much cause to commend it.'

'Tell me, Puss.'

'He drank after he lost work, had the blackest of moods.' She took a further sip and swallowed audibly. 'He began to mistreat our mother. One Christmas she'd had enough, I suppose. She'd done her best, with a chicken and so forth, but he'd consumed so much…'

Isaac remained still, and Puss told the tale of Boxing Day, when their mother had gone out, to the shop they thought, and hadn't come home; how they found a space where an old suitcase had been and saw that her clothes were gone. What it must have been like for her to leave seven children, she couldn't bear to imagine. When their father died a few months later they had counted it something of a blessing.

'Truth to tell, Mr Keff. He went to church, my father: he wasn't a recommendation for it. And we don't want to be stuck in Gloucester Road for the rest of our lives. We're happy to seek out different worlds.'

'Well, your Mary made an impression on our little world. You can be sure of that.'

The Keffs had taken to Mops and set her on straight away. The elder sons were enchanted by the well-spoken girl whose daily commute brought her from further downtown. Solomon had seven years on her; a green woollen waistcoat, grey Harris tweed, and an ebbing hairline, contrasted with Alex, whose Brylcreemed hair and well-pressed suit shaped an altogether more fashionable figure. Neither betrayed a hint of an infancy spent in the ferment of Łódź.

'One evening she arrived home rather giddy, Mr Keff. She'd dusted the house down and was completely worn out, she said. The boys had teased her endlessly. Apparently Alex took a mop-stick out and waltzed it around the floor.'

Puss declined to report her own contribution to the conversation. 'You do know that Sol's the heir to the business?'

'It was *Purim*,' Isaac said, 'when he spoke to her alone. We had a house full of guests. Now, how do you say it?' He put a finger to his forehead. 'The flamboyance! The flamboyance was high; the wine was flowing. Alex put a *spiel* on with his friends; you'll learn about those things one day. He was joking with your sister again. I had to remind him: you must still be respectful.'

Puss nodded, unwilling to break the spell, deriving hope from the intimation that she'd grasp it all in time.

'Sol caught her eye.' He chuckled. 'I think it was the competition. They both have the wit of the old East End, you know. Maybe a little bit too from their *tateh*. He picked up a plate – just the one, mind you – and took it through to the kitchen. My *froi* you have met, she spoke to him the next day.' Isaac leant forward. 'He blushed.'

'Mops coloured when she told me.'

Mops had been wary: Sol dropped a good many

consonants, she was obliged to confess. Puss had taken her sister in rather fondly, even so, bestowing her reassurance with the gentlest of nods.

Chapter 4

The boy sat on the window side so, when the bell rang, Zara had a head start at least. The volley of hyphenated half names made no sense, but they were meant for her and for her alone, as far as she could tell. Was 'Moe' one of them? She had an Uncle Morris, and her aunts called him Moe, but surely the boy didn't know that? The rest were a gaggle of twisted vowels of the kind that her teacher corrected, and she was past combining them to form words that she might recognise. Whatever they were, whatever they meant, he hadn't aimed them at the other girls. He was all hoicked-up shorts with his friends, king among the cluster of grubby knees, but he'd found time for her, too, at dinnertime, as he was passing. He'd been on top form, with his nudges and tugs of the chin, and that meant the storm clouds were gathering, so she was out of the door as soon as her chair was up, onto the high-windowed corridor and into the cracked schoolyard, trotting out to Barn Street and left to the main road. She'd been safe in class, for though he wasn't beyond a sideways look, they'd to keep their heads down, but she was panting now. What does it mean? Why does he say this to me? She was past the stockinged frontage of Marks and Spencer, and the deep young bricks of the Red Lion, slowing now to a stiff-legged march. Then over Lordship Road and left at the Clarence, that mystique of frosted glass at the corner of her own road. The door required no key, and she was up the stairs to her room, to her bed, the bookcase, her sanctuary. She leapt to the window, elbows to the sill, fists against her cheeks, and looked toward the alphabet of treetops in Abney Park and the octagonal steeple in the distance. It hid graves below the sightline, she knew, and secrets long locked away.

* * *

It offered you a long hallway, the house on West Bank, and it was tiled in red and black, accentuating the gloom emanating from the dark doorways that led from it. Yet open one of the doors to the left, and you were through to a light-filled living space, which ran from the array of panels at the front of the house – culminating in arced tops below two rows of squares, designed to present status to the street – to the simpler formation at the rear which performed its primary function equally as well. Inside, you would find Isaac cushioned in leather presiding over the transactions of the moment, whether that be lunch with friends in business or, today, a visit from his favourite grandchild. It was but a short walk from her own house, from Zara's that is, on the safety of a Saturday. Mops had held her hand as she danced toward the gate in the way she always did, and once inside she was faced, as she was every time, with the dilemma as to which of the doors she would open to surprise him.

Zara chose her door and peeked in; Isaac pretended not to have noticed till she was horizontal from the waist, straining to keep hold of the handle.

'Zuzzi,' he cried, 'have you come to see your Zaida?'

'Yes, for always,' she said, as her mother beamed behind her.

'Well, come here then, come tell me about things.'

Zara ran to him, and he swept her onto his knee. She twiddled with his beard and peered into his sparkling eyes, undaunted by the flaps of age that enclosed them.

'And how was school for you this week?' he asked.

Zara thrilled to the 'zz' with which he pronounced 'this'. 'Zaida the zz,' she called him. She was often so entranced by him that she failed to grasp what he was saying.

'Did you hear what I asked you, Zuzzi?'

'Probably yes, probably no,' Zara said, with a shrug, imitating one of his enduring idiosyncrasies.

'Ay-yay-yay, but you're a cheeky little *maideleh*, aren't you?'

Zara had once whispered something to Zaida, about the remarks of the boy in her class. He had enveloped her pigtails in his huge old hand, run the middle of his forefinger down her nose, and explained that the world contains some highly unusual characters. Another time, the boy had simply stared at her, stroking an imaginary beard. It had puzzled her. Did he somehow know that she loved to stroke Zaida's? It made her curious about his beard, and here she was, pulling it this way and that, playful and quizzical.

'I wish I'd been to a school like yours,' he said, gently taking her by the upper arms and easing her down. 'One day I'll tell you about the *kehilla* schools.'

Mops caught his eye and received a wink by way of acknowledgement. Zara wondered what a 'killer' school was, figuring there must be crueller elementaries to be attending than St Mary's in Stoke Newington.

* * *

Mops closed the door and held Zara's hand as she hop-scotched onto the pavement. They turned into Heathland Road, with its double-fronted villas and stump-arm trees, while Zara hopped and tripped, and a sequence of tableaux appeared to Mops, as they often did, an everyday sort of version of those stained into the glass of a parish church. There she was, serving at a festival, the breakneck humour of the boys, the house busy, the coming and the going. Again on the day when at the closing of the door she turned to see Sol, the courage the wine had lent him regained. Then the bashful betrayal of her conjecture, the reddening of her cheeks, the upward incline of her gaze as she was able to say that, yes, she would like very much to accompany him the next day. There were the young trees of Springfield Park, the band stand and new bowling green, Sol all-a-gangle and clasps of the hands; the light hand upon her own at the end of the afternoon. Then discovery – Sol's journey, his birthplace, its incongruous pronunciation – and the labour of learning their love required. And now a fine mid-terrace on Bouverie Road, with their two girls, Zara and Daphne, who had better learn to call her father-in-law 'Zaida', as all such grandfathers were known.

'I'm off to Dalston,' Sol would announce with a wink on a Friday afternoon, his skull-cap folded in the pocket to one side of his best suit and a packet of Players in the other. Each was kept ready for business, too, to be deployed in the most advantageous combination, along with the bottle of Red Label in the office desk.

When her presence, too, was called for, Mops would drop the girls off and play her own part at the tables to which she was shown, the study she had undertaken during the months of her conversion having allowed her to say to Isaac that 'your people are my people, and your God is my God'. Rare was the occasion when all four joined the wider Keff family. The Dodd sisters, after all, did not have religion – any religion – and Mops could be sure that displays of conformity demanded of her did not make similar calls on her children.

Zara basked in the attention lavished upon her by the aunts and cousins on her mother's side of the family.

'Dougie! Dougie! Lift me up. Please.'

Puss's son needed no second invitation to hoist her onto his shoulders.

'Zuzzi, shall we go flying?'

Dougie Coe would arrive in his sharp-cut RAF uniform, three stripes and all, as slick as he was in the photograph on the sideboard, with his wings and double-buttoned side cap angled to reveal a fresh face under jet-black hair. He had his mother's fulsome mouth and her wide-open eyes; his own expressed the uncomplicated statement of intent that was the hallmark of the Dodds. Another day, Zara and Daphne might be seen cross-legged on the living-room floor, trying to grasp the rules of the various games their cousin Lauren brought round, while Mops and their Auntie Rey set the world to rights in the kitchen.

'Can I come too, Mummy?' Zara would beg, by the time she was five, the swift tying of the headscarf the most obvious sign her mother was preparing to go shopping.

'What does that say?' Mops would ask, as they passed the building at the bottom of the road.

'F, A, R, R, S – Farr's!'

Zara could spell the name of the local – but 'far-famed' – school of dancing in advance of most other words. She had more trouble with the grocers and mongers on Stoke Newington Church Street, but 'rose' and 'crown' came more easily courtesy of the art deco façade that met them when they walked toward Clissold Park.

'But Mummy, what's a rose got to do with a crown?' she would enquire, at the age of six, before they were diverted by the clusters of older gentlemen in the park, sporting their pipes and moustaches. When Mops had Daphne too, she would take the pushchair up to one of the benches so they could make a fuss of her, and Zara would stand, a little withdrawn, at the handle.

Back on Church Street, at the age of seven, Zara would exclaim, as her eyes followed them, 'Mummy, those men have such long coats, and they have beards like Zaida's.' She would add, on second thoughts, that Zaida's was grey, and he didn't have the long curly bits down the side. Mops would give her a tug and a hurry-up-darling, and await the next of the many distractions to be found on the busy north London thoroughfare.

'Twenty Senior Service please, Mr Cohen,' Zara would say, by the time she was eight, having danced into the newsagent with a satchel over her shoulder.

'So you prefer them untipped, Zara?' he would tease by way of reply.

'I know,' he would swiftly assure her, as she began to protest. 'And for yourself, madam?'

Responsible enough to leave the house on her own, skipping to Cohen's to buy cigarettes for her parents and a few sweets for herself, she'd go on to the library, return the books she had borrowed and hasten home with a bagful more.

'Goodbye, Mr Cohen,' she called as she turned for the door.

'Give my regards to your mother.'

'For always, Mr Cohen.'

This time the door was being pushed too, and Zara found herself face to face with the boy from her class. She ducked to avoid him and slid onto the pavement.

Retaining his hold on the handle, the boy leant back out.

'Keff, Keff, Keff,' he called to her, and she stood for a moment, puzzled by the satisfaction he derived from the simple repetition of her name.

Chapter 5

'You're a sight for sore eyes, Abraham Kevlov.'

'Friend – you're never too old for the smelly trade.' He pulled one of the remaining jars of chestnuts from the shelf. 'Fredek left with a spade over his shoulder this morning.'

After the Century had brought Isaac to London, it had taken a brother to Ellis Island, and their sisters to husbands and fresh battles with the odds. Fredek it had kept, to take on his father's mantle. He had children of his own, and his wife worked at home with Roza, finishing caps off by the window.

'He read Kwapiński's appeal? Good for him. Fifty thousand dug yesterday – Poles and Jews – even the Hasids. But anti-aircraft defence won't help if they take the city. They don't bomb their own.'

Abraham gestured at the half-empty shelves. 'It's coming, old soul. Like 1914, it's coming. There'll be nothing but veal-head soup and bean cake.'

Next in the queue, a Polish widow beshawled against the years snarled, 'We should've cut the Kraut's throat in the cradle.'

'Ribbentrop and Molotov saw to that,' the first put in. 'Some friendship that is. You heard from Isaac?'

'Back in the spring. Do you know it's been more than thirty years now? He'll be handing on his own business shortly. Solomon's wed to an English girl, did I tell you?'

'D'you ever wish you'd gone?'

'Roza and me?' He shrugged. 'We had this place.'

'We have to beat them now,' urged the Polish woman. 'The trams are chock-full of soldiers on their last vodka.'

'Madam,' Abraham replied, with a grand sweep of an arm, 'what shall you have from this fine selection?'

She held a few coppers out. 'I'll take what I can get for these.'

Abraham picked a coin from her palm. 'They'll have trouble cutting off the vodka,' he said, catching his old friend's eye.

* * *

Isaac, decades from the day he had stood among the chaos by the Thames, had retired to Southend and a bay-windowed semi-detached a stone's throw from the beachfront. Sol took Mops and the girls there every second Sunday, swirls of unfiltered cigarette smoke competing with fumes from the engine as they drove. Zara hid behind her parents when they rang the bell, still teasing Zaida, still longing to be enfolded in his embrace.

Zara was set for her own journey, for once war was declared, the boroughs saw their children fanned outward, entire schools dancing to the rhythm of railway schedules more precise than any Mussolini could have hoped for. She stood with a tearful Daphne, among hundreds at Stamford Hill station, labels tied to their coat buttons, gas masks dangling from their necks, grasping battered suitcases with teddy bears strapped to the lids. Zara gripped her sister and scanned the crowd, losing sight of the teacher set to travel with them, catching instead the eye of the boy from her class who telegraphed superiority with a mocking grin. Hemmed in, she suddenly saw her mother at the top of the steps, surveying the assembly, her eyes at first flickering with resolve, then sure of her bearings. Mops had seen them now; she had changed her mind; she forced her way through and took her children back.

They called it the phoney war, the false dawn that broke then, and it nagged away as the enemy swallowed the lands on its flanks. Posters appeared, a stiff-armed caricature exhorting parents to reclaim their offspring, alongside a warning from the Ministry of Health: 'Don't do it, Mother – leave the children where they are.'

* * *

Debate raged in the dark of a courtyard tenement. The facts were clear: western encroachment, Russians in the east, a gauleiter installed in Gdańsk. There was the dread, for many, of a Polish *Kristallnacht*, but the army was dug in at Westerplatte, and there were the pleas of Fredek's son that he must stay for school, for it was fourth grade and they had the entrance exam for the Lyceum. Then there were the alarms, the air-raids and the gas, and those whom the shifting grounds had persuaded to stay saw the Wehrmacht on Piotrkowska and the General Staff bedding down at the Grand.

Fredek was instructed to open on Rosh Hashanah. A few days on and the schools went back, and his son burst into the shop. He'd been taken on the way, he gasped, they'd taken maybe twenty, made them sweep the square, then strip and face the wall. They'd fired into the air and laughed, with the Łódź Germans watching from the sidelines.

'You want to keep with the school, Jakub,' his father said, 'we have to find some way you're going to get there.'

Fredek arrived home that evening to news of a raid on the Astoria.

'Dousing the torch?' was all Abraham could offer by way of motive. He shook his head. 'Shooting practice? The chandelier went, for sure. They confiscated their papers, said to report in the afternoon.'

'Did they go?'

Abraham looked ahead, impassively.

'I guess they thought they'd be safe in numbers.'

'The first opera, the first Yiddish opera, they cooked it up there. They would've rivalled Warsaw someday.'

* * *

Zaida was to move again, as he had from Łódź to the East End, and from Stamford Hill to the seaside, for no sooner had he settled by the coast, than it was no longer thought to be safe, even for one who had lived so long in the land. It was to Woodford now, the anonymity of a London suburb the new reward for his years of entrepreneurship. It was by no means the worst place to wind up, for woods galore there were, it was a hop and a skip to the grocer's, and the Castle held promise for a man who fondly remembered the barrel-laden carts of Shoreditch, headed for Truman's on Wilkes Street. He still liked a beer before Estera's *knoblzup*.

'So, you've come to see us in Epping Forest?' Isaac said as he opened the front door.

'Is this a forest?' Zara replied. 'Where are the trees?'

'Perhaps we should go and find them, Zuzzi.'

They drove to Connaught Water, where Sol grabbed a couple of deckchairs from the boot and lifted out some argyle blankets; he waited for Mops to take hold of a hamper and knocked the lid down with his elbow.

They found a shady spot by a copse, and Estera laid out a red-checked cloth. She took the accoutrements of the picnic from the basket: white serviettes with embroidered edges, blue-rimmed enamel cups and thermos flasks, along with bread, butter, potted spreads and jam, a fruit cake Mops had baked for the occasion, and a type of cracker Zara had encountered only at Zaida's. They would disintegrate before her, however much care she tried to take when she broke them.

'*Whatsa Matzo, Zuzzi?*' Isaac would tease, one of the many phrases she came to think of as belonging to his special language.

Sol put the chairs up, and took Mops off for a drive through the countryside, while Zara spread blankets out for herself and Daphne, and picked up a flask to serve tea to her grandparents.

'Thank you, Zuzzi,' Estera said, her rarely used English carrying the sibilance of Łódź.

Zara watched her face light up, feature by feature, like the bulbs on a Christmas tree. She opened a second flask to pour squash, and tucked into her treats, such they were as the times permitted, while gathering up the courage to put a question to her grandfather.

'Mr Cohen said the phoney war's going to be a proper war soon. Are they going to fight in London?'

'You've heard about Hitler, Zuzzi?'

She had seen the boys at school imitating him, the goosesteps higher with each passing day. Daphne giggled at Zara's sedentary impersonation, ill-equipped as she was to make sense of her grandfather's gentle response.

'Hitler isn't so funny, Zuzzi. Those boys, they don't actually understand. But, you know, it isn't easy to invade an island like ours. Nobody has managed it for... oh, for hundreds of years. Hitler will attack us one day, though.'

'Why, Zaida?'

'He wants to control the world, Zuzzi. Every now and again somebody gets that crazy idea into their head.'

'You mean like Caesar?'

'Maybe like Caesar.'

'A boy at school said, "Keff, Keff, Hitler is after you".'

'Hitler is after many of us, Zuzzi, but we shall keep you safe. Trust your parents – and trust your Zaida.'

He looked at Estera, her comprehension sufficient to grasp the gist of it. They'd escaped from one emperor, he muttered.

'Shall we have to go away this time, Zaida?'

'Zuzzala, I think you will.'

Estera cut the cake and offered a piece from the flat of the knife. 'Your mother makes well,' she said.

Zara reached for her slice. Sunlight burst through the copse and made a dappled shade of her thoughts.

* * *

The Century gave the bustling city a new name, Litzmannstadt, and directed one part of its mix, debarred from the fabric industry of this Manchester of Poland, to an encirclement it called the ghetto, the ultimate objective in the words of its occupying governor being to 'burn out this plague spot'. Any Jew spotted outside its walls would be shot, he said, and the shrinkage began. Now marked by armbands, and soon by yellow stars, a hundred and fifty thousand were brought to one square mile and a half, the factory owner together with the textile worker, doctor with patient, the theatre director and the girl who swept the auditorium.

David Beigelman was among the influx, clean-cut and lean, dark eyes deep-set, hair brushed back in a crescendo of waves. His zeal as a maestro and virtuosity as a *klezmer* had found fame beyond his homeland, a land where he had once joined the Ararat, performing on the same bill as Dzigan and Szumacher, the Yiddish Laurel and Hardy. Beigelman had traversed the continent, had played the halls of New York. Crammed now with his wife and children – like every family, illustrious or ordinary – into a single room in a creaking ghetto tenement, a grime-covered parody of the bedroom at Arles, still he composed music. He established a playhouse, conducting concert after concert, directing dance upon dance, to bring fleeting transcendence amid the long, slow obliteration of the senses. Time was when his father Moishe had pressed passers-by to come and listen to him, a few blocks and a world away. '*Nit kayn rozhinkes, nit kayn mandlen*', was the song he wrote now. No more raisins, no more almonds.

A decree ordered the inhabitants to turn in their musical instruments, and the bittersweet songs of the *klezmorim* sound-tracked a new sadness as violins for the generations were brought down from their walls and thrown on the trucks that the occupiers had sent to collect them. A strained, acapella note now accompanied the pageants of ghetto life: queues for the weekly loaf of bread; the ersatz luxury that was boiled potato peel; the dismantling of a bed for firewood; women still scrubbing their doorsteps; a boy sharing a morsel of food with his sister, who had kept the bow in her hair; and the ignominy of the father who, famished beyond measure, stole up in the night and ate the ration his wife had put aside for their children.

No propaganda was required here, in this Jerusalem revived on Polish soil but a generation ago. A wooden fence, and then the barbed wire: the gates were closing on the Łódź ghetto.

Chapter 6

Solomon Keff sat at the wheel of his Austin Seven saloon, filled with the last of the petrol ration, preparing to drive to the assembly point for the evacuation. It had been different the previous time, amid the organised chaos of the first days of the war, with his daughters booked onto one of the trains scheduled to depart every nine minutes. This time he was to take them, labelled again, string-tied luggage in hand, to board a bus at the town hall.

'Mummy, do we have to go?' Zara asked as they packed for a second time.

'You do, dear. But be brave, and we shall see you again soon.'

'And Daphne will cry all the way, I suppose.'

Zara gripped the banister and pulled her suitcase down, to the regular beat of the knocks of the bottom corners against the stairs. The sun fell aslant onto the herringbone tiling of the hallway, where Mops was coaxing Daphne toward the door.

* * *

The single-decker followed the A10 along Bruce Grove and rattled through the towns of Hertfordshire. Soon Royston and Trumpington, too, were left behind, while the young travellers cheered and waved at the military vehicles juddering towards them, delighting in the hoots and hurrahs that came their own way. They turned off the trunk road north of Cambridge, whereupon a succession of country lanes brought the bus to a village, and to an abrupt halt by its church hall.

From nowhere, a cluster began to form, of brisk country types in pleated skirts or well-ironed slacks, who scrutinised the occupants as they disembarked. Zara stood motionless, a palm firmly on Daphne's shoulder, the two huddled among the children of Tottenham. And then she heard a familiar voice.

'Daddy!' He had appeared from behind the group and angled his head to beckon them over. She tugged at Daphne. They saw their mother in the passenger seat of the Austin and were tearing to climb into the back when a stern-looking official marched in their direction brandishing a clipboard.

'Just a minute, sir. You must await your turn.' She took Solomon in for a moment. 'And you're not from our village, are you?'

'I'm sorry, madam; these are my daughters. There's been a change of plan.'

It was most irregular, she said, but with an exaggerated shake of the head she crossed off their names.

Solomon had not been sure whether what he had had in mind would work, but, knowing nobody outside of the wedge from Bethnal Green to Stamford Hill, and little of the country beyond London, what he had seized upon doing was to discover a place regarded as safe by the government, make a swift appraisal, and, if the lie of the land looked promising, take matters into his own hands. He had driven discreetly behind the bus, absorbing the unfamiliar landscape, and within a few minutes of arrival had more than found what he was looking for. Having reclaimed his children, he drove straight on to Cambridge.

'Abbotts – established 1850. Victorian. We can do business 'ere.' Sol leant for the car door. 'Come on, Zuzzi. Your mother can look after Daff.'

'Sol,' said Mops. 'Don't forget your h's, dear.'

Sol guided Zara into the estate agent's and picked up some printed details from a table. A notice directed them upstairs to a wood-panelled room. There, a grey figure in a wide-lapelled pinstripe was stooped over a pile of index cards, his own the one desk among three showing any sign of recent activity. He looked up, surprised.

'Please accept my apologies, sir. There isn't much call for us now. How can I help?' Before Sol could answer, he saw the leaflet in his hand. 'Ah, the row of semis on Church Lane? We've had such bad luck with them. The work was delayed, the war started, demand dropped off a cliff.'

'In that case, sir, I think we can 'elp each other.' Blimey, Mops, he thought, that's another one gone.

'Do take a seat, sir. You sound as though you're from – London perhaps?'

Sol laughed: he was normally pinned down to the Bow Bells. 'It's a long story, guvnor, but I'm 'opin' to relocate a few people – some place clear of the bombs if I can. I'd like to take out a couple o' leases on the 'ouses, if you don't mind.' He held up the brochure and stabbed his index finger against it. 'These two, next door to each other.'

Zara looked at the piles of manila folders, which occupied every spare corner of the room, from the tops of the cupboards to the grate of an unused fireplace, wondering what they could possibly all contain.

'And will you be occupying one of the houses, sir?'

'Business is going to keep me down the Smoke. But I can tell you who will.'

'Right you are,' the estate agent said, picking out two blank index cards.

'Number twenty-six: Malcolm Imlach, 'is wife Rey, their daughter Lauren – and this one, Zara Keff.'

Zara turned to her father with a huge smile. She loved her Aunt Rey and found herself drawn to Lauren whenever they came to Bouverie Road. But surely her sister would be here too?

'And number twenty-eight?'

'Gus and Puss Coe, their son Dougie when 'e's on leave – and my second daughter, Daphne Keff. They'll probably take in a couple of evacuees too.'

Zara's mouth fell open at the prospect of being freed from her responsibilities. She could imagine the new life already.

'Puss, sir?'

'Make that Elizabeth.'

'And the gentlemen, if I may ask, they're not required…?'

'Mr Coe fought in the first war, sir, and Mr Imlach's just the wrong side of forty – married late. They 'ope to find work up 'ere. One's a builder – and a businessman; the other's an accounting clerk.'

'Send them here, Mr Keff. I'll point them in the right direction. With so many called up already, it shouldn't be difficult. The bank needs somebody, I know that for a fact. Now, can I take the deposits?'

'You certainly can, sir.' Sol reached into his jacket, pulled out a clutch of notes, and with a lick of the fingers swiftly peeled off the requisite number.

* * *

The Dodd sisters were gathered at Bouverie Road, as they did, for drinks, every so often. They remained a formidable combination and, though only one was named for the hair, they all possessed a good head of it. Puss, grey in her forties, swept hers back either side of a parting; an inveterate smoker, she was gaunt and prematurely lined. Rey, approaching forty herself now and the tallest of the three, was fuller in the cheek and brushed her dark-brown hair upward and outward from the centre. Mops, at thirty-two, favoured a parting to the left and auburn hair rising far enough in the opposite direction to begin to tumble toward her right eye, all of which did more than enough to justify her nickname. Each of them had the rounded lips of their family, which would make as if to whistle when they were acting mischievously and revealed prominent upper teeth when they smiled – and smile they often did. They were masters of the raised brow, too; their wide-set eyes spanned the spectrum from amber to grey. They got themselves up to meet each other, Puss today in a light shirt dress with black collar and cuffs, Rey and Mops in turtle-neck and white blouse respectively, combined with a pair of three-quarter-length skirts. They were in their pomp, these three women, their confidence fed by the hurdles they had overcome, the acts of their lives measured against the value they might have for the others. A rare bottle of sherry occupied the Queen Anne table in the front room, a pre-war gift from one of Isaac's suppliers.

'But the name, dear,' Rey was saying, tapping the arm of her chair. 'What about the name? What shall we say if somebody were to enquire?'

'The first thing to say is – the name has to remain,' Puss replied, looking at each of her sisters in turn. 'Everything's being checked against last year's survey. No school's going to take them without the required documents. The second thing is, I'm not sure Keff is all that identifiable. As Hebraic, I mean.'

'Yes, that's true,' Rey conceded. 'Aside from Zaida and his family, I don't think I've met another Keff. And let's face it, an unusual name didn't do the Schlegels any harm in *Howards End*.'

'They were German, though, dear. I'm not sure that helps.'

They turned to Mops.

'I've always thought of Keff as Dickensian,' she said. 'You know how he loves those short names with their double-letter endings.'

Puss smiled. 'Rather like our own, you mean?'

'Of course!' said Rey, 'And with Dickens, you have Fogg and Wegg…'

'And there are plenty of Goffs around here.'

'I think Keff stands up, so let's not worry ourselves.'

'Another sherry, girls? It could be our last for a while.' Mops topped up their glasses.

'The most important thing,' Puss continued, 'is that we go as two straightforward English families – and that includes your girls, Mops. We're there as the Coes and the Imlachs – and our nieces are with us. I don't think that's going to cause any trouble.'

'And the girls themselves, they have no real idea for now. Sol keeps all that away. He never comes home with his *koppel* on.'

Puss remained practical. 'All of that can wait. We have to protect them. If the worst were to happen… you know what they're saying about the Nazis.'

'The past is rather invading the present, dear, isn't it?'

'It's all so silly. Let's get the two of them through, along with you all.'

'We can do more than get through it,' said Puss. 'We're Tottenham girls, yes, but I'm sure we can blend in well.'

'There'll be all sorts of ways we can play our part,' added Rey. 'The boys can join the Home Guard…'

'You two must make your pies – they'll relish your pies.'

'And as for Lauren – there's bound to be a good school.'

'She'll move up a tier, won't she?'

Rey nodded. 'And so shall we all.'

'Let's drink to that. And to keeping safe, Mops. You must get yourself on a train if it all goes haywire. There'll be more than sufficient room.'

'Only if I can persuade Solly. While he stays, I shall stay. But he's pretty good at bagging a tank of extra petrol, so we're sure to visit.'

'To the Dodds of Tottenham.' Puss raised her glass. 'Good health!'

'And God's speed to Dougie, Puss.'

'We'll see you in a couple of weeks – when school's finished and we can bring the girls up.'

'Until then, Mops.'

They sipped at their glasses, their eyes alight. Puss had brought them a long way, and the seeds of the alliance she had planted on the day when she first walked up to West Bank had borne fruit with Sol's very own evacuation plan. It was sufficient for her, and she hoped for a quiet war – and for the preservation of her son. As for Rey, she could see the village in her mind's eye and envision her place there; she hoped to contribute. She was not altogether sure how, but imagined the busload of young Londoners whom Sol had followed could do with a little help. She would take Lauren up straight away, before the schools closed for the summer, to secure a place at the secondary level for the following term. Her head rose above the others; she scanned an imaginary horizon and, in the moments when her sisters caught her eye, they saw her stature appear to rise before them. And then Mops. To be safe and well guided, looked after by those who in time past had raised her: she knew what she had gained for her own daughters. More than that, when the whole business of the war was over, she hoped they would emerge with the countryside in their hearts, the ways of the Home Counties in their bearing and, pearl beyond price were it to be done, with the souls of true Englishwomen: a Schlegel or two indeed.

* * *

Zara dragged her suitcase upstairs to the small back room she had been shown, declining the offer of help from her aunt. A blue fine-checked cotton dress kept her cool, pulled in tight by its matching belt. A few months from ten, she could trade an exchange about emperors with her grandfather, be trusted to look after her sister – too often up to this point, she thought – and a spark of obstinacy was manifest in her insisting she carry the case herself, which she accomplished, a little breathless. She looked around at the sparse furnishings and out at the landscape, drawn by the open vista, curiosity as to what lay outside competing with belated anxiety at the prospect of life without her parents. Yet she called to mind the conversation she had had with Zaida at the picnic and felt certain of being safe from Hitler here. Alone in her thoughts, she swung round and saw Lauren standing in the doorway. Their eyes locked.

Zara liked having a sister well enough, despite the duties that conferred, but had yearned to find a companion with whom she might hold a proper conversation. The children at St Mary's had roped her in to their playground games, but none had become a true friend. She had played with Lauren when Rey brought her over: the polite kind of play you have when you know that your mothers are watching. Now here she was, light-brown hair cut above the shoulders, an upright stance, head held still enough to suggest confidence and an interested countenance broadening to a huge smile when she looked upon her cousin. She had a restrained panache, which Zara could not articulate, but could discern, nonetheless.

Lauren Imlach was very much Rey's daughter. Born Audrey, her mother had become Rey more subtly than her sisters had acquired their own pet names. Rey had not carried the burden of responsibility in the way her older sister had, but she'd been at Puss's shoulder in the enterprise, reading to the younger ones or supplying knowledge via the multi-volume encyclopaedia they'd bought in instalments. She joined her at the talks that took place in the local hall; they attended political hustings, to grasp the issues of the day and to listen to how the candidates communicated. They transmitted a form of speech to their sisters, and corrected them when necessary, such that it might be thought by the passing observer that they hailed from the Home Counties or Hampstead.

'Do you like my uniform, Zara?' Lauren was saying, dismissive of the need for pleasantries. 'Isn't it splendid?

It's the first time I've tried it on – apart from at the shop obviously. I love the beret. You should see the school. It's moved to a brand-new building, and we shall have so many subjects and mistresses. It's the best thing ever.'

Zara made to speak but reached in vain for the words.

'Mummy took me to the council, and they said my place at Tottenham County for the autumn holds good here. I shall be attending the Cambridge and County School for Girls, and we have an introductory talk tomorrow.' She paused. 'Oh, but you've just arrived. Shall we unpack?'

'But where shall I put everything?' Aside from her bed, there was simply a low chest of drawers in the room.

'Look, let's put your jumpers and the small stuff in here, and hang the rest up in my room. I've a huge wardrobe.'

They set about their task, chatting away, these children of the Dodd sisters, borne to the village by the Century. From time to time Zara stole a glance at Lauren, two years her elder, and, though her parents had not long departed, she sensed in this inconsequential activity the prospect of the new, of something beside the oblique strokes of the playground.

'There; that's everything. Now, as soon as we have the chance, we must explore the village.'

Zara followed her cousin to the landing and stretched for the banister.

'Yes, we must. We must.'

She caressed the rail with the lightest of touches, and her twin braids tripped with each stair that she took.

Chapter 7

Zara stood at the front gate, watching Rey and Lauren disappear in the direction of the bus stop on the Cambridge Road. Church Lane, she noticed, was quite unlike the other streets she had known. Bouverie Road, where she had lived until now, West Bank where she used to surprise Zaida, even a good stretch of Montalt Road in Woodford: each had a particular type of house replicated along an entire row. Here, she looked either side and, it was true, there was a line of six smart new semi-detached houses, all of the same design save for the mirror images the three pairs made, but opposite was a row of small terraced cottages, each with a long front garden, and to the left she could see a large detached home in its own grounds. She had read adventures from the children's section of the Stoke Newington Library, and their stories of fields and woods and country manors had been a world away. Yet here she was for as long as it might take to deal with Hitler, and, secure in Zaida's assurance that she would be safe, she stepped along Church Lane for the first time.

It occurred to Zara as she took those first tentative steps that she was alone. She could not remember having been on a street by herself before. Often, she had been with her mother, and when she went to Cohen's for her parents, or to the library on her own, there were passers-by to be seen, spread out more widely on Bouverie Road but milling along Stoke Newington Church Street as far as the eye could see. She would pass black-clad men in wide-brimmed hats, plain-stockinged wives and well-behaved children in tow, women tied in austere headscarves to shield them from the wind and men of working age in dark-grey suits or dungarees. In those first moments on Church Lane, Zara came across no such archetypes; a blackbird chirped, a squirrel scuttled out from under a bush, and she smelt something she couldn't place, even from the picnic in Epping Forest, but assumed was an essence of the countryside she had yet to discover.

Zara passed another imposing detached, which proclaimed itself to be The Rectory, and on past a narrow footpath, some houses rather like her own and pieces of rough-hewn grass displaying no obvious sign of ownership. She was approaching a road sign announcing the most unlikely and wonderful name, 'Duck End', when a man called out, 'Good morning, young lady', in a voice the like of which she had never heard before. She turned to find a tall, upright figure standing at the gateway to a cottage, older than her father, younger than Zaida she thought, with a rough, weather-beaten sort of face, a deep-green cardigan that had seen better days and trousers sagging all over the place, the whole topped with a misshapen flat cap that shaded the glint in his eye.

Much to her own surprise, Zara found herself saying, 'Good morning, sir.'

'What brings you to Duck End?' he asked.

'Oh, it's my first day in the village, that's to say the first day I've woken here. I was on my own, so I thought to explore.'

'My, what a mouthful, young lady. You do speak well.'

'Mummy says to speak properly; that way you have the best prospect, she says.'

'Well, well. Are you one of those evacuees?'

'My sister and I, we were in a way, but my father rescued us.' Zara sketched out the living arrangements, aware that her account failed to fill all the gaps, but judging it sufficient to be going on with.

'Young lady, I am Farmer Chardler. I live here with my good lady wife, and I farm those fields you can see yonder,' he said, indicating past the house and along Duck End.

'I am Zara, Zara Keff, of 26 Church Lane. I am pleased to meet you.'

'Likewise, Zara. If you're here for the duration, I reckon we'll be seeing a lot more of you.'

'The duration, Farmer Chardler?'

'It's how we talk about the war, about the length of time it might last. Nobody knows how long Mr Hitler's going to keep us, so we call it "the duration".'

'I see; then I imagine I am here for the duration.'

'Zara Keff, I'd better let you go now: I've a farm to run. I shall see you anon, I'm sure.'

'I shall bring my cousin to meet you.'

Mindful of Rey's instruction that she was not to stray too far and was to be next door by one, Zara skipped back up the lane and found cupboards for most of the breakfast things. Upstairs she hopped absentmindedly between Lauren's room and her own before alighting on the *Topping Book for Girls* that lay beside Lauren's bed, an edition she had not seen before. She picked it up by its green cloth binding: the life held out for the girl on the front cover, with her wavy black hair, orange pinafore and hockey stick, hooped scarf trailing in the wind, might be hers, in time, she thought, if she were to follow in Lauren's footsteps. Before long, she was propped up on an elbow at the top of the staircase, deep in a story of dormitory life. When the time for dinner came, Puss had to knock at the door.

* * *

At teatime, in command of every detail of the chat she had had with Farmer Chardler, Zara told of the day's events without stopping to draw breath. She tugged Lauren in the direction of Duck End the following morning, and when, to her disappointment, he was nowhere to be seen, she was able to explain that he had a farm to run so could not always be around for a natter. They walked on and reached a half-beaten track towards the bottom of the lane; at its fore was a clearing surrounded by bushes that transported Zara back to the day of the picnic; a single horse chestnut stood green at the edge. At the bottom of the path was an open field she supposed must belong to Farmer Chardler, with shocks of corn arranged in regular rows. Zara wondered what mysteries these simple backdrops held, tales that might be told in a future edition of a girls' annual.

'You should have seen Miss Field, Za, she's a proper beanpole,' Lauren said, out of the blue. 'You don't mind if I call you "Za" do you? It sounds so sophisticated.'

'Rather!' said Zara, echoing the stress on the second syllable favoured by her mother and aunts. 'But what's short for Lauren?'

'You can call me Lori if you like,' she replied. 'It's not shorter to say, but, the way I spell it, it's two letters shorter to write. Anyway, Miss Field: she's the headmistress. As I say, she is a proper beanpole. She's so bolt upright you'd think a mere prod on the nose would send her flying!'

They laughed. Zara was fascinated by these first glimpses of a world of headmistresses and berets.

'Miss Field says we're fortunate to have been admitted to the school. The time for young women is coming, she says, and that when the war's over there'll be countless opportunities for us. The best of the Cambridge and County will go on to the top universities in the country, in the world, Za. Wouldn't that be brilliant?'

They retraced their steps, and saw Farmer Chardler this time, at his farmhouse window, and Zara waved at him with gusto.

'Good morning, Zara Keff,' he said, as he came out to greet them.

She basked in this confirmation of their acquaintance and replied, 'May I introduce my cousin, Lauren,' uncertain as to whether to use the diminutive on this occasion.

'Good day to you,' he said. 'Now, what do you both have planned for this lovely summer's day?'

'We're going to have a proper look round,' Lauren replied.

'Now, if you stick to the loop as I call it, you'll be fine, there's no chance you'll get lost. Go on by the old chestnut tree off to your left, down to the bottom of Duck End, and up the high street; you'll pass the WI and the Old Rectory, which they turned into a school for boys who aren't quite all there if you know what I mean, but they're harmless enough. Carry on as far as The George. Turn right and you have the village school and the church on your left. Church Lane's on your right again, and you're back home. Take your time and take it all in.'

'Can I ask you something, Farmer Chardler?' said Zara.

'Please do, my dear.'

'I was wondering yesterday. How did this road come to be called Duck End?'

'Well you see, dear,' he replied, 'it's where the poultrymen used to live. Come near to Michaelmas time, they'd get hold of the ducks and geese, pluck their quills for those clever blokes at the university and fatten them up for sale. It was Duck End all right, in all manner of ways.'

Zara looked at him, open-mouthed, and with a momentary shake of the head.

'Can we come back and see you again?' asked Lauren.

'Well, it's a busy old time, you know; you'll likely find me out on the fields this afternoon, got the rest of the winter oats to get in. But you'll be seeing more of me, I'm sure of that.'

They set off to discover the loop. They adhered to it most of the time; at all events they kept it in sight. They could imagine Rey's reaction if they found themselves lost on their first outing together. They passed the twisted limbs of the chestnut, its spiny defenders swathed in dense foliage, and their first detour led them down Washpit Lane to a flat wooden bridge straddling a brook. On the far side, their shorts yanked up by overstretched braces, a trio of young boys were playing with a makeshift bow and arrow; one, to cheers from his friends, took aim at a cow, before scarpering at the sound of a farm labourer's fury.

'He must be one of the London children. He hasn't learned about country life yet,' Zara said, assuring herself that not even the boys' version of the Topping annual told of English cattle cast in their own Wild West film. 'I hope people don't think we're like those boys.'

'They come from close by us, you know. Mummy says the village hosts over a hundred now, from places like Hackney and Stokey. Most of them came at the start of the war: they've been away from their families for so long, poor things.'

Turning onto the high street, they paused outside the Women's Institute, where the noticeboard announced talks ranging from 'jam-making' to 'supporting our troops', a meeting for evacuee wardens and an invitation to take part in a survey, 'Town Children through Country Eyes'. They wondered how much this would all become part of their own lives; they were young women, after all, and were sure they could make jam if somebody showed them how. They passed the Old Rectory, now Middleton House School, promising 'every care for the boys who need it most', and on to The George. There appeared to be a second pub further on, but they stuck to the loop and found the village elementary, which Zara was pleased to see was even closer to home than St Mary's had been. A woman came by in a matching grey jacket and skirt, rather buttoned up for July, and Zara caught her attention in the way she often did. She thought she might have been a less fearsome incarnation of the official with the clipboard at the bus, but if she were, the recognition was not returned.

'Good morning, girls. I don't think I've met you before.'

Lauren said, 'We're quite new. I've been here a fortnight, my cousin Zara for a day and a half.'

'We're here for the duration,' Zara said.

An aeroplane buzzed overhead, and they looked up.

'That's from the Oakington aerodrome; it's one of ours I can assure you. I'm Mrs Barnett from number six, Church Lane.'

'Lauren Imlach.' She offered her hand. 'That's ten from us.'

'We're having a good look round,' added Zara. 'We saw a boy being scolded for shooting a cow with a bow and arrow.'

'You speak beautifully,' said Mrs Barnett, accommodating this offbeat tale without comment. 'I specifically asked for well-spoken girls, because of my own children, and they said there weren't any.'

'We live with our family,' explained Lauren. 'We're not the same as the other evacuees.' She exchanged a glance with Zara to confirm that was about right.

'I must call on your mother and ask if she'd like to help with the war effort. Now, ten along; that'll be…?'

'Number twenty-six,' confirmed Lauren. 'Mr and Mrs Imlach.'

'Right you are, girls. I shall be seeing you.'

They proceeded up to the church with its imposing gravestones, high elms and grand clock tower, and on past a set of allotments and a corrugated hut labelled baldly as an ARP post, whatever that might mean. They came across a disused army ambulance, abandoned on rough ground, with canvas flaps serving as doors to the rear. A group of children were gathered, and, amid a flurry of excitement, three more emerged from inside and pulled the flaps back. The first began, 'When shall we three meet again?' and they acted out the rest of the scene to great applause.

'That'll be an 'apenny each,' the second witch said, as the boy playing her sprang down and threw off the blanket that had served as a cloak.

'But we've only just arrived,' protested Lauren.

His skinny, freckled face jutted its jaw at her. 'I dunno, you come 'ere, you want yer entertainment and yer not prepared to pay.'

'Look like locals to me,' another witch said. 'Bumpkins are yer?'

Lauren put her hands out, inclining them helplessly, and looked at them in turn. 'Honestly, we only saw a minute or so.'

'A minute was what there was. Who do you think we are – the Globe?'

Zara looked at the dozen faces upon them and froze.

'We don't actually have any money,' said Lauren, and searched for something by way of mitigation. 'We only came up from London a few days ago. We're still getting used to the place.'

'You call this up? You sound mighty posh for a gel from the Smoke.'

Zara judged it probably not the time to give a second outing to her mother's injunction.

'Forget it, Joe. We'll catch 'em another time.'

'Go on then – be off with yer. And no more freeloadin'.'

'I'm sure we didn't mean to intrude,' said Lauren, whispering as they walked away, 'Well that was a close shave.'

'You got us out of it, Lori. How on earth did you know what to say?'

'You have to keep your wits about you, Za. Think on your feet.'

'Oh, I hope I don't meet them at school.'

Hungry now, they were soon home to find that Mrs Barnett had dropped by, and that Rey had acquired a veritable panorama of their new surroundings.

'They don't have to choose between jam and sugar.

They all take the sugar and use the fruit they grow to make preserves. It's marvellous. Half of them have chickens so they're not forced to make do with the one egg in their rations. And I've agreed to become an evacuee warden. We must make sure those poor children get the most from life here; we certainly shall.'

Lauren looked at her mother, and Zara did too, before they glanced at each other as if to say, well, that's quite something. Zara climbed the stairs to the landing and looked out of the window into the gardens beyond. She had never known, close up, so many different shades of green, and the closer she looked, the greater was the panoply. And when she stooped to peer through a solitary pane, she was struck by how much more was unveiled, even than she had seen through the whole.

Chapter 8

The children new to the village shivered slightly as they stood in line for the church hall. Each was listening for the announcement of their name and their assignation to the spot where they were to sit, cross-legged, on the parquet floor, to hear their headmaster speak to them for the first time.

Jimmy Garver was conscious of the role the Century had brought him without wearing it with ostentation. He had fought for king and country, forty years and two wars ago, and carried the life-saving injury he had sustained without complaint. He thought it no sacrifice to be advancing his country's cause in this altogether different way, lacking the self-importance of those of his fellow villagers for whom the current hardships were their first.

He raised himself as far as the advancing years allowed, and the hall fell silent. He greeted the assembly, extending a particular welcome to those starting the term with him for the first time. He prepared them for more crowded conditions and the need to form an extra classroom at the Village Institute, where they would take it in turns to have their lessons.

The door crashed open, and two of the more established pupils – brothers – stood embarrassed and out of breath, unkempt, their grubby shirttails exposed.

'And more arrive by the minute,' observed Mr Garver, with the angled glance of the schoolteacher, to chuckles from the staff, as he directed the boys to their places.

'We must all enjoy getting to know each other. If you're new here, you'll soon learn what country life is all about. You'll be eager to join in, too, and I don't mean as Robin Hood and his merry men.' There was an outburst of good-natured laughter at this, for the tale of the boy with the bow and arrow had percolated through the village. 'The cow was to be redistributed to the poor, I presume,' he added, to a further ripple of enjoyment. 'We do farm our food here, but we try to preserve the beasts that provide us with milk. I shall say no more about that.'

He went on to speak of the nuts and bolts of war, those which secured the home front at any rate, and to praise them for bringing their gas masks. He didn't believe the Germans would bomb their little village – after all, children had been evacuated here – but preparation was essential even so. There were the cloakrooms to know about, and the sandbags that surrounded them, assigned the role of protecting his scholars, dispatched to sit on the shoe lockers with their schoolbooks, should the air raid siren go. He checked that everything was clear to them, and there were murmurs of comprehension from the floor.

'Remember, we may not be in the trenches with our soldiers or in the sky with our airmen, but we can all play our part. We must help the Home Guard, pay heed to the Air Raid wardens, and work hard to keep village life going. We shall try to keep the school as normal as possible.'

And with that, Jimmy Garver directed his small band of non-combatants to take their charges back to class.

Zara felt a yank on her cardigan sleeve. 'You was on the bus with us, weren't yer?' The hand belonged to a girl she recognised from the journey, no taller than her, though ganglier, with black hair tied back in a ponytail. She was Joy, she said, and the friend by her side was Maureen.

'You should see my guardians,' said Maureen. She was two or three inches shy of the other and still had some puppy fat, her dark-brown coat a little tight, with hair cut to the collar. 'They've lived in the village so long they even have grandchildren here.' She spoke with the straightforward tone Zara knew from the shopkeepers back home.

'We got to go gleanin',' Joy said, in an accent closer to that of Zara's father. 'You scramble for the grains in the corn stubble after the wheat's been stacked. It adds a bit to yer rations.' She had a jaunty way of swapping over her stance as she talked.

'Did you hear about the seven sisters of Islington?' Maureen asked.

'These were yer seven actual sisters, I promise you,' said Joy, after Zara had replied that she'd always believed that to be a railway station.

'You were the quiet one,' a freckle-faced boy said, wagging a finger as he passed. He leant towards her. 'But don't forget you owe me an 'apenny.'

They looked at each other, but Mr Garver hurried them on. Zara had the story of her own guardianship off pat now, and, with half an eye over her shoulder, was ready when her friends asked at playtime, and they had their first experience of the wooden seats between thin partitions, with their strips of newspaper hammered into the wall.

By the time she returned home that evening, Zara's memory was struggling to retain everything she had to tell. The seven sisters of Islington proved to have been no exaggeration: taken into quarantine when infection was detected among them, they disappeared one night never to be seen again. Lauren was full of her first proper day at the Cambridge and County and the characteristics of the various mistresses she had encountered. She had acquired a new way of speaking. 'Double Lat, with Miss Sturridge. It'll be the end of us.'

Mr Garver himself took Zara's form every Tuesday, heralding history after dinner, provided they had worked well in the morning. On such afternoons Zara would race back to the classroom, impatient for stories of Elizabethan times. She would find herself lost in the world of Tudor houses, fashion, and the various forms of entertainment. She could imagine herself a lady at court, or one of the Queen's servants. The world of the here and now was present on the class wall chart, teams competing for the coloured stars they could affix if their work or their contribution were deemed to be of sufficient merit. Zara leapt to hand out the books and concentrated keenly on her handwriting, her eye drawn to the constellation pinned to the wall. In assemblies, Mr Garver roughly distilled for them how the war was going; it puzzled Zara that he was so polite about 'Mr Hitler', while her classmates mocked him without mercy, despite being reprimanded whenever they were caught. She listened to the locals and Londoners swapping tales in the playground, the ritual of two-course family sit-downs comparing unfavourably with chip sandwiches munched on the doorsteps of Hackney. Joe gave her a nudge now and then, but he was in the older class, and she stuck close by her friends during breaks from lessons. She did wonder, though, what she'd done to attract a rogue boy's ire again. Joe didn't call her names, but his eyes darted her way if she slipped into his field of vision.

Fifty couples hosted evacuees, the arrivals often constituting a ready-made family, labelled, string-tied, and hand-delivered. The boroughs had promised teachers and welfare officers, but none materialised, the Century depleting such reserves while it drove its children out of town. A great stove strained to warm the village school, exerting an influence beyond its walls, and potential tensions were defused by the acquisition of a common enemy. As London burned, the night sky glowed red in the distance.

* * *

Zara hauled her gas mask onto her shoulder daily, its cardboard container quickly disintegrating and being replaced, as those of her school friends had been, by a hardier but no more accommodating mackintosh case. The mask and satchel formed something of a load, but she skipped to the rhythm of the double burden as it thumped against her side. Each morning, the schoolyard resounded to the events of the previous evening, the war their constant companion.

'It was the end of his shift in Bolsover, and he was instructed to mobilise there and then,' Zara explained to Maureen, mastering phrases she had never heard before, somewhat to her own surprise. She was rather proud to be helping to look after Lance Corporal Davison from the Derbyshire Territorials, a section of whom had arrived in the village unannounced the day before, having made their way to a map reference. The evacuee wardens had sorted out emergency billets, and Zara had taken their allocated soldier next door.

'Auntie Puss. Pleased to meet you, ma'am.'

'You remind me of our Dougie,' Puss replied, turning toward the frame on the wall. She introduced him to the household. Daphne was kneeling on the rug, her limp hair cut neatly to a bob, and two evacuee boys the Coes had indeed taken in were curled up together on an armchair. They occupied Dougie's room with an obligation to swap it for the couch when he came home on leave. Gus had come through from the garden, the broad shoulders acquired by the physical work of his younger self, adding to the well-groomed appearance of the businessman he had become. He studied those he met with interest, his expression defaulting to a smile while he listened.

'So, you're a miner? That's some work, young man.'

'Yes, sir. But eager to serve, sir. They're speaking of keeping miners at home, so I'm glad to get the call now. You've fought yourself?'

'Joined up in 1914; kept going till Passchendaele. Copped a blighty one. Past it for this, though.'

'What line are you in?'

'Building – homes fit for heroes. Lost the business after the crash like so many others. Was up and running again when this palaver started. They'll need us, though, soon enough.'

'The lasses were telling us how you folks came to be here. It's quite a story.'

'He's quite a brother-in-law.' He looked toward Zara. 'We've got this one's mother to thank for that. She's a remarkable woman.'

Zara searched their faces; she'd never heard her mother described like that, nor herself as a lass for that matter.

Gus gave her a fond smile. 'All in good time, young Zara, all in good time.'

'Gus,' Puss put in, with the lightest of touches.

'Understood, dear.'

'Now, I've managed to get hold of some extra sausages. How's that for your tea?'

* * *

'That one's damaged,' Lauren cried, as they craned their necks in the garden, plane-spotting, with their adopted soldier the following evening. 'Look! Look! At the back.'

'Let's hope the rear gunner's made it,' he replied.

'Oh, I hope that's not Dougie,' said Lauren. 'Or if it is...'

The next interrupted as it flew back intact, and they all cheered.

'Now that's a Short Stirling. Am I right, Lance Corporal?'

'Think on, Lauren. What are you looking for?'

'The engines,' said Zara. 'The engines.'

'It's a Wellington then?'

'Do you know, or are you guessing?'

The girls sighed.

'Twin-engine.'

'Wellington!' they replied in unison.

'Wellington,' he confirmed. It was the last to return. A clamour of rooks flew by in the direction of the church, seeking their treetop home.

Zara pointed to a length of rope that was lying on the grass. 'Show us some more knots, please, Lance Corporal.'

'Come on,' he said, grabbing the rope and marching them to the back gate. 'Let's go down to that bench by the green.'

As they approached the churchyard, Zara suddenly tugged on his cuff.

'That's the one we told you about,' Lauren whispered into his sleeve.

He moved Zara's hand gently away and went to stand by the boy, looking twice as high and several times the bulk. 'Well, hallo, lad. I understand you three know each other.'

'I wouldn't go that far, Corporal.'

'What's your name, lad?'

'Joe. What's it to you?'

'Well, Joe. You and I speak a bit different, don't we?'

'I s'pose so. I ain't really thought about it.'

'What do you think we've in common, lad?'

'I dunno. Tell me.'

'Hitler, Joe. He'd have us all: lads and lasses, north and south.' He shook the rope. 'Now, do you fancy learning a thing or two?'

'Don't mind if I do.'

'First things first, though, lad. I gather my friend owes you an 'apenny.'

'Er, not exactly, Corporal. I reckon she can 'ave that one for zilch.'

* * *

The gusts of early October blew hard around the village scholars, assigned a fortnight to help with the main potato crop, and Zara's first contribution to agricultural life was stamped by the frost that seeped through her mittens. The evacuees, po-faced against the cold, came from her neck of the woods, but she saw herself less and less like them as the days went by. There had been the boy: there was always a boy. But the lance corporal had taught him the knots, and Joe knew that Zara could tie them too. With the harvest over, her gas mask flapped again inside its mackintosh drum, while the short walk to school put a spring in her step.

Chapter 9

Jimmy Garver would not have chosen the war, but he was wise to the good that could come of it. His charges delivered leaflets for the parish council, designed posters advertising War Weapons Week, and collected books to be rebound for servicemen. He had each class write to the forces, showed the newcomers how to make jam, and urged his scholars to enter the children's categories at the autumn fair.

Around the village it was plain to Zara that the various groups of children generally got along, or at least put up with each other. There were occasional disagreements, even so. One of the Londoners might take exception to being ribbed for their dropped h's and chase after the mimics with their fists pumping. They in turn might prod the locals for sounding simple, or even snooty to their ears, as she and Lauren had discovered. Zara began to see, too, that the evacuees themselves didn't always stick up for each other and that arguments broke out between them now and again.

Zara was determined to make sense of everything, but even approaching the end of her tenth year found that events could defeat her. When a sailor came home on leave, the lemon he carried with him was the talk of the village and was to be raffled off at the school. It was best won by one of the Londoners who could make use of it in their tea, Zara heard one of the guardians say. She had no recollection of tea and lemon being spoken of in the same breath, and, although she comforted herself that it made no less sense than the pairing of a rose and a crown, she remained mystified; it was the kind of thing she would have asked Zaida about.

An autumn Thursday, the day before the half-term holiday, brought the turn of Zara's class to be taught at the Village Institute, and when Mr Garver directed them to stand first at the end of assembly they began to comply a little disconsolately. Zara liked the appearance of the VI, with its white picket fence and mock-Tudor façade, but it was not popular. Decrepit desks and chairs had been retrieved from storage to furnish it, and a row of toilets built with haste from buckets, the staff regarding it as an overflow location all round. Often the class was not taught: if the school were a teacher light for the day, the children due for the Institute would be set to work in the garden.

As the group were about to be dismissed, Joe, in the oldest class, sniggered and mouthed 'VI, VI' at them. Turning round, a local boy in Zara's line pointed down at him and said, 'Don't laugh at me, Ikey-Mo,' whereupon a hush ensued, a silence magnified by the spotlight thrown on to the two. There was rarely trouble at the school, beyond an unkind word here or there, or a scuffle over something and nothing, and certainly not in Mr Garver's assemblies, at the close or otherwise.

Joe put the heels of his hands to the ground, and, with a furrowed brow and pursed lips, leant forward, weighing up the possibilities, casting around, restraining an instinct perhaps. He pushed up, still frowning, breathing more audibly, until, half risen and distinct from his class, he started to point back.

'Who you callin' Ikey-Mo?' he demanded, as he assumed his full height.

They were facing each other, a yard apart, the scene frozen like a game of musical statues, the children holding their breath while their eyes sought each other, their headmaster, the pair, or the floor. Mr Garver, having picked up his Bible from the lectern and now in crouched conversation with a child at the front of the room, registered the change in atmosphere and was half-sprung when the other responded, 'Whaddya gonna do about it?', his blent country consonants at odds with the omissions of the boy who had stood from the floor.

Joe retorted with, 'I ain't no Ikey-Mo,' and defied the other to make something of it. A friend of Joe's began to rise, and a second from Zara's line stepped forward, another of the refugees from London, opting for sarcasm.

'Shu' up, Abie, 'ope you won the lemon.'

Hands on hips, angled against each other, they held their ground as Mr Garver straddled the crossed legs toward them.

* * *

'What did 'appen between those boys?' Joy asked, as the class prepared to file back to the church hall at the end of the day. It had remained an unsolved puzzle for the intervening few hours.

'It came right out of the blue, whatever it was,' said Maureen.

'I don't know,' said Zara, 'but that word, "Ike", I've heard it before – I'm sure I have. I remember talking to my grandfather about it.'

'What did he say?'

'Oh, it was a good while ago; not to take any notice, I should think – that sort of thing.'

'Well, it made Joe mad,' said Joy. 'And 'is friend was gonna join in too.'

'Thank goodness Mr Garver reached them in time.'

''e was ever so upset, though, afterwards.'

'Joe?'

'Mr Garver. It was like 'e was looking for 'is kind old smile, but 'e couldn't find it.'

They formed a line behind the second class caught up in the morning's altercation, who had emerged to wait at the church gate.

'They're looking at us,' said Zara. 'Over there.'

Two women had their eyes on them, mothers of children at the school, Zara thought.

'They are,' said Maureen. 'It's like they're looking down their noses at us.'

'Or they're sort of disappointed,' said Joy. 'They must've 'eard – maybe from the kids who duck out the rissole and mash and go 'ome for dinner.'

'They're pointing at Joe.'

'He didn't start it, though,' Zara said. 'At least I don't think he did.'

Looks were exchanged between the boys involved as the two classes entered the hall. In the main, though, they held their heads steady, acknowledging rather than accepting responsibility for what had happened. For her part, Zara was alert and upright as Mr Garver steeled them for what was to come: it would likely be the most important talk he would ever give them, he said.

'A war like this brings many things to a country,' he continued, 'many sad things. Soldiers and pilots have given their lives in battle, defending our great country. Cities have been set on fire, bombed by the Luftwaffe. Many have left home to take refuge with us, here in our village. We're so short of things that we celebrate when a lemon comes to town.'

Jimmy Garver could be relied upon to locate a note of gentle humour in even the most difficult of times, and soft laughter, short-lived, rippled through the hall. A war could bring good things too, he told them, though it sounded strange to say so. They'd rubbed along well most of the time, city and country folk, considering that so many had been squeezed into the school. They'd worked together, delivering leaflets, raising money: he was proud of them. Zara met his eye and smiled; several of the boys lowered their heads.

'When this war comes to an end, as every war does, we must remake our lives together. Mine is but for a few more years; yours will be for the whole century. Now listen carefully. I'm going to give you something very serious to think about over the next few days.'

* * *

Lauren had come home from the Cambridge and County that afternoon to find her cousin at the landing window, rolling an ancient grey tennis ball along the ledge, wondering how much of the future a single pane might reveal. 'Come on,' she said, grabbing the ball, and they made off towards Duck End, while Zara related the day's events as best she could.

'What did he say exactly?'

'He said,' and Zara slowed, trying to get it right. 'He said that he hoped he would never hear words like that spoken again, at school or anywhere. Ever.'

'Not Mr Garver, silly. The boy.'

'I didn't really hear. Just the shouting afterwards. And Mr Garver marching a boy across the hall by one of his earlobes.'

'Go on. What happened after that?'

'Well, nothing really. He just scolded him and said we'd to come back at the end of the day.'

'Oh.' Lauren sounded mildly disappointed.

'We've got to write this thing on Tuesday. About the future. About the world – what it could be like one day. By the time we're old. That sort of thing. Oh, and he promised a prize for the best.'

'But that's brilliant, Za. You have such imagination:

you're bound to impress him. I wish I could do that on the first day back rather than double algebra.'

'But there's the rest of our lives to think about.'

'Look, there's a game we play at the County. It's called "catch it and say it". You think of an idea, say it aloud, and throw the ball to the next person. They must add to the idea or contest it. Let's try it with the two of us. Here. You start.'

They were approaching the horse chestnut, its softened pods now cast to the ground. Zara flipped the ball from hand to hand. 'Just imagine...' She tossed it to Lauren, with her arm held high.

'Imagine what? You'll have to think faster than that.'

'Ouch! You almost had me there.' Zara stumbled, then righted herself. 'Well, no more war – that would be a start.'

Another sharp return. 'Oh, what *rot*. They said the last one was the war to end them all, remember?'

'Oh, I don't know then. Perhaps a scientist will discover...' she flung it further this time, '...how to stop thunder.'

'Pfft. How to fly around the globe in a jiffy, more like,' snorted Lauren, laughing as she stretched to send the ball soaring back over her cousin's head.

Zara scrambled to rescue it, breathless, one knee grazing the dusty farm lane. 'Or up to the moon and the stars,' she replied, with a high, but ill-directed lob.

The ball fell to earth and nestled, camouflaged, among leaves and conker pods. As the girls hunted for it, a cloud covered the sun. Suddenly chilled, they straightened and turned to gaze at the sky above the chestnut: the churchyard rooks were calling time on the day against a reddish dusk.

'Really, though, when he said to imagine the future, I don't think he meant flying to the moon and that sort of thing.'

'You said he was upset?'

'*Rather.* About the words. I've never seen Mr Garver like that. Honestly, he was shaking.'

Lauren spotted the ball and bent down to retrieve it. Then, with a mischievous grin and a fair imitation of her cousin's headmaster, she began to declaim, 'We must make a world where ugly words are for-bid-den.'

'That's just like him!' said Zara, wagging a finger in turn.

'Where little children are kind to each other...' added Lauren.

'...and everybody performs their plays for free!'

They laughed at this reminder of their first day together, and dawdled on toward the clearing between the trees, tossing their hopes between them. That weekend the beaten tracks were Zara's partners in contemplation; by Monday evening she had the notion of a plan; the fine detail would come to her in class, she was sure of that. She fell asleep with an idea starting to take shape, a belief of sorts, about the century for which Mr Garver had predicted they would live.

* * *

'You'll all recognise this,' Mr Garver said at last, eyeing his scholars over a pair of half-moon glasses.

They had taken their places in the hall, that crisp sunlit morning, with exaggerated shuffles of their legs, watching him mull over for longer than usual whatever subject matter it was that lay on the surface of his rickety lectern. He lifted the framed photograph for them all to see.

'Our village memorial: below it the names of eight young men who left to fight in the Great War of 1914 to 1918. I taught every last one of them – at around the age you are now.'

He looked down, for a moment, at the unpolished floor. 'They promised us a peace to last for a hundred years, children,' he said. 'It lasted only for twenty.' He paused and swallowed. 'We may have our playground squabbles every once in a while, but I never – *never!* – thought I would hear, in the sanctuary of our school, the kind of words that have brought so much trouble to our world.'

Zara looked at Mr Garver, watching his mottled hands tremble. Was he really addressing his remarks to her?

Mr Garver replaced the photograph on the wall, standing back to ensure that it hung perfectly straight. He turned towards his pupils. 'Listen to me now. The task I instructed you to think about on Thursday. I need you to put your very heart and soul into it. It will be the one activity for both classes until playtime.'

It was the day for Mr Garver to take Zara's class and he walked them back, his fine limp the relic of a wound sustained long ago, before he had seen his former charges leave for battles that would take so many of them.

'You may present your work in any way you choose,' he explained, once they had reached their desks, 'just so long as you describe the world that you hope to live in by the time you're my age.' He added, with a dry smile, 'If you can think that far ahead.'

Warm laughter broke the tension, and the class settled down. Zara was not sure how old her headmaster was. His back was quite bent, his face deeply lined, his thin moustache grey: she must look an awfully long way forward to imagine any future as old as he was, she was certain of that. Sensing the importance of the occasion, she was determined to do her utmost to make him proud. She opened her book at a fresh double page and smoothed down the centrefold with her palm.

Chapter 10

The chestnut trees turned golden and soon began to bud, and the Battle of Britain bled to the Blitz. When that, too, was done, a number among the newcomers returned to their boroughs, though the strong bonds many had forged with their guardians brought them back in the breaks to see them. Those who stayed in the village thrived: the healthy air and home-grown produce sustained them, and Mr Garver would tell them how lucky they were to have been evacuated. The tales told by those who visited made the evacuees rather wish that their parents could join them in the village, as Lauren's had, than to be back in the city themselves.

* * *

Abraham Kevlov had not even the advantage in his own displacement that David Beigelman had, of retaining a room for his family. As the shrinkage intensified, and the westerners came in by train, he and Roza, and Fredek and his family, made the most of a solitary bed. They had the floor, too, and the landing, and the effluent-infused courtyard when it was fine, though when the rare leaves fell and the cold set in, the fence was soon dismantled for fire. There was work to find, for that brought you food, though it quickly gave out, and a school for Jakub, for the lyceum was his goal, chronic though his cough had become, remote as the prospect of that future remained. But they were not dead yet, not dead like the ones who had starved, or been shot for the sake of some hens, or machine-gunned after demonstrating in the street.

* * *

Zara noticed how often Mr Garver talked about their futures. He would say, 'Now when you go up to the Cambridge and County, as I hope many of you shall, you'll need to set your equations out like this...' or provide another such example which held out a bright prospect for them. For all Lauren's faux complaints about high school, the Cambridge and County was the future Zara saw for herself; she might still traipse and trail, rather in the shadow of her cousin, catching her face in the stream, but giant leaps were there to be taken now. Lauren had discovered as much, bringing to Church Lane Latin conjugations, Wordsworth, and the order of the elements. Zara looked forward to seeing more of her parents one day, and to picnics in the forest, but the Century had brought her to this village, and the argument between the boys a sense of the place she might start to find, among those who had embraced so warmly the extended family the war had thrust upon them.

* * *

They were ambitious for work in the ghetto, for though they were shopkeepers, and their shop was within its confines, they lacked cash to make down payments on provisions, and the authorities repurposed their store. So work they found, for Abraham called upon his credentials in textiles – and these things ran in the family. The linen workshop on Dworska did for a while, for the months he stayed strong, and he produced white and grey shirts for the Luftwaffe. How fortunate they were that Chaim Rumkowski, who had supplanted the elders and was the eldest himself, had made arguments for their labour, that use might be put to their bodies, until nought but their bodies remained. Fredek obtained work in fur, on Ceglana, and toiled with a gaggle of fellows to patch coats from the scraggiest of pieces; they made greatcoats out of horsehide, too, for the Blackshirts. Fredek's wife stitched alongside Roza on Brzezińska crafting hundreds of hats, and their daughter, too, was packed in tight, crocheting insignia for the complete range of garments the imprisoned were manufacturing for the enemy. For this rescue by work imposed no age bar, no pitiless discrimination to prevent you playing your part, in hope of a hunk of bread from beyond the fence.

* * *

The sticky buds of the chestnuts began to melt, and, as their plates fell to ground, unveiling slender leaves that hung like unripe bananas, Zara found herself observing the characters who stood tall in the village. Mr Garver commanded respect for experience and wisdom, qualities she could admire without emulating, the redoubtable Mrs Barnett exercised a brisk energy, and Zara saw that modest people like her Aunt Rey could also make a difference to people's lives. When she put that to Lauren, as best she might, her cousin replied that she thought the thing to do was to get involved, that Miss Field had said as much, had said to work hard and all that, but to be involved in sport or plays or debates if one could: it lent strings to the bow. Zara began to take more of an interest in the world around her and, one early spring day, she asked Farmer Chardler whether any games were organised around and about. His reply, that the football team played, over on Barker's Field on Saturday afternoons, and that, having won a lone match in the last five, he was sure they'd welcome support, wasn't what she'd had in mind, but Zara began to take the evacuee boys from next door along to give Puss and Gus some peace. Then, as spring gave way to summer, the children scoured the common land for medicinal and culinary herbs. They collected nettles, raspberry leaves, foxgloves and rose hips, striving to meet the target the Women's Institute had been set, so that less fortunate parts of the land might have access to such familiar ingredients. In turn, when the holidays came, Mr Garver and the WI brought milk over to every house with a child at the school.

* * *

They scrambled for wood, in the ghetto, and demolished the sheds. The lines for food stretched around the block, in huddles of caps and shawls, and old coats and yellow stars, and two hundred gravediggers could not keep up with the dead. They queued for bread in meagre proportions and for salad salvaged from scraps in the vegetable yard. 'Give up your selfish interests or invite disaster,' the eldest had said: don't strike or connive, or be late to work. 'Dictatorship is not a dirty word,' he was later to add.

* * *

Zara's breakthrough came with the paper salvage operation. Mrs Lambert, from the parish council, was speaking at the school assembly.

'Do you see that poster, children, which Mr Garver has been kind enough to put up for me?'

It showed a Tommy calling out, 'I need your waste paper,' which, the poster promised, could be fashioned into bomb bands, shell containers and cartridge wads.

'Now, I'm your salvage warden. Paper salvage is expected of every household in the land, every business and every school – and our village is no exception. Even Princess Elizabeth is Buckingham Palace's very own salvage steward.' She thumped the lectern – 'We must turn raw material into war material!' – and paused for effect, to stunned silence. She moved to the practical. 'So please, every one of you, remind your parents about the importance of the collection and the location of our depot in the outhouse, here, behind the hall.'

Zara leapt to speak with her friends as soon as Mr Garver dismissed them, and they badgered Mrs Lambert as she was detaching the poster from the wall.

'We'd like to take part in this scheme, ma'am,' said Zara, breathless by now. 'Is there nothing we can do apart from talk to our parents?'

'What did you have in mind, girls?'

They spoke over themselves in their rush to reply, Joy that they could involve their classmates, Maureen with an offer to collect on Saturdays, Zara adding that her Auntie Rey could surely persuade the village guardians to encourage their foster children to join in.

Mrs Lambert was sceptical of the girls' interest. She had struggled to drum up support, a problem replicated the length and breadth of the country, prompting the announcement of fines and spells in prison for those who refused to participate.

'It's a chance to become involved, ma'am, to do something for the village.'

'I'll talk to Mr Garver,' said Mrs Lambert. 'Let's see what we can do.'

It may not be sport or debating, Zara thought, but it was surely far more practical. Mr Garver kept her behind at the end of the morning, and Zara was keen to impress upon him that others, too, had their hands up to be counted, but he had seen how much she liked to help, he said, making sure the books had been collected and the coats securely hung.

'I'm sure that's not just for the stars,' he added. 'And that day when I had the class write about the future. I remember your piece. Now's the time for you to start to live up to that. You can make this scheme a genuine success.'

'And my friends can help too?'

'You're the one who will involve them. This is your project, Zara Keff.'

She took a deep breath. 'Righto, sir. How do I start?'

'Talk to your aunt. She'll help you to organise things.'

Zara began the next day. She stood at the front of the class, Joy and Maureen alongside her. She spoke of the efforts of the grown-ups, with their jam-making, their raffles for War Weapons Week, their make do and mend.

'This is our chance, as the children of the village, to play a part.'

On the Saturday, no fewer than twenty volunteers turned up to see a copy of the village map on the classroom wall, which Zara had used Mr Garver's spectral array of crayons to shade in. Each pair was to take a section, their mission for the morning not to collect but to explain. They were to promise to return a week later, asking that in the intermediate period the householder undertake some sorting and have their contribution ready. If doubts were raised, they were to describe all the different uses to which the salvaged paper could be put and refer to the WI noticeboard where a copy of the poster had been pinned. Their own task in the meantime was to lay hands on sacks and wheelbarrows. Zara was conscious of having been rather bossy, propelled by her anxiety to live up to Mr Garver's trust.

The following Saturday, still eight pairs set out in pursuit of their goal, steering their wobbling carts by the crocus shoots that had started to flourish and the blackthorns and violets nestling in the hedgerows. The next week, they set about sorting their collection into the categories required. Zara had seen a leaflet doing the rounds, 'Look before you throw': she was eager to make sure that valuable records were not discarded in the rush to salvage. She checked documents of possible interest and set aside the ones that might benefit from an adult opinion. They covered the entire village at least twice during the ensuing weeks, and by the time they finished had amassed two tons of paper.

Zara contemplated the achievement and recalled how quiet she had been at St Mary's, that she had been prone to teasing, not least by the boy who called her names. Zaida was right: that had not been important. Here she was, a Stoke Newington girl in a Cambridgeshire village, her village now, helping to provide much-needed material for the troops.

Mrs Lambert appeared once more at the church hall. There were a few murmurs as the pupils filed in, wondering what lecture they were to receive this week; there must be a limit to the amount of paper they could be expected to collect.

'Several weeks ago,' she began, 'I came to speak to you about paper salvage.' Zara straightened her back. 'Today I have come to express the gratitude of the village for your help.'

Mr Garver stepped onto the compact stage behind

him and drew back the curtains to unveil a sizeable cardboard package, secured with string. He scanned the hall for a volunteer, and though a couple of dozen hands shot up, his eyes alighted on Zara. He motioned her to the front, and she stood beneath him, her arms held rigidly by her side.

'I had to wait for a meeting of the parish council,' Mrs Lambert continued, 'and I am pleased to report they unanimously agreed to my request.' She pointed toward the parcel. 'Miss Keff.'

Zara took the three steps to the platform, so far above those on the parquet floor now, and saw Mr Garver, with a twinkle in his eye, give an imaginary tug. She pulled at the string, and the sides of the box fell to reveal a polished mahogany wireless. There were gasps of astonishment, an eruption of applause; a tear rolled down Zara's cheek. Maureen and Joy forgot themselves and rushed toward the stage, Mr Garver being compelled to restore order by pointing them back to their places. A soft hand on her upper arm emphasised that Zara was to stay with him.

He hadn't been altogether sure, he said, how much would become of it, when Zara and her friends had offered to help with the paper collection.

'But week in, week out, Zara, you organised the work of your volunteers and accumulated a remarkable success. And now, thanks to Mrs Lambert,' he concluded, to further applause, 'we have a wireless for the school.'

The assembly began to file out, and Mr Garver looked to his side. 'I have a feeling, young lady, that one day this wireless is going tell of the Century of Zara Keff.'

'You know something, sir, you never did announce the winner of that competition.'

'Well, it's a good job, isn't it?' he replied. 'We can't have you winning all of the prizes.'

Chapter 11

Though he hadn't much to sustain him, Jakub got to return to school, through the rain and the mud, as his shoes gave way, with but months to cover the grade. He tilled the soil, too, in the section assigned to his class, but the tilling could not remedy the shortfall, and the form shrank as the scholars began to starve. He came home to tell of a boy who had stood his ground, intent on convincing the authorities the dying ought still to be fed. The boy had said to come to their group where they studied Lenin. Abraham warned him that his uncle's back had never recovered from that sort of thing, that he'd carried the scars to London, though in the ghetto the Jewish police were the ones who stamped down on communism. Jakub worked on his algebra and geometry, his Cicero and his German, and stood tall in the class bath, raging against Catiline, while the doctors still feared for his lungs.

* * *

Mr Garver took Zara's class more frequently in her final year and often brought them the more accessible scenes from Shakespeare. They started with the entry of the witches, and Zara saw that it was one of his lessons which must have inspired the rogues in the old ambulance. She and her friends performed it without charge in the playground. The boys poked fun at them, but their stock was high, and the teasing soon faded. The school library held the complete works, a gift from a hopeful benefactor, and Zara searched for the passages they had read in class, aware of the limits to her understanding, in awe of the language and impatient for the day when she might get to grips with it. More suited were the range of classic books abridged for children: the landing at Church Lane hosted Dickens and Robert Louis Stevenson, and saw the reader fall in love with the March sisters. And every so often, it was the turn of her class to go to the hall and listen to one of the concerts the BBC broadcast on the Home Service.

* * *

There were concerts in the ghetto, for those who could meet the dress code, and Jakub slunk in from time to time. He found his semester truncated, as more resettled from the west, to join the Jews that Jews had looked down on, requiring the schoolrooms as places to live. He signed the class letter to Rumkowski, to thank him for all he had done, and was dropped from the communist cell. A tooth gnarled at him: the dentist slashed the gum and said to pull it when the abscess allowed. Fredek's needle dropped from his fingers, without cause that he could see, for his hands looked strong as they swelled and swelled. As the boils began their advance upon a face of old leather, he forced himself to the workshop to prove he remained of use. Abraham was exhausted, too, but he and Roza clung on, somehow; unable to work now, unproductive but unspotted, they collapsed onto the bed while the offspring were earning their crust.

* * *

Zara was ready for the Cambridge and County when she went, as Lauren had been two years earlier. She took a test, was interviewed alongside Rey, and spoke with such enthusiasm about the books she had read, the music she loved and the ideas she had stored away for becoming involved that, with Mr Garver's recommendation to boot, her place at the Long Road school was never in doubt. She and Lauren boarded a battered old bus at the church every morning. A converted troop-carrier from the previous war, it crossed the bridge over the River Cam and drove by the colleges of Magdalen, Sidney Sussex, Christ's, Emmanuel and Downing. Zara had seldom been to the town, and it was on the rare occasions the family used their clothing coupons, rather than rely on the exchange scheme run by the Women's Voluntary Service, that Rey and Puss took the children there to utilise them. Now, the twice daily journey familiarised her with the façades of the great institutions and prompted intrigue as to what lay within. The scores of undergraduates, gowns billowing in the wind, may have been diminished in number by the war, but the young women among them represented something the future might hold. Miss Field had said as much, as she had to Lauren on her own first day, and the several years of girls older than Zara, filling the long corridors with their animated conversations, strode the living bridge between her present and those colleges by the Cam.

* * *

Jakub saw the last of his father, or his father the last of him, from heart failure the paperwork said, for none died of hunger in the ghetto. The Century had delivered its concatenation: the movement, the shrinkage, the sealing; the pretence that education, the economy and culture persisted; the fading of hope that liberation was knocking at the door. The smack of firm government meant edicts nailed to the walls, that order might prevail within them, and death proceed according to plan, under the loosely coupled hierarchy of Litzmannstadt.

* * *

'My father works at the university,' Hilary Burgess said to Zara on their first morning. 'He lectures in chemistry. I want to become a physicist myself, though Pa says I must improve my maths if I'm to do that. Personally, I don't think it's all that bad.'

'Do you live in town, then?'

Hilary nodded vigorously: 'In Cranmer Road, near Selwyn College. It's a fascinating street. All kinds of interesting people – even a don from Germany. At least I think he's German – Polish maybe. You must come around.'

Zara rattled off the details of her own whereabouts – and her evacuation.

'You're a Londoner? Mind you, there's been bombing here. Bridge Street took a hit, and the union building was damaged. She's a bit of an old stick, isn't she?'

Zara: soft olive, mid-brown, anxious, inquisitive, eager. Hilary: full of gusto, pale-skinned, with straw-coloured hair that fell to a fringe and deep-blue eyes. They had geography, history and music in common. Zara was undeterred by the fusty wartime substitute who taught English; the sciences offered Hilary the chance to shine.

They both volunteered for the junior play, scheduled immediately before the half-term break, and were given parts among the general workhouse crowd in their all-female production of *Oliver Twist*. Rey, Puss and Lauren brought Daphne and the two evacuees to see it, forming their own Church Lane row toward the back of the stalls. At the curtain they rose as one, in arch-backed acclamation, to the startled looks of the parents around them. Zara went to the practice sessions for the under-thirteens hockey team and was thrilled to be selected as halfback for the match against Impington Village College, for whom Joy played as a forward.

Though the Cambridge and County occupied much of her time, Zara was determined to play her part on the Home Front. There was plenty of encouragement too: from Farmer Chardler, whom she bumped into sometimes on her weekly walk to Duck End and beyond, ever hopeful of more ideas such as the one which had inspired her Century; from Mr Garver, whom she might catch when the bus dropped them off; and from Mrs Lambert, who had a 'Good day, Miss Keff' for her whenever they passed each other on the street.

It was her aunt who gave Zara the idea for Christmas. The WI announced a party for the children of the village, inviting former evacuees to come back for the event. Having rehearsed the argument with Rey and co-opted her friends, Zara convinced the committee to allow a short play, and, armed with copies from the Cambridge and County, conducted auditions at the Village Institute. Joe pitched in for Mr Bumble, and Zara cast him with a gulp. Come the day of the party, the hall was festooned with homemade decorations, and three lines of trestle tables were covered in white cloths and the victuals that wartime permitted. At the door, Joy was dispensing bags containing four ounces of boiled sweets.

'Australia, would you believe?' replied Maureen, who was sharing front-of-house duties and fielding the questions.

'You're kidding me. Come on – honestly?'

Mrs Lambert stepped across. 'The British Children's Comforts Fund. Australia. Via the County Youth Organiser. So no complaining next time Bradman runs up a hundred.'

'You bet. The Aussies – who'd've thought it?'

'You know there's only fifteen of us now,' one of the returnees was saying, of St Mary's. 'They put us in one class, every age an' all.'

The play started with the workhouse scene, Joe's booming lines giving way to an apparent hiatus.

At the back of the hall, Zara was placing an empty bowl into the hands of a nervous young boy. 'It's your cue. Slowly now.'

'Shush! Look!' said somebody close to them.

'Hey,' whispered another. 'It's Oliver.'

Row by row, they turned to see him edge toward the stage.

Zara's cast concluded their *Oliver Twist by Charles Dickens: selected scenes* to much applause, the accents of Joe and his co-evacuees lending the proceedings an air of authenticity. Mrs Lambert stood up to 'thank Miss Keff and her friends for another fine contribution to the life of our village in wartime'. Joe gave her a playful wink and told her she'd not done bad for a posh gel. Mr Garver placed a hand on her shoulder as he was leaving, saying simply, 'Well done, Zara'.

As she climbed into bed that evening, Zara cast her mind back to the day, more than two years earlier, when she had outlined her Century. She was more hopeful than ever that the world could be a better place, and, if the play were something to go by, she might have a hand in achieving that. She didn't dare to guess how many years would pass before countries stopped fighting each other: she had learned enough history. The Wars of the Roses, of the Austrian Succession, the Napoleonic Wars:

these failed to offer scope for optimism, and perhaps she had hoped for that too soon. On the other hand, even the longest of wars ended, and her cast had performed so well together that she thought she had been pessimistic about the time it would take for people to stop 'using words that make trouble in the world'.

Zara's parents came for Christmas itself, and, with her aunts brimming with confirmation beside her, she deluged them with tales of the previous few weeks, and of the school carol service at Great St Mary's, where the hymns had been sung with a passion that made her spine tingle. The new year saw Lauren bumped up a class, on the fast track to university; Miss Field extolled the triumphs of her alumni, either in pursuit of the war effort or as exempted students; and, while the politicians promised a second front and the Century sought the reckoning, Zara Keff found herself closer to the brow of the bridge than she had ever been so bold as to imagine.

The Professor II

Camden, 1999

There was little doodling, out here on the bleachers. A pen might be held lightly between forefinger and thumb, resting gently against the lower lip and the upper incisors, or a digit point toward the temple while another reclined like a caterpillar moustache beneath the nose, and a pair of elbows might rest on the desk part, their crossed hands forming a steeple below the jaw. The headteacher could see that the freshman student with the glossy folder had her first sheet partly covered, making intermittent eye contact with the professor at forty-five degrees, while one hand sketched an impression in half-phrases and the other restrained the file. A few, it was true, were scribbling to take down every word, but these words, in the main, she thought, made best sense spoken, in the way an actor brings meaning to iambic verse. This was the lifetime of the grandparents of these students now, just about, that he had reached: the roaring twenties, the Great Depression, the precipitants of war. It was the period of their school examination courses, the rise of totalitarianism having outfought the Tudors and the long nineteenth for their teachers' affections – and to boost the uptake. It was the epoch of the films her parents had talked about, passed on to them in the age of the founding channels.

'It had been conflicted, the Century,' he was saying, 'with its aspirin age: raging uncertainty tempered by the pill of liberalism, the trumpet call of democracy counterbalanced by the trial of Sacco and Vanzetti, emancipation threatened by the Ku Klux Klan, Bauhaus by the dead hammer of the state. And it sowed seeds for the apocalypse. The *fasces* hailed the politics of demagoguery and marched on Rome. A man of steel worked his way to the top of the Soviet machine. In the Weimar Republic, the demands of the victors laid waste the reconstruction, and its people pushed wheelbarrows to buy bread. A failed art student sought a party, attempted a *putsch,* wrote an unremarkable book and eked out an existence on the edge of society.'

In such ways, he put it to them, the Century prepared the ground for its own bold statement while keeping everybody guessing.

'At the intersection of its life now, it wanted more, wanted intensity, extirpation, the ultimate resolution. A great crash deadened the pan-Atlantic roar. Dictatorship rehearsed in Iberia. Blitzkrieg shocked awed opponents into submission. Inside the new Reich, those brought to cities beforehand were pulled inward and prepared. Those enjoying freedom and high culture in sophisticated capitals were forced outward, all in the same struggle, borne by the winds of history to the reckoning.'

The old historian looked inquisitively at the middle rows, undergraduates shortly to pass that most redundant of markers, the millennium, a construction without substance, built like a vast dockland edifice without reference as to what might occupy it. For those out on the bench seats, he thought, to frame an era would be challenging enough, a mere decade more than half the span of their lives. They have seen wars fought, to be sure, wars to which they can bear no witness, even when their country was involved. Their governments have changed naturally, by way of the settled score of the ballot. History may have been their ticket to Bloomsbury; it had not yet been their lives.

'And then,' he continued, 'the Century turned the tide of the war. In the turmoil of its midlife, torn as to legacy, it had its protagonists fight to the finish, defending cities with liberation at the door, defending islands before ultimate acts of destruction gave them pause. But after the tanks had steamrollered the east and the partisans had been given their head, the long-awaited second front had brought the conviction that it was all downhill from there.

'What may we hypothesise, at this point in our period, with dictatorship's violent fire so long in the burning out, its eager feeding so slow to choke the feeder? That light doesn't exist in its own right? That it can only ever follow the darkness. Is this what the Century is saying, if only the Century could talk?'

Lamentations

1944–1951

Zara spots a problem with her idea now. She wants to set down her ambitions for the duration, but with each line on the page counting for five years it's an impossibly tight fit. To change the scale, though, would mean a lot of rubbing out, she realises, with her forehead cupped in a palm, as the clock ticks by in the silence. She straightens up. Her first paragraph ends a line shy of 1940 and, with the aid of a large curly bracket of the kind she has admired when studying charts in the school library, she decides to devote this and the following pair to the whole decade, by squeezing double the number of rows into the space available. *I shall do everything I can to help with the Home Front,* she writes. *There is jam to make, and there are clothes to mend and money to collect for the soldiers to send them parcels. I hope to attend the Cambridge and County School, and I would love to go to the university to learn more history. I long to wear one of those gowns and to feel it flapping in the wind behind me.*

Chapter 12

In the village, the Century had brought sandbags and gas masks, salvage and the wireless, and it brought news of Dougie Coe, listed missing, his Hampden shot down above Almelo on the German-Dutch border. Wracked with grief like so many, Puss and Gus ploughed the love they had to burn into Daphne and their two evacuees. Thus did it wrestle; riven between competing versions, the Century hurtled forward, in parallel with Zara but ahead of her, bringing devastating impact in its wake.

To Łódź it brought darkness, unforeshadowed by precedent, unpredicted by revelation, unimaginable, even in the ghetto. Here, the dispossessed could be drawn nowhere; they who had taught and become eminent, those who had studied or become craftsmen, be they teacher or tailor, chemist or carpenter, mathematician or metal worker, those who had built the world with brain and brawn, they could be drawn nowhere, nowhere, that is, except in shoes wrapped in rags to the prison and thence to Radegast station. Or they might be drawn direct to the transport, volunteering, in the belief that nothing could be worse than here. That, or to the wire, so the guards could finish them off.

'The tailor – did you hear about the tailor?'

Abraham Kevlov, long into his eighth decade, had passed the usual cast of characters: the walking corpses, with their drawn looks and sand-timer faces, vacuum-sucked in the heart of Europe, death's kingdom, eyes peering from the deepest of hollows; the stooping children, with the yellowed visage of the old, mining for the discarded coal dust to be found in pre-war dumps, ghetto-diseased with a unique form of consumption; the faecal workers, living a death sentence, cranking their tanks of excrement to the edge of the ghetto; and those who lay prostrate, adrift, having given up their ghost to the street. He was walking to hear Chaim Rumkowski, stained with the taint of collaboration, unanointed leader of the ghetto, rich despite it all, carving a path amid the Holocaust for himself.

'I can guess,' he said, to the bony acquaintance who'd approached him.

'This was novel, even for them. They collared him for theft – a single thread draped on his shoulder after he'd finished for the day.'

'You know they've emptied the hospitals? No last goodbyes: you couldn't even get close. The Jewish police were at the back windows.'

'And the old folk's place on Dworska. Piled onto trucks. Hide well, old man: they might leave you. You shouldn't be here.'

They reached the square.

'Fathers and mothers, give me your children,' Rumkowski was saying. Disorientated, senses distorted by deprivation, the words tumbled between Abraham's ears without making landfall.

'Give me the sick. In their place we can save the healthy.'

Asked to hand over Roza, weakened by malnutrition, short days remaining, constantly in pain from waterlogged lungs, and to become complicit in the gathering of his grandchildren, it was more than he could bear.

'You should kill yourself before taking our children,' he cried.

Rumkowski's logic carried no weight with him. Strengthened by the knowledge that Isaac and his family had been prospering when last he heard, he was fearless enough to utter that small cry of resistance.

He saw David Beigelman in line for the march to the station, for all the ravages of his four years in the ghetto, recognisable, undiminished by the thinning of the waves at his sunken temples and the cracks that had formed on his skin.

'Do you have anybody in the other world? I'll send them your regards,' the musician said.

For this most consummate of the *klezmorim*, who had brought solace to the trapped with the gentle pluck of an instrument salvaged from the pyre, for him to be reconciled to the end extinguished any hope to which Abraham Kevlov might himself against all hope have been clinging.

* * *

Yet in nemesis straws were dropped to the wind. Word escaped, if only there were those with the prescience to act. Forewarnings were conveyed, broadcast in exile, the Warsaw ghetto infiltrated. The world's leaders responded with no more than a press release.

The news found its way to the Cambridge and County.

Hilary said to Zara, 'You know that college don who lives on our street?'

Zara nodded vigorously.

'He knows what's going on in the places the Germans have captured.' Hilary hesitated. 'It's tough to say this, Zara, but the Germans are rounding up the Jews, all of the ones they can find anyway.'

'What happens to them?'

'They make them wear yellow stars, apparently, and force them to live in the most cramped of conditions. They pretty much make slaves of them.'

'How does he know all of this?'

'I think it's his work, you know; he's in the law; he has contacts. I think he may be Jewish himself.'

'But what have the Jews done to be treated like that?'

'I don't know, but the Nazis hate them so. My father says they were once accused of killing Jesus. But Pontius Pilate was a Roman, wasn't he? It's all so complicated.'

'It's too awful, isn't it?'

A handful of Jewish girls attended the school, though Zara had not come to know them well; they came into assemblies at the end, along with the Catholics, for the notices. Zara wondered if they knew, and if, like the lecturer may have done, they had relatives in places the Germans had occupied.

Lauren heard similar exchanges among the older girls at the Cambridge and County. They brought snippets of news picked up the previous evening: the remarks of their parents, the chronicles of returning soldiers, conversation among fellows at the university. One expressed relief that, with Germany set to be defeated, the local evacuees would be safe from them.

She said to Rey one evening, while Zara was at tea with Hilary, 'Are the evacuees here… Jewish? I've heard such horrible things at school.'

'I think many of them are, Lauren. But it's not been part of their life up here.'

'We were evacuees, too, don't forget.' Malcolm looked up from the newspaper he was engrossed in, his ruffled hair and glasses hinting at a life more academic than that of the Cambridge bank clerk he had become. 'But let's hope we can stay now.'

Lauren took this in, but found herself starting to add, 'I was wondering, is Zara…?'

'Why do you ask, dear?'

'I don't know. It's something one of the girls at school said. We had a newspaper in the library, and it was about… I just wondered.' Lauren was reluctant to repeat that one of her friends had thought Zara 'looked' Jewish. She was unsure what that had meant, but it sounded less than complimentary. But if Zara were Jewish, wouldn't she be? And yet her parents went to church on occasions.

Rey looked at Malcolm, who closed his eyes and

nodded. Lauren would understand what she now had to tell her: of Zaida's journey from the Irongate Stairs to Stamford Hill, of the unlikely union of Zara's parents, and the supposition that Zara was Jewish, by virtue of her mother's conversion.

'Being Jewish… is a religion?'

'Yes, dear. They believe in most of the Bible, but not the New Testament.'

'So how can you look Jewish? A girl at school said somebody did.'

'I don't know, dear. But generations ago they came from a different part of the world. If you think about the evacuee children, many of them have darker complexions or perhaps curlier hair, don't they? And they do have a certain look about them: it's nothing to be ashamed of, but it's a bit distinctive.'

'Why do the Nazis want to kill them?'

'You only have to look at what the Nazis have done,' said her father. 'How they invaded country after country so we'd no choice but to go to war with them.'

Lauren took a moment to think. 'But what do they have, in particular, against the Jews? It doesn't make sense.'

'It doesn't,' he said, 'but throughout history the Jews have been picked on. This country's been better than most: we've had a Jewish prime minister, though he had to convert to be accepted. They have a habit of sticking together, living in the same areas. Solly and his brother Alex, they get on with everyone, their father, too, in his own mischievous way. But they often keep themselves to themselves.'

Lauren looked intently at her father, her cheeks suddenly cold, a taste of acid trickling up from her throat. She wanted to know, though.

'I think people are envious of them. They work hard, like your mother says, and they make something of themselves. Many of them are poor, but the money they do have they don't drink away in the tavern. They may dress in an old-fashioned way: you've seen the long coats in Stoke Newington?'

Lauren had a recollection of that.

'Remember how good the Keffs have been to us.' Malcolm was conscious of his good fortune: he had earned a small promotion at the bank.

Rey added, 'When Mops fell for Solly, they sort of adopted our family. Our father had died by that time, and we hadn't all settled yet.'

'Does Za know?'

'She's been away from home for four years. At nine years old she was too young to know about these things. They don't keep a Jewish house if you take my meaning.'

'But Za hears everything that's said at school, and she feels so sorry for the Jewish people. Do you think we should talk to her?'

'We have to leave that to Sol and Mops. I'm not sure what they plan to do when the war's over. But up here in Cambridgeshire, there's no need for Zara to know. She fits in so well. And she feels such responsibility for the evacuees.'

'But if she asks...'

'...then we'll sit down and speak about everything.

But Mops is clear. She's not religious, and she sees this… this picking on people as… silliness. That's the word she uses. She's done well in her marriage, and it's helped us all, but she wants to bring up her children free of religion – of any religion. It was easy for her to convert; she did so for love, not faith.'

'I think that's about right,' Malcolm said. 'We must leave it to Mops and Solly.'

They heard the front door close, and Zara burst in, full of the tea table. She dropped her satchel in the hallway and exploded into life.

'Hilary's father says the end of the war's in sight. He says the Germans are retreating on all fronts, that it's only a matter of time.'

'He's right,' said Malcolm, 'but I'm afraid they'll keep us till next year at least. There's fighting to be done yet.'

'Oh, for life to return to normal after these five long years,' said Zara.

'Rather,' said Lauren, though the word carried little of its customary emphasis.

'A hot drink before bed, dears?' Rey offered. She turned on the gas and made busy with the saucepan.

Chapter 13

The chestnuts gave up their gold and bled red to the roadways; cold, incessant rain submerged the potato crop; the church clock stood by while the rooks battled wind in the evenings. Frost danced with the sunshine at the crispest of Yuletides, until the snowdrops and crocuses flowered once more, and the hedgerows began to spring back to life. Then winter lashed out again, an angry flail sent to chide the beguiled, before the twisted branches above sported yellow and white, and were dyed pink by the work of the bees.

Victory drew nearer with each passing day; rumours abounded of a date that had actually been set. At morning break, amid this optimism, a group from the lower fourth at the Cambridge and County were engrossed in the previous day's newspaper, the *Daily Mirror* of 20th April 1945. The secondary piece, below its thin wartime masthead, recounted Heinrich Himmler's attempt to bolster the resistance of his crack troops while the Allies marched on Hamburg. A half-page photograph illustrated the lead story: humanity at its most desperate, emaciated, exposed and half alive, passive, haunted, incredulous at the point of rescue. The girls read of the sixty thousand found perished or diseased at this place, of those destined, even now, not to survive, their 'only crime' having been to be Jewish. An advertisement for Fry's Cocoa supplied contrast with the lives of the paper's readers, even in wartime.

When they turned the paper over, though they could not have bargained for it, a yet more horrifying scene met their eyes: the pit of Belsen, piled high with protruding ribcages, the rag and bone of laconic limbs interlocked above sunken trunks that breath had abandoned; in all, a mass grave paying fitting tribute to the 'German triumph' given expression by the words of the *Mirror's* sardonic headline.

'They must all have been gassed,' said one of the girls.

There was a crack in Zara's voice; at the second attempt she asked, 'How can you tell?'

'Our neighbour, the don...' started Hilary.

'But how does he know?' asked another.

'Messages were smuggled out somehow; people occasionally escaped; he's certain the government knew. He said that Jews were forced into... ghettos, he calls them, where they'd become thinner and thinner, and they'd have to march to a railway station, however weak they were, with only their spindly legs to carry them – no help, not even from each other. It was desperate: they'd be shot if they couldn't stand up. They were taken by train to one of the camps; they were told they were going to work, but it was a place to gas them.'

They were silenced by the story, these wartime girls, used to their privations, the air raid sirens, the exertion of total war and the loss of fighting men, now starting to comprehend the force their country had been combating. They held the work of the devil in their hands that morning. Nothing had prepared them for it.

Tears had begun to fall onto Zara's cheeks.

'They must just hate the Jews,' said one of the girls, somewhere on her own transition from the gradual onset of shock to a more obvious distress.

'It's time for class, ladies, and you know what I say about gathering on the corridor.' Miss Field had all but passed the group when she caught a glimpse of the newspaper. There was a measure of steel in her eyes, and she beckoned them to her office.

'I read that yesterday,' she said. 'You're thirteen or fourteen years of age. I wouldn't expect you to see such pictures normally. But as the paper says, it makes no apology for publishing them, and you must find the capacity to take them in. Girls, there's been manifest evil at the heart of this war.'

Zara looked at Miss Field, despondently. 'But why have they done this?'

'Gassing people?' was the incredulous remark of another.

'I don't think this was a place where they gassed people, from what I have read. But I believe that did happen elsewhere.'

'Is that why we had to carry the masks?'

'They were for the kind of bombs the Germans might drop, but it's all part of the machine we've been up against.'

Miss Field had never talked to them like this. She was a formal figure, seen most often from the floor of the school hall. They strove to extract as much as they could from the conversation.

'But why?' repeated Zara.

'Some things are hard to explain,' said Hilary.

'That is true,' said Miss Field. 'A friend and I holidayed in Germany one summer, oh, twenty years ago. It was a place of such culture. Art, new fashion, music, Richard Strauss, great silent films. It was at the centre of civilisation.'

'So why did…?' The voice of one of the girls trailed away.

'The Germans were sold a story by Hitler. He said they'd been hard done to after the last war. For some reason he blamed the Jews for that. But the other countries' leaders weren't Jewish: it was a prejudice he had. The Germans can't have had any idea he could do this sort of thing.' She paused to assure herself of that. 'Do you remember when I talked to you, in assembly on your first day?'

Zara wiped her eyes with her handkerchief. 'You said our time was coming.' She had heard the words first from Lauren.

'I did, Zara. The one good thing about these pictures is that they demonstrate that the war's nearly over. That's how the newspaper could acquire the photographs, and the troops bring hope to the survivors. Read on, and you'll learn that German radio has called for an end to resistance. They're preparing for defeat. Girls, you must grasp this chance to build the world of the future, one that will stop wars like this from occurring.'

Zara brought to mind Mr Garver's talk, more than four years earlier. A connection was beginning to dawn on her when a knock at the door intervened.

'That'll be my scholarship group. But let me say before you go, ladies: never doubt your capabilities. You too have university to look forward to if you're ambitious. You've seen how many women are at Cambridge now? Yes, that's in part to do with the war, but there'll be room for you when it's over.'

For an instant, Zara touched the good that might come from this wickedness.

* * *

'That was a serious natter your bunch were having with Miss Field this morning,' Lauren said on the bus home. 'She doesn't often keep us waiting.'

Zara could bring back every detail of the exchange, but found she could not explain events in quite the way that her headmistress had done.

'Why would they do such things? Miss Field said that when she went to Germany, the people came over as so... cultured, you know, so interested in art and music and everything.'

Lauren knew that if she answered Zara's question, her cousin might one day ask how much more she had known at this juncture. To claim that she'd been ignorant would add to the lie of omission she was forced to endure for now. What her mother and father had said did make sense, though. It was for Zara's parents to talk to her: she had to remember that.

'You should have seen those photographs, Lori. There was a girl staring straight at the camera, dazed, forlorn, yet somehow with the barest glimmer of hope. She could have been one of us.'

Lauren held her breath.

'They piled body upon body into this huge open grave. How on earth will their families find out about them? And yet there were thousands still alive. Would they all have died if the Allies hadn't come? Miss Field said the Germans didn't gas people there, but would they have forced them into marching, with their starving bodies hardly able to walk…?' She was powerless, deep in the seat, looking to the countryside beyond for hope or salvation. Lauren could not provide it; she was sinking herself, as the bus clattered home to their adopted village.

Opening the bottom drawer of her chest, Zara sifted through the items she had kept from her time at the village school. There was a letter from Mr Garver thanking her for the salvage operation that had won the wireless. There was her last arithmetic book, not her main strength, but, in its carefully ruled columns, a source of pride, nonetheless. Then there were the writing books, with her short stories, descriptive pieces and grammar exercises. And in one of these was the Century of Zara Keff. She turned to the page. She had produced it four and a half years ago, when but a month shy of ten. She read it, proud of it still, deflated as she was by the course that history had taken. She had written that children might become kinder to each other and could see that was the remark of a younger girl, but, even so, it had happened in the village, hadn't it? They had collected the paper together, they had put on plays, there had been no repeat of the words that Mr Garver believed had brought so much trouble to the world. And then a thought, which had begun to insinuate itself before Miss Field was interrupted by the fast-stream, struck her directly. Had those words been said to Jewish children? Is that what her Century was to be for? Was that her task for the future? Was that the opportunity Miss Field was speaking of: to make the world safer – for those people, of all people? She saw how distant lay the hope that those words would no longer be used: that must come sooner. Yet she *had* seen children being kinder to each other, and the way they handed their clothes down, the swapping of fruit and sugar for jam, the various collections for the war effort, were cause for optimism, surely. Together, they brought her a moment of light – before the power of the photographs, past forgetting, simply overwhelmed her.

Chapter 14

The signs of light were clear to Zara and Lauren as they ambled around the village during the final weeks of the war. The evacuees, Joy and Maureen among them, were trickling back to Stoke Newington and its neighbouring boroughs. Italian prisoners of war, billeted on a farm, marched by under guard, welcomed, bringing trinkets they had sculpted from scrap metal. The noticeboard at the Village Institute advertised a dance, concerts and a whist drive, all to raise money for a homecoming fund. Bananas arrived in the local shop. The barren wastelands of the longest winter humanity had faced were succeeded by the ghosts of golden daffodils that greeted the girls as they chattered.

They circulated the loop as they often did, freelancing along footpaths by and by.

Zara said, 'Auntie Rey thinks the evacuees have taught the village so much.'

'They've learned about the children of England; that's what Daddy said. He's counting on us staying here after the war.'

'Oh, I expect we shall,' replied Zara. 'And I have so

many friends at the County. But do you know something? I still can't stop thinking about…'

'I know, Za.'

The Century had made an angel of Zara Keff and clipped her wings as she learned to fly. It was unforgiving but applied that unforgiveness, too, to those through whom it had brought catastrophe. It set destruction upon them and left them vanquished: wrung, worn and slaughtered behind the scorched earth. With phials of poison plucked from underground hideaways, it cheated the victors of some and saved others to face the new forms of justice being crafted in Cranmer Road.

* * *

'I've had a bit of a fall, dear,' Mops said to Zara. 'I'll be right as rain before long. Thank goodness for Alex – all that lovely space in the rear.'

Alex Keff had driven up for VE day, with Mops and Sol in the back. He'd sold his share in the family business, the taxi acquired with the proceeds now freed from its commission as a wartime ambulance. The sight this Hackney carriage made as it sped to Church Lane on a sun-drenched late-spring day was a wonder to behold, a marker itself of the changing of the times. Mops stayed in the car for the final stretch, while Sol, the Imlachs, the Coes and the Keff sisters strolled to the village green. A huge pyre awaited them, primed to burn long into the evening, to celebrate the end of the blackout and to stand as a handy spit for scores of jacket potatoes; striped bunting hung in irregular shapes; the entire village had made its way there. Alex helped Mops out of the cab and passed her a walking stick.

'Well, you've a fine daughter here, Mr and Mrs Keff, so you have.' Farmer Chardler strode toward them and took their hands, while Zara proudly made the introductions. 'I met her on the first day she was here, and it's been wonderful to see her flourish. Are you still following the football team, my dear?'

Her parents looked at her enquiringly.

Zara gave an outing to the terminology she had picked up. 'It's been rather off and on recently – they've not mustered eleven for the past few matches – they'd been third with a game in hand, with a chance of winning the league.'

'No wonder they could cut their shirts up for the bunting,' said Farmer Chardler, before turning to ask Sol how long they were planning to stay.

'Oh, just the one day,' he replied. 'We're busy readapting the business, and Alex can't afford to lose too many fares.'

'We heard the weather forecast this morning,' Mops offered.

'The first for, oh, for how many years, Mrs Keff?' Farmers, like the rest of the population, had been thrown back on their own invention for fear of broadcasting vital intelligence.

'Yes, what a treat that was,' Mops replied. 'Seventy-five degrees. We jolly well had to come. And it's always nice to see the girls.'

'Oh, they're doing so well,' he said, acknowledging Daphne, too, as he took the group in. She was in her final year at the nearby school, a little shy still, with a single fine-stranded ponytail, and every prospect at Impington to come.

'They certainly are,' boomed the voice of Mrs Barnett, overhearing as she and Mrs Lambert approached. 'Miss Keff here has given as much to the home front as any one of us in the village – and rather more than many.'

Zara demurred, giving a light shake of the head, but Mrs Barnett was having none of it. 'My friend here will tell you: young Zara took on the salvage collection and turned it into one of our great successes.'

Mrs Lambert responded with a firm nod. 'And you, Rey, as my own friend will testify, have been a first-class evacuee warden,' she said, adding with characteristic bluntness, 'despite being an evacuee of sorts yourself.'

Looking first at Malcolm and then at Lauren, Rey replied, 'Once perhaps, but we're pretty settled now. The town will have work for my husband after the war, you can be sure of that.' Sol and Mops exchanged a glance.

'You've definitely earned your place in our village,' Mrs Barnett began to continue, before their attention was diverted by a sudden buzz of excitement.

A posse of boys, whom Zara knew from her time at the local school, were dragging a huge Guy Fawkes-style effigy roped to their hands. They began by turn to push it and haul it towards the top of the pyre. The gathering cheered once they recognised it.

'You may think you've taken your life in the bunker,

Adolf, but tonight you'll be burned in every village and town in this country,' said Farmer Chardler, his geniality supplying contrast to the message, to the general approval of the group.

On next to The George where, heady in the crowd, beers in hand, they joined millions up and down the country, and strained to hear the prime minister emit from a loudspeaker standing high in the courtyard. 'Unconditional surrender' gave way to 'land, sea and air forces', 'today is Victory in Europe Day' to the reminder that Japan yet remained to be defeated. Rousing applause put them in the mood for the evening, when Zara helped Mr Garver reel up Laurel and Hardy shorts for the children, while the WI hosted a dance for their parents.

They all came out for the bonfire. For Zara, the stuffed pelt on the pyre stood for all that she and her friends had read about.

'I can't imagine him human, Lori,' she said. 'I don't care for this.'

Lauren put an arm around Zara and allowed her to rest her head. Puss and Gus stared into the distance, the burning of this replica tyrant no consolation for the loss of their son. Their thoughts were on the German-Dutch border, their belief that he had gone without pain, their consolation the airgraphs from Lance-Corporal Davison which adorned the mantelpiece. Malcolm and Rey were full of the future: the war had made them in a small way, transporting them from a once anonymous life in a sprawling metropolis to become figures of stature in their new world; each put an arm around one of the

Coes, optimistic about the days to come. Mrs Barnett and Mrs Lambert were dignified in celebration, their confident Englishness in no need of reassertion, having carried them through the darkest of ages to the light.

The bonfire was alight now, wood and straw, every flammable material to hand, doused in spirit put by for Molotov cocktails no longer to be kept in reserve. Its crackles rose to the height of the church spire, its Hitler and huge swastika ablaze, burning away the pain of the past six years, for those who could entertain that, as the village danced around the pyre. Zara pushed the *Mirror* pictures to the back of her head; children like these, here at the bonfire, she thought, would never encounter an outrage to match those.

* * *

Abraham Kevlov and his wife Roza had walked in line on the march to Radegast station, among the last of the two hundred thousand Jews to leave the city. Abraham knew enough not to believe the postcards bringing news of the safe arrival of previous deportees at the city they'd been informed was to be their destination. He'd heard tell of a ghetto inhabitant who'd met a Polish carpenter: he had worked at Auschwitz, he'd told him, and they're gassing the Jews. Chaim Rumkowski had spared no effort to suppress the news; now, escorted by motor car, he was driven past the holding area and assigned with his family to mount a slender gangplank. In the crowd a voice rang out as he boarded, 'Give up your selfish interests.' On a par with his people, one barred vent in a truck for dozens, he was in line to share their fate. The great grandparents of Zara Keff, in the oldest of old age, stood hunched in the midland heat of the Polish summer, indistinguishable from the hundreds kettled in with them, borne by the Century to this antechamber of the apocalypse.

The short-lived Litzmannstadt was shunted out, and Łódź returned, a city without Jews now, bargained away, Russian again. The victors shared the spoils and brought reoccupation to a place where those who had despised the Jews might see a twisted version of something they had not even dared to envisage.

In the village, VE-day yielded to the summer; by the end of the novel she was reading so voraciously by the landing window, Zara could not help but concur that the letters M and A spelled perfection. She wandered the country lanes alone, while her cousin was cramming. The tennis ball had disintegrated; she had handed her gas mask in. She was fourteen years old.

Chapter 15

Zara Keff had been to The George and the pyre; she had helped to conduct the celebrations; she was at one with the village as it looked to victory in the Far East. Now fourteen, she had begun to understand the significance of the year's events, over and above the fact that the war was ending. They had not learned further of the details at school: Miss Field's assemblies focussed more on the bravery of the soldiers and pilots, the enemy two dimensional rather than some entity that existed with its own characteristics, for vilification or otherwise. As Zara walked the corridors of the Cambridge and County and looked up to the sixth-formers striving for tomorrow, she knew that by following in their footsteps she might grasp the Century of her bold imagination.

The summer term came to an end, and Miss Field stood to address her pupils, saying this was the final assembly she would give at the school. Muted conversation broke out, but she quietened the girls, reminding them of the forthcoming changes to the education system: the Cambridge and County would become a grammar school, with every place provided free of charge by the council, as part of the new tripartite system. She had therefore chosen this moment to take up a new position. She was moving to the town where Joseph Priestley had first isolated oxygen, she told them, and she hoped the academic atmosphere at the school would be similarly rarefied. She concluded:

'During the period I have been at the Cambridge and County there have been two world wars. We did not imagine that there could be another to rival the first, but the second has exceeded it and introduced new forms of barbarism. The Japanese will go the same way as Germany, but they'll defend to the last, and it may take months. Your generation must build a new world, one that will never again produce such a war. Education is the path to power and prominence that women must be prepared to take.'

'She's been at the County since a few years after it opened,' said Lauren, as she and Zara took the air, straight off the bus that midsummer's afternoon. A faint rustle blew through the trees and the breeze sliced an edge off the heat.

'I know she can be a bit of an old stick, but she has so much wisdom. And that joke about Priestley...'

'That time she talked to us...' Zara checked herself. 'I do hope Miss Battensby's going to be as strong.'

They speculated on the future as they walked, Lauren full of her Oxford candidacy, electing a life away from home for the duration of her degree at least, Zara uncertain that she was up to university herself but eager to learn how you went about it. They arrived home, giddy on their prospects, to find that Zara's parents were paying a visit. She had not seen them in the weeks since the war in Europe ended, and she ran to each of them in turn. She had so much to say – about school, about Miss Field, about Lauren's entrance examination – that she practically forgot to ask them how they were.

Mops changed the mood with a momentary closing of her eyes. 'It's time to come home, dear.'

The firmness of the phrase, though it had been quietly said, was in such discord with the previous hours – the final day of term, the assembly, the have-a-good-summers, the elation of the walk with her cousin – that Zara failed at first to take it in. She noticed Rey beckon Lauren to the hallway.

'I'm sorry, what did you say, Mummy?'

'Zara, your father has to wind things up here.'

'We're to leave the village?'

'Zara, dear...'

'But it's our home now. I'm so happy here, so happy at school: I've so many friends there, I'm so involved in the village...'

She listened to her mother: they lived in London; they'd taken the houses for the duration; Sol must now invest in the business. Of course she was to return, she realised.

It occurred to her. 'But what about Lori? She has a year to go, and she'll have her exam and everything.'

'I know, dear,' Mops replied. 'Rey, your Uncle Mal and Lauren are going to stay on. They're going to move permanently from London.'

'But...' Could she not stay herself, she wanted to ask.

'Life 'as to get back to normal, Zuzzi,' her father said. 'We're not country folk.'

'But if Lori can stay...' It was lost, and she sought the will to feel hopeful – of seeing Zaida again – but could not command her spirit such as to find it.

She ran upstairs to her room, her wartime billet, and turned to see Lauren standing behind her, as she'd once stood before, in her uniform, a waymark on a footpath she could follow.

'I can't believe that you're not going to be here, Za.'

'Nor can I, Lori. Only this afternoon, we were talking of...' She saw her aunt come up the stairs.

'Your parents are leaving now. They'll be back the day after next.'

'You mean Za has just one more day here?'

'She does, dear. Zara, your father's done so much for us. I can't criticise his decision.' She brought the girls toward her. 'We'll miss you so much.'

'Za, this will not be the end of us,' Lauren said, after Rey had left them to it. 'These five years count for all time. We'll be friends for the rest of our lives.'

'I hope so, Lori. I've followed your every step. I've read your books and borrowed your notes. I'm even wearing your old school clothes. We'll stay in touch, won't we?'

'We must. Cambridge to London isn't far, you know.'

'I shan't even be able to say goodbye to my friends.'

* * *

The ending of her village life was to be as sudden as the beginning had been, Zara thought as she went to bed that evening. She could picture Stoke Newington, but her fond memories were here, in this place, where she had completed her elementary studies under Mr Garver and to which she had clanked back from the Cambridge and County every school day for three years.

Now, on her penultimate morning, she set off to roam with Lauren, as they had five years before. They turned right along Church Lane, as they did then, thoughtful now, no excited chatter, no thrill of the new, no anticipation of tomorrow beyond the dull certainty of its imminence. They turned to look at each other, every now and then, these cousins given life by such different unions, their breathing uneven, as their cheeks absorbed the slow irregular tears of their disappointment.

They reached Duck End and, mid-morning as it was, hoped to find Farmer Chardler tucking into the early lunch he was in the habit of taking at this time of year. He saw them first and, seeing them hesitate at the front of his cottage, made for the door to greet them.

'This is Zara's last day with us, Farmer Chardler.'

'My last full day, anyway,' Zara clarified, echoing her first conversation with the man who'd done so much to ease her into her new surroundings. She had come across him but a dozen times or so each year, busy as he was with the schedule the farming calendar demanded. He was always pleased to see her. Even when returning from The George with a couple of farming pals in tow, he'd have a 'Good afternoon, Miss Keff' up his sleeve, which he would deploy to the benefit of her sense of standing, his tenderness, compassion and wisdom all wrapped up in his baggy country clothes.

'So, you've finally had enough of us, Miss Keff,' he said.

She looked at the greenery around Duck End. 'One could never have enough of this, Farmer Chardler. Besides, I've grown up here.'

'And so you have, Zara Keff. I remember the first day you came by, so breathless in your excitement you were. And you've spent the entire duration with us. We've all grown up these past five years, you know, even old buffers like me.'

The girls laughed, grateful for the chance to, and Farmer Chardler became in that moment, as people do when you're leaving a place, a manifestation of the life Zara would lose.

'You won't forget us, Zara, will you?' He had the humanity to have her reassure him.

'Wartime can make strangers of people, Zara, but that didn't happen here. We even found a fan for the football team, didn't we?' Zara laughed again, gaining respite from the tightness she felt. 'Things will change again now: no gas masks, no air raid shelters; people say even the government may change.' The polls had closed, but the count awaited the gathering of the armed forces' ballots.

'And as for you, Zara, you'll have your old life back, shortly enough. Now, what are you looking forward to?'

She lit up. 'To seeing my grandfather.' She threw her arms around him.

'Go on now, Zara, before you start me off.' His farm-battered palm cupped the crown of her head and glided over locks held loosely now by a crimson ribbon. He brought his hands gently to her shoulders and stood back from her. 'You make sure to write now.'

They walked on, Lauren and Zara, by the horse chestnut in all its summer glory, down to the lane where they had seen the bow and arrow shoot. Then on past the Women's Institute with its array of notices, by the old school from which Mr Garver would surely be retiring soon, and along by the church. Each had vowed to write to the other, yet they sensed an alliance forged amid total war must now change in some way unforetold.

* * *

Zara lay the last of her books in the suitcase and letters to her friends on the chest. She had conjured her Century in the village, and, for all the peaks and troughs, had begun to fashion it. Now, she could not but wonder whether the dreams she had harboured, for her own life at least, were to be left behind, here, in a place where memory might falter, allowing those once embraced to recede.

Chapter 16

Zara was slumped in the back of the old Austin, which Sol had replenished with a tank of extra fuel he had bartered, now that a ration of sorts had been restored to civilians. As they slipped from the village, and picked up towards Cambridge, she craned forward to catch the great colleges that had fired her yearning, Hilary's house on Cranmer Road a short way beyond, the world of her war years receding into the distance. She knew one could live elsewhere and still attend the university – after all, Lauren was heading to Oxford – but in this moving away she read a portent of a time to come, reinforcing the dull ache inside her, as they steered through the peace the Century had brought to England.

The villages of Cambridgeshire gave way to Hertfordshire and the suburban sprawl of Middlesex. They drove through Ware, Broxbourne and Hoddesdon, their streets bereft of repair, populated by grubby boys astride oft-mended bikes, all a-swagger with their trousers and sleeves rolled up, sisters playing mum with pushchairs, hitching lifts on each other's tricycles, and shopkeepers still rationing wares according to rule but advertising bargains, nonetheless. Onward through north London with its bomb-ravaged streets and ersatz recreation grounds, where scrawny wartime children searched for crumbs of comfort; to the density of Tottenham where crowds made their way home from a warm-up game for the Football League South, and Hassidic Jews ploughed a hang-dog furrow, snug teams yoked in the heat of this urban safety; and to Stoke Newington itself where they pulled up outside the mid-terrace that Zara had left five years earlier. It had taken little more than two hours to bring her back to her pre-war world.

Zara was numbed by the arrival, the foreboding that had gone with the journey replaced by a feeling that time had been rewound, back to the day she and her sister had stepped onto the bus at the town hall, and had stood still for the duration, that the young woman she had found herself becoming over the past five years was but a wartime substitute for the girl from Bouverie Road who had kept herself to herself and was happiest in the arms of her grandfather.

The house was not dissimilar to the one in Church Lane: it had two fine reception rooms, a substantial front bedroom, along with a further room and a box to the back. Zara had the larger of the rear-facing pair, the first sight of which nudged an uplift in her spirits – her clothes could be kept in one place here – and Sol showed her with pride the whitewood desk he had made for her schoolwork: a tear slid down her cheek when she saw it. She announced that she was going to the library to renew her membership and discovered, among old favourites, *The Swish of the Curtain*, a tale of American children and the derelict church where they produced plays, overcoming the many obstacles placed in their way. It reminded her of one of her triumphs and part plied her optimism with flickering reignition.

Over the next few days, the life Zara had led as a nine-year-old brushed against her teenage self and demanded recognition. She accompanied Mops to the shops, the daily round taking them past the dancing school, still far-famed, to the high street for Slatter's fishmonger and poulterer, or to the far end of Church Street for McCree's butchers, calling all the while at the awned fronts of the baker, grocer and greengrocer as required. Cohen's, closer to the bottom of Bouverie Road, was the final calling point, for cigarettes for her parents and, on Saturdays, chocolate for the girls.

How much more she knew now than then – the rose and the crown made complete sense – and how much more there was still to know. Zara was intrigued to learn from the librarian that Daniel Defoe had written *Robinson Crusoe* when domiciled on Church Street. She read the adaptation over and over, imagining her window looked out over palm trees. Her parents had a telephone installed and she rushed to answer it with the sharp-spoken clarity of 'Clissold 627'. There was school to be arranged, too, a glowing report from the Cambridge and County aiding her admission to the Skinners' Company's School for Girls for the start of the autumn term. The ghost of a boy's voice whispered beside her, taunting her with a distant memory.

* * *

Zara used to scamper to pick up the mail in Church Lane, eager to check for a letter from Mops or from one of her aunts. Here, a few of her friends had written already, and one morning, when she heard the flap of the box, she darted towards it only to see that a folded newspaper had dropped onto the doormat. Zara had no recollection of any previous delivery of this kind; curious, she picked it up and opened it out. In her hand, its title spanning the full width of the broadsheet, its ascenders and capitals straining to outgrow the shrugged shoulders of their lower-case companions, staring out at her, was the masthead of the *Jewish Chronicle*.

Zara paused, her mind blank. She took the paper through to the kitchen, and, after looking down at the linoleum, she lifted her eyes, her mouth part open, hands half risen, formulating the silent, puzzled beginnings of a question.

'Oh yes, dear,' said Mops, 'Your father reads that – or pretends to. He must have forgotten to pick it up from Cohen's.'

'But why?' Zara replied, the question that followed representing terminal, demi-conscious hope. 'Is it because of the war?'

And then, from her mother's look, part distant, part present, imploring her in some undefined way, it began to dawn on her.

When she looked back on this moment later, Zara recalled how many snapshots of scenes from her young life had streaked before her: the studied reactions of the girls at school when she expressed revulsion at the photographs in the *Daily Mirror*; Lauren's taciturn response on the bus home that day; the boy from St Mary's who had teased her at school or on the street. There was the time she'd wondered whether the words Mr Garver said had caused so much trouble in the world were related to the evacuees, and had they been Jewish, and had everything been about that? And there was Hilary's hesitation; she had said, 'It's tough to say this, Zara...' before repeating what her neighbour knew of events in occupied Europe.

The short conversation she had with her mother was to come back to her in fits and starts. They had been waiting for the right time; the Imlachs were Christians in a general sort of a way, and she was part of their family for the duration; during the war, these differences were not important. They were themselves Jewish by her father's background and, though they never wanted to let Zaida down, they didn't keep a Jewish house and went to all the usual shops and so forth. They wanted to raise her with the freedom to choose; 'All this religion is frankly nonsense in my opinion, my dear, anyway.'

Zara had struggled to form the questions that occupied her part of the exchange: her interjections had been half formed, her dazed queries submerged in a fug of puzzlement and a sense that she had somehow been betrayed. Church Street was sixty miles from Church Lane, but they were worlds apart. She heaved herself upstairs and stood bent by the window, her chin on the sill, looking out toward Abney Park. What other secrets will you spill, she wondered, of the sylvan array in the distance. She lay on the bed, and took in the desk her father had made; the third drawer on the left contained the cahier in which she had cast her Century. She made half a move to retrieve it, but sheer burden of thought pushed her head to the pillow. She saw the front page of the *Daily Mirror* and heard the outraged voices of the girls at school; the masthead of the *Chronicle* flashed before her, repeatedly. She brought back the image of that Belsen pit and the heartbreak she had felt for those sunken-eyed survivors. Was she herself now, had she always been, one of those for whom she had felt such devastation and about whom she had demanded: why them? what had they done?

Chapter 17

There was no update on family matters in the letter Zara
Keff wrote to her cousin in August 1945, no remarks
about her new environment, no excitement about her
acceptance at Skinners'. She saw no virtue in describing
her new bedroom, the handmade desk, the bustle of
life on Stoke Newington Church Street or the renewed
routines of daily life. Brief and to the point, it was the
most perfunctory letter she had ever committed to paper.

Zara was insistent that she travel to see Lauren: it was
the first time she had said something of such apparent
importance to her parents with so little equivocation.
She brooked no argument, and they asked no questions.
They provided her with the fare, and one Saturday she
caught the local chugger to Hackney Downs and picked
up the Cambridge connection. She had arranged to meet
Lauren at the station, and they walked up to the town,
dawdling around, settling for small talk, half-admiring
the colleges that Lauren still passed every day. For the
Cambridgeshire autumn term had begun already, and
Miss Battensby, Lauren was proud to say, had made a
strong impression as the County's new headmistress,
speaking of the 'post-war generation' who must rebuild

the country in every respect. Zara ached to live again the energy of the classrooms, the crowded corridors, and the consciousness she had of the opportunities open to her. Lauren carried that conviction with every stride; Zara knew it to be history for herself now, but weeks ago, though, it was.

They stopped by a tea shop and ordered scones from a surly waitress, nibbling at them by a concave window, attracting the interest of a late-summer wasp.

Lauren said, 'Za, do you need to tell me anything?'

They settled up; the wasp followed them onto the street, much to the waitress's amusement, and they flapped it away before turning through St John's to the Cam. Zara composed silent half-formed sentences that failed to open the conversation they had to have. As they drifted along the riverside, the kingfishers, moorhens and swans must have appeared to the involuntary eavesdropper to be the primary objects of their concern.

'Lori,' she began, distracted by a frog amid the reeds nearby.

'Za...' She hesitated, unsure how much to encourage or what to prompt, used as she was to the free-flowing nature of their exchanges. And then Zara began again, and they talked till the sun fell below the college rooftops.

'I jumped up to grab the post the other day, and it wasn't a letter; it was a newspaper called the *Jewish Chronicle*.' The words tumbled out; they sounded strange to her. It was the first time, she realised, that she had used the word 'Jewish' aloud. She had formed it inside her head; she remembered that. She had asked fervent questions about the treatment of the Jews. But this was the first time that longer word had left her lips: it had been an unspoken question mark during the conversation with her mother. It was challenging for her to say, in every sense. To form it in her mind, knowing the word applied to her, was hard; to propel it into speech required particular effort, the fudged consonant leading uneasily to the long vowel, her mouth dry by the time it essayed the trailing sibilant. For that matter, she couldn't recollect having used the word 'chronicle' either.

'Oh, Za.'

'Lori, I...' She recovered: she had to complete it. 'I froze, you know. The very name of the paper. There were those photographs in the *Mirror*: it all came back. And then I thought, but why is that newspaper here? Why was it posted through our letter box? What did it have to do with us? And I took it through to Mummy and...'

'Za?' Her mouth remained open as she looked at her, before dropping her gaze to the towpath.

'And she said...' Her own head followed.

'What did she say, Za?'

'She said.' She paused. 'She said,' and slower now, 'She said that's what we are.'

Lauren held her breath, and they met each other with half an angled eye.

'I had no idea. I thought I was the same as... all the other children.' She looked up. There was a choke in her voice. 'Lori, did you know?'

'Za, I knew...'

'Then why didn't you tell me?'

'I only came to know...'

'When did you know, Lori?' She was agitated; it was urgent for her now.

'You mentioned those photographs, Za – the ones that were the talk of the County?'

Zara lowered her head again and shook it.

'Two or three weeks before that, our regular bunch were reading a paper in the library. There was an article about the events that were happening in Europe. One of the girls asked if you were Jewish.'

'They asked if I was...? Why did they ask that?' Even with the knowledge she now had, Zara could not comprehend it.

'I don't know, Za. They just did. So I asked Mummy and Daddy about it.'

'What did they say?'

Her loyalty uncontested now, Lauren conveyed what her parents had told her.

'Your father's a great man, Za. He helped us all; he brought us to the village. He may have saved our lives.'

'But you knew. Why didn't you tell me? We've always shared everything.'

'Mummy said it was for your parents to tell you, that we shouldn't interfere. Unless you asked.'

'But why would I do that? How on earth could I have known to? Ought I to have woken up one day and said to myself, "Am I one of the people the Germans want to kill?"'

'Za, I...' She stalled. 'Za, if somebody had said something to you, then maybe you would have asked.'

The fog started to clear. In the kitchen with her mother, she'd recalled Hilary's hesitance to burden her with the testimony of the lecturer who lived on her street. Had she known? She was sure now that she had. And who else? Who else had known?

'I didn't know myself until a few months ago. All those years that we've known each other, I thought you were just like us.'

'But I am like you. How am I different? Who else knew? Did Farmer Chardler know? Mr Garver?'

'I don't know, Za. I don't think so. Nobody said anything. Mummy said a good number of the evacuees were Jewish, but one never heard them described so. This was the war: people were sticking together. These things didn't matter.'

'But why should they matter?'

'They shouldn't. I hoped you'd stay with us, and it might never come out.'

'But that sounds...' She rallied again. 'Is it bad? A thing nobody can talk about? I don't understand.'

'I don't either, Za. It's a religion, you know, like being C of E or Catholic or Methodist...'

'So, why...? Why did they do those awful things to them? Is there something about them? Is there something about me?'

'No, Za.' She was firm in that but straddling the border between confirmation of the facts and the devastation of her friend. 'Daddy said the Jews have been picked on throughout history.'

'But so have the Christians. The Romans threw them

to the lions. And there was Elizabeth and the Catholics, the gunpowder plot...'

'It goes back to the time of the Bible, apparently. I don't fully grasp it, Za. I don't regard you as different from me, honestly I don't. Our mothers are sisters; we can't be that different. We're *not* that different. We've been through the war together; we have the same ambitions; we're Miss Field's girls.'

'I'll never be one of Miss Battensby's though, will I?'

Lauren reached into her pocket. She brought out a packet of Kensitas cigarettes, tipped, illustrated by a butler carrying a silver tray.

'I didn't know you smoked, Lori,' Zara said, unsure whether to welcome the distraction.

'It was time to try, you know, over the summer. Most of the senior girls at school do; the undergraduates are bound to. I thought I should get into the habit: it does help to calm you down.' She pushed a cigarette out with her thumb.

'I don't know, Lori.'

'Our parents smoke. They won't mind you trying one.' She lit the cigarette and passed it to Zara. 'You must be careful at first though: the shortest of draws and breathe it out straight away.'

Zara coughed and sputtered, and handed it back.

'You can try two drags next time.' They laughed and began to absorb once more the twisted trees bending over the riverbank and the amphibians that leapt between the reeds.

They telephoned Mops from the wooden call

box at the station – she was delighted, naturally, that Lauren might stay over – and they cast an eye over Stoke Newington the next morning. With every awning they passed, every shop sign they read, each accent they heard, the very shuffles of footsteps around them, with every ragged group of children who scrapped before them on this late-August Sunday, they could feel the displacement, the drawing away, the gnawing disappointment, the small gains and significant losses that supplied the life of Zara Keff in her post-war world. They had walked the Cam, feverishly along the backs, and they walked now, muffled as the trolley buses that glided by, to Clissold Park and back along Church Street, on to the High Road and Manor Road, forming a new but far less compelling circuit. They skirted the deep-lying roots of Abney, protected from intrusion by the backs of terraces, its memories securely stored by an alphabetic code of its own. They had discovered the village loop five years before: the war had forged the bond between them, and the peace was pulling them apart.

Chapter 18

Three days after Zara had accompanied Lauren to Hackney Downs for her cousin to catch the fast train home, came the news that there were to be trials in Nuremberg. At the Cambridge and County, they were the subject of much talk among the upper-fourth girls who knew from Hilary that the don from Cranmer Road stood commissioned to advise the prosecution. A highly-regarded American lawyer had arrived, she said, to plan how to bring the Nazis to justice.

'But how do you know, Hils?' asked one of her classmates.

'Well, one of Mummy's friends' daughters – she's about eight years old – she wandered into his garden – you know that's so easy where we live, and he has this beautiful, manicured lawn – anyway, she wandered in, and her mother saw her from the window and went to fetch her, and this huge American voice asked the little girl's name and said, "Well, young lady, you have walked in on one of the most important conversations of the century. Now, you won't tell anyone, will you?" Honestly, her mother repeated it word for word. Anyway, Mummy met the fellow's wife in Fitzbillies – we all love their cake – and asked her about it; she said, well, she couldn't say too much, but yes, her husband was going to help prosecute the Nazis.'

'Well, that's living in Cambridge for you,' said Hilary's friend. 'You're never far from history.' It was no surprise that confirmation should have come from the most select bakery in town and its queue for the prized Victoria sponge.

The local take on the story reached the sixth form, and Lauren sought Hilary out.

'Oh, I wish I'd known,' she said, when Lauren mentioned that Zara had come up the previous weekend. 'She wrote me the most wonderful letter the day before she moved to London. I replied, but I couldn't match her beautiful writing.'

'I don't think she could have faced people. She's discovered that…'

'…that she's Jewish?'

'Did you know?'

'One of the girls said something once; but it was when she went back, it sort of clicked with me; I don't know why.'

'She's devastated.'

'Oh, Lauren. When those photographs appeared a few months ago…' She paused at the significance of what she was about to say. 'She'll be thinking, "I could have been one of those bodies in the pit". I know she will.'

'It's broken her heart. No, she still has her heart. It's her spirit that's broken. It's more than that: it's being back in London. She loved the village; she loved the

Cambridge and County. She loved you, Hilary; she felt so lucky to have you as a friend.'

* * *

Hilary's next letter lay uncollected on the doormat before Mops rescued it. Zara picked it up absent-mindedly from the kitchen table. Hilary had been as direct as she always was. 'You're still what you were when you were here, Zara, in the place where you really began to grow up. Carry that with you: don't be defined by the worst that has happened to the people you now find you belong to. Remember you belong to Cambridge too, to the village that made you the girl you are, to the school where you made the best friends you have. And don't lose your spirit, Za.' She added what she knew of the role the college don was taking in bringing to book the perpetrators of the enormities they had read about.

Zara joined the upper fourth at Skinners' the next week. The twenty-minute walk took her past West Bank; she looked to the left as she crossed the road and saw the house that Zaida used to live in, the second along the one-sided street that abutted the railway line. It brought back the days when she skipped up the steps and ran to him, and the comfort he used to bring when she talked about the boy who tormented her. The words made no sense to her still, but she understood something of what they betokened now.

The crimes of the Century, impossible to contemplate, were laid bare before the world when the prosecution commenced. A burning topic they were at Skinners', too, where Jewish girls rubbed alongside the daughters of Tottenham. If the aspiration to greatness were not the default position it had been at the Cambridge and County, the girls shared an appreciation of the good fortune they enjoyed in being at the school, their places having been gained through examination or the moderate prosperity the times provided for some. The news from Bavaria gripped them, assailing their sensibilities as the year raced by.

Hilary had written again, late in 1945, after an evening out with her parents. Their neighbour had given a lecture, speaking of crimes against humanity and insisting the Nazis would not be permitted to hide behind the leader they had served. These were new ideas in the law, he said, and he had worked with the chief British prosecutor, though the real complaining party was civilisation itself. The trials were to punish the men who had persecuted the Jews; justice would be done, Hilary assured her, and she must walk tall.

Zara had looked forward, on first moving back to London, to corresponding with Hilary. In the back of the Austin, on that July day, the idea that they might become young women of letters had attenuated the knot building within her as the car sped south. She had imagined they'd write about books, and debate the merits of the new Light Programme, and share thoughts about topics they were taught in history or the French vocabulary they were accumulating, that they might wax about plays and clubs and halfbacks, that she might experience at least vicariously the life of the Cambridge and County in the age it had entered without her. But when the letters came now, though she knew that her friend meant well, Zara baulked at the compartment she felt pressed to occupy, and rather glossed over the remainder.

The newspapers published their reports. Hilary and Lauren at the Cambridge and County, and Zara with the girls at Skinners', learned of the narrative from ghetto to gas chamber, of casual slaughter put on by cunning and forced cause. They read of round-ups, of stations given over to transportation and those erected like film sets to mock the coming of the trucks in which the infernal journey was undertaken; of selection, entrance, undressing, a shuffle forward; of sudden realisation and the hiss of the pellet; of the defiant desperation of the last to draw breath; of death accompanied on occasion by the taunting symphony of a discordant orchestra, on another by the screams of children thrown into furnaces alive when the gas had run out; of the removal of bodies by inmates forced into the privilege of a life retained for the undertaking of such work, each bureaucratically commissioned mass execution succeeded by the extraction of gold, the piling high of spectacles and the mountains of shoes; and down the line, in the manner of a noble native American exhausting every possibility presented by the life-sustaining buffalo, the ignoble, contemptible conversion of human skin into lampshades and the paperweights wrought from the shrunken heads held aloft as trophies.

The reports, and the debates that reverberated

through the schoolyard, left Zara numb with outrage. She had been shocked by Belsen and moved by the haunted stares of the rescued; now she had learned of those from the camps in the east, consigned a fate the more shocking for its scheduled simplicity. The images fused: the cast of survivors on that newspaper front page, their weakened legs unable to carry them, fighting for every last breath until the air was gone. And she said to herself: this was also intended for me.

By the autumn of 1946, when the verdicts were handed down, Lauren was at Lady Margaret Hall, nudged toward the study of law by the stories Hilary had brought from Cranmer Road, her interest piqued with every step the trials took to bring the offenders to justice. Zara stayed on to the fifth, propelled by a residual optimism, encouraged by the ideals of a headmistress who, like Miss Battensby, was bringing Skinners' into the post-war age, one careful step at a time. By contrast with her cousin, though, she felt the nag of something missing, and withdrew at the close of the academic year, armed with a school certificate pass and a hard-won distinction in English.

Chapter 19

Zara spent a year at the local technical college mastering her Pitman and, having achieved sufficient speed and accuracy, emerged into the London of the late 1940s a fully qualified shorthand typist. The ribbon had gone, her hair styled instead like Ingrid Bergman's, and her rouged lips had formed the habit of making symmetrical marks on the filters of her cigarettes. She obtained work at a leading livery company and watched Tottenham Hotspur once a fortnight, burrowing her way to the front of the Park Lane terrace, bolstered by the turns of phrase she had absorbed supporting the village team.

She had finished a game of tennis at Springfield Park one Saturday, with three of the girls from Skinners', when they passed a group of onlookers, one of whom called out, 'I've seen you on the bus,' in an accent Zara reckoned to be from somewhere in the north. He was leaning on a gnarled oak tree, catkins at the ready though yet to leaf, slim, bronzed, in his late twenties, with a pencil moustache. He was half familiar, like a darker, deeper version of a particular Hollywood archetype. She had seen him on the bus, too, when she'd leant across the aisle, as the number 73 took her to work, and asked for a light. He had regretted he didn't partake but smiled when their eyes met for a second time, and she reached work attended by the first darts of disarray. One of the young managers, Martin, had asked her out, and they were going to the cinema that evening; the butterflies had gone by the time they left to see *Passport to Pimlico*. She saw the sullen, early-day version of this handsome man once or twice again. And once or twice again their eyes had met, and she had reached work possessed of the same light flutter.

'I'm Harry,' he added, stepping forward.

She half giggled. 'I'm Zara. Zara Keff.' She had tacked on her surname; she was not sure why she'd done that.

'Shall we walk?'

She looked from her friends to her tennis racket and back again. One was shrugging, another was laughing at the cheek of it and the third had broken into a broad smile as if to say, 'Go on, Zara, you know you want to.'

The late-spring weather, the virtues of racket sports and the glory that was Springfield Park competed for the honour of being assigned to their first clumsy attempts at conversation, but, in common with Farmer Chardler, he had the gift to put her at ease and not to tire of what she was saying. They were soon strolling the footpaths and talking together in such a natural way that Zara found herself thinking that she'd been with Lauren when last she had established rapport in so short a space of time.

'No,' she replied when Harry asked whether she'd always lived around these parts. 'I should say I was born here; I went to St Mary's up the road there until the war became serious.' She went on to tell of the village and the Cambridge and County. 'I missed that place every day for two years.'

'But you went back to school when you came home?'

'Yes, I stayed in Cambridgeshire for the duration, but...' He gave her time. 'I moved back to my parents and went to Skinners'. It's a good school, I know, but it wasn't the same. Every day a bus used to take me past the great colleges in town, and I'd see all those billowing gowns. It's not the same walking along Dunsmure Road.'

'You're more likely to see billowing silk greatcoats there,' said Harry.

They laughed. 'You're...?' It was still a word she found difficult to say.

'Yes, but I gave up the religion many years ago. And you?'

'Likewise, I suppose.'

He chose not to pursue it. 'You were talking about Skinners'?'

'I was, wasn't I?' She looked up at him. He was around six feet tall, she within three or four inches of him. 'It wasn't the same. At the Cambridge and County, one felt... part of tomorrow.' She paused, allowing herself the small satisfaction of having summed up the difference.

He smiled; she was the most well-spoken person he had ever met.

'So once I'd completed my school certificate I went to technical college.' She had no need to confirm the course. 'I work for Goldsmiths now, for the clerk's office. We're a small pool.' She added with a modest smile, 'Very select.'

'So that's what puts you on the number seventy-three?'

'I catch it as far as Tottenham Court Road and hop on the Central Line to St Paul's.'

'I go to the Angel and walk down to Clerkenwell. I work for a wholesaler; we're in cotton thread.'

'That's a distinctive accent you have.'

'I'm a Mancunian.'

'That sounds like you're from an exotic island somewhere.'

'Only Manchester, I'm afraid.'

'So what brought you here?'

She listened to Harry's story. He was born into poverty in the Cheetham Hill area, to the north of Manchester, with an older brother and sister. Too young to join up when the war started, he had been taken on by an aircraft factory. Proud that his brother was serving, he'd tried later to enlist himself, but was turned down on the grounds that, having once had tuberculosis, he was not deemed fit to fight.

'They sent me to Southport when I had that, to convalesce. I've never eaten better.' He contrasted that brief interlude with day-to-day life in a Pemberton Street terrace, with its freezing toilet in the backyard. His parents had little income; his father worked by hawking offcuts around the shops, making a few pennies here and there. He had enjoyed the factory work – it was part of the war effort at least – and had become active in the Amalgamated Engineering Union, he said, pulling out the membership card which still had a place in his wallet.

It carried the photograph of a dark, soft-featured youth whose eyes betrayed a languorous yearning.

Once the conflict was over, he'd been set upon leaving Manchester as soon as he could. He travelled south on the mail train, during the severe winter of 1946–47, squatting in the corridor to save a night's accommodation. The first bed he found was in Bethnal Green, used by a shift worker during the day while he took it at night. He spent as much time as possible, day and night, at one of the Lyons' Corner Houses and undertook casual work in the East End cloth trade until he obtained his current, more permanent job; his new employer had a room to spare at their house on Stamford Hill. That, to cut a long story short, was how he came to be on the number 73 every morning.

'That's quite a tale.'

'So is yours,' replied Harry. 'Evacuation, two grammar schools, working at Goldsmiths. Our lives have certainly been shaped by the war, haven't they?'

'Or by the Century,' said Zara.

'Or by the gusts of time.' His accent made the words sound new.

There was a downbeat way to him, she thought: their conversation had been unforced, he had listened, he had refrained from boasting of myriad achievements. Rather, he was aware of the steps he had taken to make a little of modest beginnings, and rightfully, she thought, he spoke with quiet pride about his journey from Manchester. He had alighted at a Euston station still damaged by a direct hit, cardboard suitcase in hand, hard-saved money in a creased leather wallet, and had walked through the famous portico into a city he had never seen and to a life in which he had no inkling what was to be in store. He was making something of that, bit by bit; he had made friends; they liked to stroll in the park; they ate at civic restaurants, attended the occasional dance, quaffed a bottle of pale. His clothes suited him: his wide-lapelled jacket could have been made to measure, and, pushed back to one side by the hand in his pocket, it revealed twin buttons for his braces and the relaxed pleats of well-tailored trousers, though the material was somewhat substantial for the time of year. He wore a tie, too, even on this casual Saturday. She found him enigmatic but not secretive; the sullenness she thought to have seen on the bus was but a humble, honest melancholy. There was a shyness about him, but he had stepped forward as she passed him, even in front of her friends. She wanted to get to know him, she thought. They had walked from the tennis courts along the Lea towpath, the flaked paint of its dozens of barges hinting at lost glory, different to the Cam, by the pond and past the bandstand, revisiting each as they willed the conversation on, until arriving as if by unspoken agreement at one of the entrances on Spring Hill. Harry walked her as far as the top of West Bank, and, looking at Zaida's old road from this unfamiliar end, Zara said it was fine: she was all right from there. A train hissed and slowed for Stamford Hill station, all but drowning out Harry's parting words. 'Shall we meet next Saturday?' he managed to call after her.

Zara looked back and smiled. 'Let's do that,' she said. 'By the same old oak.'

Chapter 20

Dressed in a buttoned white one-piece, the crisply ironed skirt shorts of which splayed a little wide, Zara examined her reflection, framed by the teak-mounted oblong in the hall, and put the finishing touches to her lipstick.

'Is Martin joining you for tennis today?' her mother asked.

'No, no, Mummy, it's the usual gang,' she replied, spotting a pimple on the end of a nose that she could have sworn had become more angular since the last time she'd checked.

'He's such a nice young man. We did enjoy meeting him last month.' Mops nodded firmly to herself, musing on the role Puss had played in her own life, in all their lives, nurturing the fledgling alliance with Sol.

'I know, Mummy.' He had gone down well, for sure.

Zara reached the Lea side of Springfield Park to find Harry leaning once more against the oak, his black hair Brylcreemed, his moustache newly trimmed, wearing the same jacket and tie but a different shirt, she noticed, one with a faint grey stripe. He offered his arm, and she took it, while the sun warmed them through the sparsest of spring mists. The racket slung across Zara's back prompted talk of sport for a while, the verbal exchanges swinging between them, their groundstrokes extending each other while keeping them both in the game.

'I loved hockey: I played for the County and Skinners'; halfback – a super position – always in the game. Netball, naturally. But guess what my secret love is, though I've never played it?'

Harry was wrapped up in this girl who said 'super' and had played for the County. 'You'll have to tell me, Zara.' His 'have' was shorn gently of the h.

'Call me Za. My best friend – and cousin – does. Go on, take a guess.'

'I'm guessing you're a Compton fan – cricket?'

'You're close: the same number of players. We must go to Lord's sometime. You won't believe it – football!'

Harry looked at her, sideways on, breaking into laughter. 'Tell me more.'

It had started in the village, with a dear old farmer, she said, and then there were the girls at Skinners'.

'They were mad keen. One would bring in the Sunday newspaper, and we'd pore over the results and tables. We supported the Spurs, though we'd never been to watch them. They're up the road here, after all. They finished sixth on goal ratio – it was the first season they played after the war. Once we started earning, a few of us decided to go along. We've been seven or eight times now. We're bound to be promoted. Eddie Baily is quite brilliant. It's great fun.'

'I went to Maine Road as a kid, for City.' The last

ended with something like a French acute. 'My hero was Frank Swift.'

'The goalkeeper with the huge hands! He retired at the end of last season.'

'The older fans passed us boys over their heads to the front, so we could see.'

'We dive under everybody!'

They talked of books and films and theatre. Zara was beavering her way through a three-volume edition of *War and Peace* she'd received for her birthday; Harry had read George Orwell, but thought the left capable of avoiding the mistakes of *Animal Farm*. He was a fan of the Ealing studios: he'd enjoyed *Passport to Pimlico* as much as Zara had. They'd each been taken by *Brief Encounter.* He was old enough to remember the great silent stars; Zara was a fan of Laurel and Hardy, he of the Marx Brothers; they shared an affection for screwball. He talked to her of Preston Sturges and Katharine Hepburn, and likened her to a darker version of Celeste Holm. He'd seen the lights turned back on in the West End, had cheered Bud Flanagan and Peter Glaze in *Knights of Madness*, put sixpence in the slot at the Royal Opera House to magnify *Peter Grimes*, and, like Zara, relaxed to the Third Programme in the evening.

A week later, when they met at the Bohemian on Church Street, Zara pulled out a packet of Kensitas to go with the pot of tea they'd ordered. It was close to home, but the lower half of the window was curtained, and a café renowned for midnight assignations was unlikely to attract her mother's attention.

'Do you mind if I...'

'It's how we first met,' he said with a smile, extending a palm to decline one for himself.

'I only smoke sometimes,' she said, picturing the look in his eyes on the 73. 'I do like to over a cuppa.'

She ventured that she was curious about the array of enthusiasms a boy from an engineering factory had developed: it hinted at a broader education. There's a story there, he said. Pressed, he spoke of winning a scholarship to Manchester Grammar School, and of his father baulking at the cost of the uniform. Harry believed that a way could have been found if his father had had ambition for him. He had gone instead to the municipal school on Waterloo Road where his class teacher, the inappositely named Mr Whipp, had recognised his intelligence and helped him to cultivate a wide range of interests. He'd continued to explore them since leaving school at fourteen, hoping one day to meet somebody with whom they could be shared. Zara saw now, across the table, the vestigial longing with which the boy from Cheetham Hill had stared into the camera as the war raged.

Zara liked Harry – she was not in doubt of that – and in the feeling she had when they were apart, thought she might be falling in love. At the same time she was wary of losing herself to him, even as Springfield became their Central Park and Leicester Square their Broadway; and, though the number of the local cafés with which they were familiar began to multiply, she avoided bringing him home to meet her parents. He was older, twenty-eight, while she was now twenty, although that was not unusual: Martin was twenty-five in any case. He was somehow 'other' than her; he hailed from the north; he *looked* different. People glanced a second time when they passed them; she read disapproval into the frequent admiration of their distinctiveness. She knew that somewhere among the feelings she was trying to distil was that Harry was Jewish.

She was Jewish herself, in a manner of speaking, she understood that, however much she had railed against it. Her mother had made an apparent commitment to the faith in order to marry, but regarded religion with disdain, much though she loved her in-laws. Zara had found consolation in her mother's background, though she was not sure that she ought to have done, and could see marriage as the answer to the conundrum of her Jewish-but-not-Jewish existence. If she married Martin, for the sake of argument, the inheritance of their children would be one quarter Jewish: they would have a non-Jewish name, they might be lighter in appearance. Was she right to be pondering such matters? Was it fair? Was it moral? What would Zaida say? On the other hand, Harry was so secure in his Jewish atheism that she pushed back against the very instinct of which she had become conscious. He'd even make a *sotto voce* remark whenever a huddle of the local *Hasidim* passed by: *frummers* he called them. She was not persuaded that was fair either, but it was reassuring in its own way.

Yet it was clear to Zara, too, that Harry *was* distinctly Jewish, in a way that stopped short of religion or ritual.

He took pride in Jewish film stars, pointing to those who had changed their names from something far less cinematic, in the eyes of the great moguls at least, and in one director of photography who shared exactly his own name. He remained as unembarrassed in his general Jewishness as he did at having a strong opinion against the religion – or a bias against its more fervent adherents.

'Did you enjoy your tea at the Lyons on Saturday?' Mops asked one evening.

'How do you...'

'One of the neighbours, dear. They do like to think they know more about one's family than one does oneself.'

'As a matter of fact, I did.'

'And who was the young man?'

Zara proceeded to field the questions that Mops inevitably had.

'And your colleague from work?'

Zara knew that Martin had the greater prospects, and that Mops envisaged her daughters marrying out as their father had done. A generation on from Isaac, her mother hoped, and the pressure would be less for conversion; those objecting to that approach could be pointed to the maintenance of the maternal line.

'I don't think he's the right one for me, Mummy. He doesn't make me *feel* like...'

'Like what, dear?'

'Like Harry makes me feel.'

'Zara, dear...'

'He's asked me to marry him, and I wish to consider it.' She had said it now, for Harry had indeed proposed, and – with menus capped by post-war rationing to five shillings – he had proposed at the Ritz.

'I think it's high time that we met Harry, dear.'

'Well – of course, Mummy.'

'And I'm sure he'll enjoy the ride in your father's car.'

Chapter 21

'Now, young man, I understand that you've proposed.'

Mops left little room for small talk when Harry called at the house on Bouverie Road for the first time, nor was it long before she insisted that he come to meet Zara's grandfather.

'He makes all of the important decisions around here.'

For Harry, whisked away after he had met Zara's parents for but five minutes, the journey felt rather like the infrequent taxi rides he had taken, with conversation reduced to incidental chatter between the front and rear seats. Sol had grabbed a fedora from the hall stand and pressed it upon Harry. Isaac likes a hat, he'd said, and Harry sat with it between his legs, playing with the knot on the band. Mops, for her part, was half hoping that Harry's lack of obvious prospect would leave Zaida uncertain about bringing him into the family. Yet she had sight of him in the rear-view mirror: he and Zara made a handsome couple, she thought. They had started out on the A10, and there was at first much polite talk about the old journey to Cambridge, and of how much less they saw of Zaida now the girls were grown up, but a strained silence ensued once they had turned through the Tottenham Marshes, before, having skirted Chingford, they pulled up by the place still known to them as Zaida's Epping Forest home.

The house was a veritable villa, double-fronted, a balcony to the first floor, with ivy crawling up the walls. From the hallway, where a fat moggy sat curled like a turban on top of the grandfather clock, Mops directed Sol and Harry to the study and ushered Zara through to the vast main room. Zaida held court by the bay window, at the old walnut table, one arm in a crepe bandage, supported by a grey-white sling, with a large Scotch in his free hand. Five or six house guests were present, members of an extended family who had fallen on hard times after the war, stooped, downtrodden types in the main, creased more extensively than the red leather Chesterfields which accommodated them.

Zara made straight for him, so much older than when she ran to him at West Bank, the first signs of frailty outcompeted by his enthusiasm at seeing her. He put the tumbler down and held her at the length of his good arm.

'You're a sight for sore eyes, Zuzzi.' He raised the bandaged wrist. 'I've been in big trouble this week.'

'Trouble, Zaida?'

'My daughter-in-law – Yetta – she's a bit of a *kochleffel*, you know, always in my business – you'd think I hadn't worked it all out by now – she tells me off for too much gardening. She says a *mensch* of my age should go slow. But time is not my enemy, Zuzzi. And what am I to do? Are the apples to pick themselves?'

'You were reaching up too high?'

'Mm… probably yes, probably no.' He grimaced at Mops. 'To be honest, Zuzzi, I was actually halfway up in the tree.'

'Oh, Zaida!' She threatened to hug him for so long that he was compelled to ask, 'Am I meeting anybody else today?'

'Forgive me, Zaida,' she replied and, after receiving a nod from Mops, brought Harry through from the study.

'Zaida, this is…'

'Harry,' said Isaac. 'Come in, *boychik*.'

Harry held the fedora close to his head that he might doff it. 'Mr Keff.'

'Zaida,' said Isaac. 'I am Zaida – to everybody who comes to this house. Remember that. Now – a whisky, young man?'

He eased himself up and poured a double from a cut-glass decanter. 'Tell me about yourself. And please do put that hat down: there's plenty of space.'

Mops and Zara withdrew; the cat leapt from the clock to the varnished zigzags of the hall and, watching them enter the study, onto Zara's lap, all in a continuous movement. Sol had disappeared within the house; Isaac signalled to his companions, who took themselves to the far end of the room.

Zara heard snatches of conversation between the purring. There was talk of walking from Poland, of Manchester, of Yiddish, even Shakespeare. She thought about Zaida, seeing him in her mind with greater clarity than she had when she was younger. She had begun to understand that it was possible somehow to 'look' your religion. She comprehended the cynical gesture of the boy from her junior school; she discerned the stereotype, but saw gentleness in that long white beard and kindness in the waltzing eyes.

Harry came out and asked for Sol, and one of Isaac's guests motioned to Zara to go back in. There'd been no chance to ask how it had gone.

'Your cat's gorgeous, Zaida. How long have you had her?'

'Oh, for a few months now. I wanted some intelligent company. She comes along when I head for the woods.' He raised his eyebrows. 'I get told off for that too.'

He looked directly at her. 'Zuzzi,' he said. 'It is time I talked to you of Łódź.'

'Of Woodge, Zaida?' She and her grandfather were alone now.

'Of Woodge. Though you don't exactly spell it like it sounds.' He decided the slash and the accents could wait for another day. 'Make yourself comfortable, *sheyne meydel*.'

Making a mental note to add that to her glossary of Zaida-isms, Zara picked up a cushion and sat by his feet.

'Zuzzi, I'm going to take you back fifty years to the place that's now Poland. Back then it was the Russian Empire. I came from a city called Łódź where my father had a smelly shop. A delicatessen to you and me. It was a city of Poles, of Germans – and Jews. We didn't get on so badly. But the Czar of all the Russias – such a big title for a small-minded man – thought his people might rise against him. He kept them down and turned them on each other.' He directed a thumb over his shoulder. 'I still bear the marks from the back of a Cossack sword. This Czar – *Nikolai* – allowed pogroms to take place. He pretended not to know, but we all knew what he wanted.'

'Pogroms, Zaida?'

'Zuzzi.' He held his head steady to prepare her. 'They are campaigns of violence against Jews.' She lowered her head. 'Harry tells me you don't like much to talk about that sort of thing.'

'It's not that, it's…'

'Tell me, Zuzzi.'

She kept her head down. 'I just didn't know.'

'Your mother, your aunts, they wanted to protect you, with all those terrible things going on. It was for the best.'

'I know, Zaida.'

'My father said to leave, to try and make good over here. I walked a long, long way, began a new life. I found this place to live on Bacon Street: that's a name for a street full of Jews, yes?'

She laughed and met his eye. 'I think that may have been Francis Bacon, Zaida.'

'Mm. Francis Bacon, Zuzzi. I can hear him sizzling. Once I was settled, my Estera came to join me, and she brought your father and your Uncle Alex. We lived in the East End for a long time, had a large family together. What a place it was. Everybody selling bagels. "T'ree a penny! Seven for tuppence, bagels!" Always they argued. *"Schreckliche frau!"* they shouted. We spoke Yiddish – it's a bit like German, a little bit Hebrew. We had a flicks on

Brick Lane – all the silent movies, Richard Dix, Douglas Fairbanks. Your father and Alex would go to Klatekin's sweet shop on Grey Eagle Street – what names! – for a haporth or two. Your grandmother made huge pancakes – *zaidalach* we called them. The whole place was a hotchpotch of life like it was in Poland before they turned against us. They were hard times, but they were good times.'

Zara distilled what she could from the rough and ready picture: the snapshots of everyday life with their odd foodstuffs and the sounds of women hurling insults.

'Your young man: his name is Landsman?' She nodded.

'I knew a Landsman in Łódź. Always he was wanting to organise against the government. Perhaps he was braver than me. He stayed, like my father. I expect the worst happened to him.'

'What do you mean, Zaida?'

'You know what happened to the Jews?'

'I know about Belsen. I know about the trials.'

'They forced every Jew into this ghetto, around the time you left to live in the village. I never heard from my father again, nor from my brothers, my sisters.'

'Oh, Zaida. But didn't they try to escape?'

'I have asked the same question, *sheyne meydel*. But it's not easy to escape who you are. Their only way out of the ghetto was not to be Jewish – or to fool the guards. You can't separate yourself from your shadow, Zuzzi.

'So tell me, Zuzzala. You want to marry this *boychik*?' He hammed up the Yiddish for her, with a sense of playfulness.

'Harry? I think so.'

'You are hesitating?'

'Zaida, I… I wouldn't want my children to be…'

'To be Jewish? There are many ways you can be Jewish, Zuzzi. Look at your mother. If you bring them up to do good, they'll be Jewish, whatever they call themselves. I am from Łódź, nothing can change that. Yes, I'm from Brick Lane too, and Stamford Hill come to think of it. You're a bit Łódź as well, but only a little. But your children: Łódź will be a long, long way from them – until you sit them down one day and talk to them like I have talked to you. Then they will be a tiny bit Łódź too.'

He took her arms in his hands and her eyes in with his own. 'I like your young man, and, if you choose to marry him, we shall help you on your way.'

She embraced him, aching for a moment to feel part of his world, and gently stroked his injured arm before she turned to go.

'Zuzzi.' She looked back to see him take in the room with its sculpted architraves, carved wooden furniture and satin-curtained windows. He gave her a wink. 'Woodge to Woodford. That's not so bad, is it?'

Chapter 22

Zara heard a familiar voice, after Mops had answered the door surprisingly late on a Friday, and rushed down the stairs in her dressing gown.

'Lori – what brings you? It must be more than a year.'

'Give her time to catch her breath, darling – and do take the suitcase: she must be worn out. Now – cocoa, dear?'

The flight from Warsaw had touched down too late to make it home, she said, draping her coat over the banister and following Zara into the lounge. So, after the train from Croydon, she'd made her way to Liverpool Street and, well, on to here, hoping for a couch for the night.

'Rather, Lori! We can spare one of those.'

Lauren had spent three years at Lady Margaret Hall, coming away with a second in law, a fashionable, short hairstyle, several pairs of tailored trousers, an adventurous glint in the eye, and a penchant for romance, tempered only by the absolute rule that *la grossesse* was to be avoided at all lengths. She had joined the British Council and been assigned the task of liaising between Polish and British scholars, the more challenging with the election of a communist administration shortly after the reopening of the Warsaw office.

Zara was due to see Harry for lunch the next day, and Lauren required no persuading of the terrific idea it would be for them all to meet. They sauntered down to the Bohemian, all sideways looks and half-whispered avowals, and bagged a table by the window, none the worse, they shrugged, for an overnight tea stain. They gave the menu a cursory appraisal, insisting that a pot for three would be fine to be going on with, before Harry turned up with a bunch of asters and a huge smile. Zara's you'll-never-guess-who found him right first time; he had heard so much about Lauren.

'Likewise, Harry. I hear that you're a Mancunian...'

'Aye, am that, lass.' He had worked long enough in the factory to build up a store of the dialect. They laughed.

'...and that you'd like to marry my cousin.'

Zara kicked her under the table. 'Harry, Lauren's flown in from Warsaw.'

'Now, there's a place I'd like to go. What have you been up to?' There was the faintest tremor in his voice: he had dared to hope this might be the occasion she answered him, but the presence of another granted a stay of execution at least.

'Academic exchanges. There's one I'm particularly pleased about.'

'Oh, do tell,' said Zara.

'His name's Lucasz. We're seeing each other. He's proposed and I've accepted.' She glanced at her hand. 'I don't have a ring yet.'

No sooner had Lauren issued that pithy biography of their relationship, than Zara was rising to embrace her. Harry stood too, aware that the currency his approbation carried was curbed by the fact that he had known her for less than ten minutes.

'He lectures in history, and that's a big deal in Poland, take my word for it. He worked for the underground university during the war; he took his doctorate in those unimaginable circumstances. He's a bit older, Za.'

'You do realise we all have Poland in common.'

It was obvious, but Zara had not made the connection until Harry spoke.

'Your Zaida walked from Łódź, he was telling me. My father did the same. These journeys...' He was shaking his head.

'The three of us,' said Lauren. 'Only history can explain it.'

Only the Century can explain it, thought Zara, as they made to go, after an omelette each and a second pot of tea. She arranged to see Harry the following week and dawdled home with Lauren. They joined Mops in the kitchen, and Lauren said more about Lucasz: he had studied under Manteuffel, a Polish historian who, with no shortage of courage, had kept his department at Warsaw University functioning for the entirety of the conflict.

'Rey must be so proud of you, dear.'

'Oh, she is. I've not done too badly for the daughter of a Tottenham girl, she says. She doesn't know I'm engaged, though. I'm here to tell Mummy and Pops, and to sneak a look at the exhibition.'

'I don't know whether Zara's engaged yet,' Mops added. 'She has more than one suitor, you know.' Lauren saw her cousin redden.

'Mummy, I...'

'Did you know, dear, she's met a fine young man at work? He'd provide rather a good living for her.'

Her voice rose sharply. 'Mummy, if I want to marry Harry, I shall.' She stood and made for the hall. 'Zaida gave me his blessing.'

They heard the front door slam. Lauren looked at Mops and received a nod, catching up with Zara at the bottom of Bouverie Road.

The bit between her teeth, she strode on, weaving between the shoppers on Church Street like an inside forward bent on goal. They had reached the gateway to Clissold Park by the time she slowed. They looked at each other and occupied a bench. Zara produced her Kensitas and pushed a couple upward, offering the first to Lauren. They had been here before, walking the loop, trailing around Stoke Newington; the bench would do.

'Lori, she married for love herself.'

'Za.' Lauren held out the palms of her hands. 'Then why don't you put her out of her misery? She believes the door's still open, you can see that.'

'To tell the truth, I haven't said yes to Harry yet. Martin's a good man, though I'm pretty sure he's not the one for me. But, Harry, I... I don't know, Lori.'

'Zara Keff! I've seen the two of you together. Once, I admit, but what a once! You thrill each other; you make each other sparkle; anybody could see that. Come on, imagine us married – to these exotic chaps. What a foursome we'd make!'

'That's the trouble, Lori.'

'What is? Za?'

'It's such an irony. Martin's the *type* of man I should marry. But I want to marry for love too. Mummy did, and her marriage to Pops brought her a new life. I want the same, but *this*...' She looked around her, gesturing at the park in general. 'This here is the life I want to be taken from. With Harry – this place, this history – it'll always be mine. I must escape it.'

'I don't quite grasp it, Za. Escape what?'

She looked ahead. 'Back in the village, I was like you. Our family – the family we had there – was like every other one. But here...'

'Za, what are you saying?'

'I don't know, Lori.'

'Are you saying... you want to escape from being Jewish?'

Zara spotted some acorns that had fallen close to the bench and began to shake her head.

'You are, aren't you? Za, your parents don't even... I mean, to go into your house you wouldn't know. And Mops is even urging you to marry out.'

'But every wedding – or funeral – on Pop's side, there they all are, with their, you know, with their caps and their strange words.' She gave an exaggerated shrug of the shoulders. 'And with their *schm* this and their *schm* that, and all their assumptions about how one's to live one's life.'

'But Harry...'

'I know. Harry doesn't believe in all that. Neither does Mummy. I don't even know whether Pops does, for that matter – I think he just keeps it all in his pocket in case of emergencies. But it's still there, Lori. It's so much easier for you. Your Polish guy: Rey will adore that. I do love Harry, but I'm not sure that I can.'

'Zara.' Lauren rose from the bench and turned to face her. 'Listen to yourself.'

Zara slumped back. 'What do you mean by that?'

'Think about everything you've ever said – about the camps and the trials – what you felt for those people – and you're telling me you can't marry a guy because he's Jewish?'

'What are you saying?'

'Zara...'

She stood herself. 'Are you saying I'm just like them?'

'Those are your words, Zara. What do you think they'd have wanted for you and Harry? I've been in Poland for a year. I've seen what they did to the place.'

Three brothers ran past them, chasing each other with their *koppels* on, the youngest losing heart and tumbling onto the grass. 'Only as far as the end of the path, boys,' their mother called out.

'It's time I was going. It's a pity I can't take news of a second marriage back to Cambridgeshire.'

Lauren headed for the street, while Zara followed, a couple of steps behind.

'It's all right for you, Lori.'

'What is?'

'You knew about me. I had to find out for myself.'

'But that was ages ago. You've nabbed a real looker, Za, and a great guy to boot, from what I've seen.'

They traipsed wordlessly to Bouverie Road and collected the suitcase. She'd walk her to the train, Zara said, if she could bear her to. Lauren shrugged and they maundered down Manor Road to Stoke Newington station.

'Za, do you remember – soon after you came to the village?' The approaching engine whistled as it heaved clear of East and West Bank on the short ply from Stamford Hill. 'You must have been nine or ten, and I was in my first year at the County. Mr Garver set you that piece about the future.'

Zara looked at her cousin, blankly.

'Don't let your Century be the monster that comes back to bite you. It's throwing everything at you, Za, but you have to push back. Imagine what you and Harry could do, how you'd bring up your children. Think of the world you'd create for them. You wouldn't involve them in all that stuff. Mops would understand; like you said, she kept it all away when you were young. She'd square Sol.'

Zara left Lauren to make the hop to Hackney Downs and drifted on to Springfield Park. She felt there the certainties that she always did about Harry, the longing and the admiration both strong as the old oak, but also the aching ambivalence, the apprehension that if she married him, her life would come to be defined by that which a few years earlier had been the object of annihilation and pity. Love for him was impossible to combine with escape from that condition. Back at home, she pulled the Century from its drawer. It had fashioned her, she saw, rather than she it; that much was plain. Her tears, gentle at first, consumed her, but somehow, through the dim-lit filter of memory – the wireless, that village Christmas, dear, dear Farmer Chardler – she strained to find a residue of hope. A trace did survive, though, for she beat back an impulse and couldn't bear to rip the page from the book.

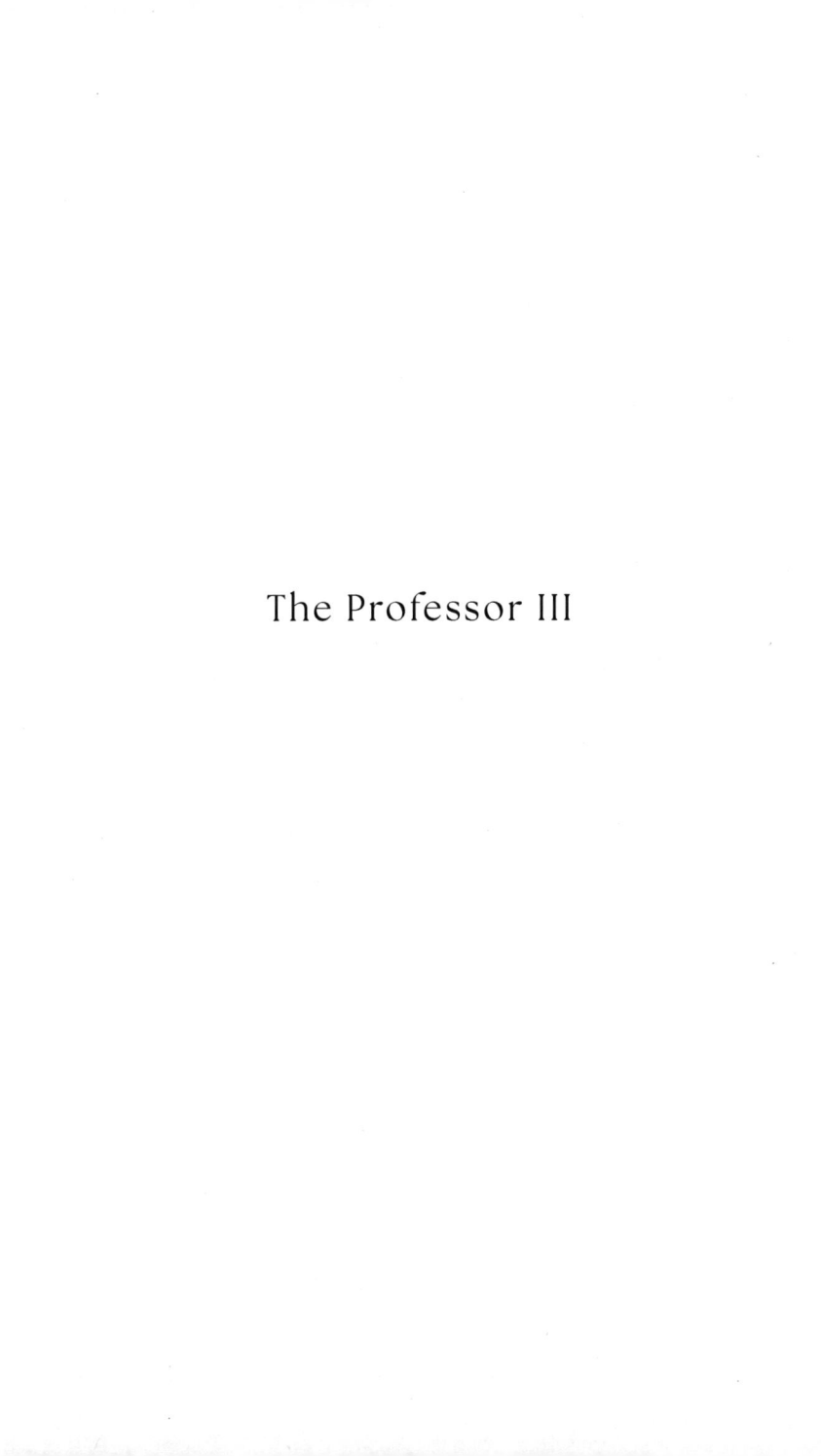

The Professor III

Camden, 1999

The lecture had passed the mid-point; he had talked of war and revolution, of economic collapse and war again, of displacement and genocide, more than sufficient, in his view, to justify William Golding's remark that they lived in 'the most violent century in human history'. He dwelt for a while, for balance, on Art Deco, the avant-garde and the fireside chat, and steered towards an unsettled peace.

'The Century brought the United Nations, a divided Germany and a new state to the heart of the Middle East. It bore midnight's children with their restless abandon. It ended armed combat, among the great powers at any rate, but fomented that which had the potential for it, a curtain descending to demarcate for its audience the several acts of a Cold War. The protagonists brewed conflict by proxy, their passive fury outstripping the old ordnance as they raced to make new weapons of mass destruction.'

It had been the time of his greatest disappointment. He had stuck to his guns after the war and imagined now that a thick manila file, stored on some dusty shelf, had mitigated against the promotion he'd merited. Still, at least nobody threw you out for your views. Would his audience appreciate the disillusion occasioned by fifty-six, and again by sixty-eight, he wondered, when all but the most disciplined were forced to moderate their support for the cause? Or understand why, despite that, he'd stayed in the Party? It was different for those who became communist in the Berlin of the 1930s, he would say. Then you were a Nazi or a communist or you were nothing. And if you don't think you're part of world history during that sort of time, then you never will. Something for later, perhaps.

'We enter the lifetime of your parents now, they for whom the worst is indeed history, not lived experience, they who missed the active fury, and were born to peace, or born of catastrophe, according to the way you see it, the generation who didn't look back, in every sense of the phrase. A Hanoverian émigré did, though, and produced a comprehensive compendium within six years. If, as Arendt contends, you're forced to be a man in the street and a Jew at home, and that's replicated across lands, there'll be a reckoning in time: it's simply a matter of when.'

The headteacher sat up at this. She'd been proud, for so long, of what she'd been in the street, abashed, in equal share, at what she'd been at home. There'd been a reckoning, it was true; there was no doubt about that. She'd barely had time to garner such thoughts when she discerned a change in the professor's tone.

'Yet now the Century lost its fire, exhausted by the whirlwind it had stirred. It permitted the decline of its latter-day Salem, denunciation of the man of steel, and a decision by nine to strike at segregation. It taught a lesson to one prime minister, who had skulked in the wings, but the next could speak of times all-surpassing. The wind of change blew through a carved-up continent, and a community forged on coal and steel began its long journey towards unification. A band led by brothers scuttled down from the hills and brought the slow-burnt rhetoric of the speech in the square. It was taking a breather, the Century now, sixty, dressed in beige, its forty-odd years in charge taking their toll.'

The professor paused, momentarily transported to the day he'd dropped into the Five Spot, on his way to give a lecture at Stamford, and had encountered the shape of jazz to come. He toyed with the notion of a digression. 'Beige?' he said, weighing it up. 'Beige, yes, but tinted with a kind of blue. Now you won't get me started on that, will you?'

Chronicles

1952–1995

Zara recognises that, as far as events in her own life are concerned, her timeline imagines no milestones to come. She adds a wedding day to the shaft of the arrow and predicts the births of a baby son and daughter. *I may become a teacher myself one day,* she speculates on the facing page, *or marry and bring up my children never to use the wrong kind of words.* My children: they will have their own dreams. Of course they will. Zara considers the flights of fancy she and Lauren had indulged in the previous Thursday. *Perhaps they will become scientists and make great discoveries. They might fly around the globe or soar to the moon and the stars.* Zara holds her pencil against her lower lip, stopping to wonder whether that's rather a tall order, as her aunt would say. She feels the faint breeze of her headmaster, spectacles dangling as he walks by, sees him glancing at his pocket watch, and adds next to 1950, *Mr Garver retires.*

Chapter 23

Zara made her entrance to the Village Institute as unobtrusively, dressed in a slim white gown, as she could, having been a bridesmaid along at the church. Harry was deep in conversation with Lucasz, and Zara saw that each was animated by the other. They'd been talking about Poland, she thought, probably about Łódź, certainly about history, for Harry would be fascinated by all that he knew, by everything he could learn of the great historian he had worked for, his interest piqued by intellect, seldom betraying disappointment at the course his own schooldays had taken. A fleet of Hackney carriages had parked on Church Lane, the Dodd sisters alighting, resplendent in fur, as their investment, backed by the Keffs, reaped dividends afresh for the next generation.

During the months since she had turned Harry down, Zara had beaten out a rhythm for her life that might with justification have been described as routine. She attacked her tasks with efficiency, made regular visits to the library and gave every encouragement to Daphne, now at college herself. She played tennis when the weather permitted and kept up a steady stream of correspondence with her friends. Mops detected a form of resolve she had not previously displayed: a commitment to the everyday, the maintenance of an even keel, an avoidance of discussion about the future. Professional with her male colleagues, she maintained a friendship with Martin but no more, stuck close by her friends at the Skinners' Old Girls' socials, and, when a light was required on the bus, leant across to one of her own. She caught sight of Harry periodically, perhaps downstairs with a paper as she took the steps to the upper saloon, or from the window, throwing an arm out in frustration as they pulled away at the Angel, or when his lean frame was threading its way through the bustle on the other side of the street.

Once he'd plucked up the courage to ask, they talked as they danced, in her case of work, in Harry's of his conversation with the bridegroom. His mentor's bravery had had an ironic precedent, Lucasz had told him, for he'd lost a hand defending Warsaw from the Soviets in 1920. When the number finished, Harry insisted that he missed her. She spun to look at him as she glided back to the table, but, content as she had been to forward Lauren's invitation, there was no encouragement in her rearward glance that they might revert to the former state of affairs.

* * *

Rey looked from the dance floor to her sisters. 'They do go well together, don't they, Mops?'

'They can dance, dear, I'll hand you that.'

'Is there no prospect?'

'I believe there's still a prospect for the young man she met at work.'

'Is that Martin, dear?' Puss asked.

'He has the advantage as far as I'm concerned, but Zara doesn't feel enough for him, she says.'

'Enough's not easy, dear, not when your gaze is directed elsewhere. Could we have steered you from Solly?' Rey looked toward the end of the table where their husbands were enjoying a beer. Sol had half heard, and his smile took Mops straight back to the kitchen at West Bank.

'You two steered me towards Solly. We all agreed on that one.' Mops surveyed the group. 'But Sol was the exception. If Zara were to take Harry, the Hebraic, would it not predominate?'

'The name, dear,' said Puss, 'I think the name's a saver. Two English words. Remember how we thought the original to be Dickensian. And I don't imagine he sees the inside of a synagogue very often. But Zara: has she taken against the match?'

'Not to judge by the manner of the dance,' Rey put in before Mops could answer. 'And he impressed Zaida, you said. There's no barrier there.'

'It may be a good balance,' Puss began to say, before she noticed Harry approach the table. There were beads of perspiration on his brow.

'Mrs Keff, I wonder if you would mind giving Zara this note? I have a train to catch.'

'With pleasure, dear. Do have a good journey home.'

'What a lovely way of speaking,' Puss said to her sisters, and to the world in general, as Harry walked away.

'We have to ask,' Rey was saying, 'what should we have wanted if our mother and father had been with us? Should we have hoped for their approval for Gus, and then for Mal and Sol? You trusted us, Puss.'

'We trusted ourselves. We trust Lauren with her Polish academic, though it'll keep her away and you would love her to have stuck with the law, Rey. I think we must trust Zara. We shouldn't push her, but she must know that we back her, Mops, whatever her decision, that we don't take against, that we're no obstacle. What do you say?'

'What do you think, boys?' Rey asked of the other end of the table.

Their husbands looked at each other, three such different men, lent commonality by their wedding suits and their attachment to the Dodds. Sol, at fifty, in timber since his bar mitzvah, had the pinched cheeks and sallow complexion of a lifetime's hard work and a faultless commitment to cigarettes. Gus appeared the more prosperous, muscular, riding the post-war boom in the business, while Malcolm, steady at the Cambridge bank, was given renewed vim by the company of his brothers-in-law.

'We think,' said Sol, 'that whatever you three are cookin' up – that'll be good with us.'

'Aye,' said Gus, 'when the hurly-burly's done...'

'And the battle's lost and won,' added Malcolm.

'What *are* you gents going on about?' Rey asked.

'Who knows?' said Gus. 'Another beer, boys?'

A waitress came by, plying her tray of nibbles, and they each picked out a cocktail sausage. Gus looked at Sol and laughed.

'Well, we scoffed a few of these on Bacon Street, you know.'

'Mazel Tov!' said Gus, with approximation, as he raised a glass.

'Mr Coe!'

'Understood, dear,' he replied, holding up an index finger and half-cocking his wrist to acknowledge the same. 'Now, where did we get to, chaps?'

* * *

Lucasz had no difficulty understanding that, even at her own wedding, Lauren was somewhat preoccupied with Zara: he had experienced the wrath of the age himself. There had been no question that Zara was to be a bridesmaid. Their conversation in the park had not ended them; they had written back and forth, rather skirting the subject, between London and Warsaw, a pact favouring more dispassionate news. When it came to the bouquet, though, Lauren's aim had been every bit as true as ever it once was with a tennis ball. Now they formed a distinctive pair, dressed in their brilliant white, circumnavigating the village green.

'There was no way through it, Lori.'

'Za, you ache for the life we had here, but those days are gone. They're gone for the village itself. The peace took you away, Za. It took me too, in time, and propelled me to see the world – or a part of it, at least. I shan't forget Tottenham – or the village – they're my roots. But I wanted the wings to fly. My degree, my job, my new husband: they're my wings. Harry can be yours. When he's with you, Za, you fly.'

'But, Lori, you must see it: we'd be rooted where we started.' The tangle of connections played with her mind; doubt defeated her impulsiveness, much though the latter fought back.

Lauren was having none of it. She'd had time to rehearse her arguments since the day of the impromptu visit to Bouverie Road.

'Harry's your escape, Za, or your best prospect of it.'

'But...'

Lauren performed a quarter turn to face her, bringing them to a halt, her wedding gown rippling gently in the breeze. 'He made his own escape, with that midnight journey, not the journey your grandfather made, but a leap in itself: he walked away from those who'd held him back. He's forging a future, slowly as you might expect – he came south with scarcely more than Zaida had when he disembarked at the Tower of London – but look at him, Za: he's a real catch. He does find escape, through his music, films, theatre, politics. He held his own in there. He and Lucasz: their intellects are on the same plane. They appreciate the forces at work, everything each of our countries had to do to get through that thing, that war, the oppression, the slaughter, all of that... stuff. Yes, they're each defined by that to a degree, but they're equipped to escape it.'

'But Lucasz is...' Zara threw her arms out, pleading. She could not bring herself to make a direct comparison, but it was still at the heart of everything.

Lauren kept her voice steady, though the law graduate inside her wanted to ram the point home. 'Lucasz is Polish, yes, and Harry's Jewish, but neither defines himself by the afflictions of the past. They don't wear their history like stigma.'

Zara audibly inhaled.

Lauren took her lightly by the wrists. 'I didn't mean that to sound...'

'I know you didn't, Lori.'

Lauren took one hand away and encouraged her cousin back to the walk.

'Yes, Lucasz is further down that path – you should see him back home, Za, he has such stature – but look at Harry. Ask yourself what you're looking for in life, Za, then see if he's not the answer. In his own way he wants to reshape the world like you do – all right, with modest beginnings. Let's face it, he's reshaped his own life. Look at where he's come from: every step of that has been his own, unaided by his home life, or much schooling, or any obvious source of backing beyond hauling himself up by his own bootstraps.'

She stopped again and placed her hands on Zara's shoulders, almost shaking her in her urgency. 'He *is* an escape, Za. And you said that even Zaida approved. He can march you to that point and take you off any way you want to go. It's not as though your parents expect observance – they don't practise themselves unless Sol's side are looking.

Marry him, Za. Move away a little. If my parents can wear Poland for me, yours can wear the suburbs.'

With that, she left her to ponder; and then, as if by command, the personification of her village past appeared before her. Zara's wartime allies had all been at the wedding: the Imlachs still lived here, after all. Farmer Chardler was the first to stride from the Institute towards the green.

'Did you enjoy the service, Zara Keff? That's a lovely hairdo, by the way. It'll be your turn soon.'

Mesdames Barnett and Lambert were next. 'We'll always remember you, Miss Keff. How are things back in the big city?'

Mr Garver took his turn, stooping now, retired indeed. 'How's your Century coming along? It's your tomorrow, Zara. We still have the wireless, you know.'

Lauren had sent them to tilt the balance, she thought. Or maybe Rey had. Or perhaps it was the Century itself.

'Would you kindly see me home?' Mr Garver asked.

She took his arm, and they walked on by the church and the school.

'That's a fine-looking young man you were dancing with.'

Zara looked at him and smiled.

'I met your father back there. He told me something of his life.'

She felt herself redden.

'To see him with your mother, it makes me so awfully glad we won the war. We fought for more than the ground we stand on.'

She lowered her eyes. 'I know, sir.'

'Jimmy, Zara.'

'I don't know that I can manage that, Mr Garver.' She laughed a little and raised her eyes again – and she felt things open up. 'You mentioned my Century just now.'

'I did. And I remember the day that prompted me to set the task. It must be a dozen years ago, but it could so easily have been yesterday.'

They passed the school, and she looked wistfully through the window of the classroom where she'd written the piece.

'I was ashamed that a child had been taught to say those things: to take great names from the Old Testament and turn them to insults. I had read of Hitler's motivations, even then. There'd have been no war without them.'

The kind of words that had caused so much trouble, she thought.

'Did you know there were two children who'd come to us from Germany?'

'No.' She looked up at him, surprised.

'There was a programme to rescue Jewish children, to find them homes in England – before the war started. Thousands came. We took Frank and Robert; they lived at Haydon's Farm. A scruffy pair, often late to school.'

'Frank and Robert? They were brothers. They volunteered for the paper salvage.'

'They did. They'd been with us for two years by then: you wouldn't have known they were German. You gave them a chance to play their part.'

'And they helped to win us the wireless.'

'Those words, Zara: I couldn't bear it, that they'd heard such things in the village. But I'm proud that we looked after them – alongside you Londoners. And that we gave you the chance to start to make your Century come true.'

He stopped, supported himself and turned to look at her. His eyes glistened, and then his features broke wide, taking longer than once they did to complete their journey to the smile, separating the remaining strands of his moustache as they did so.

'You will make it come true, Zara.'

He took her arm again, and the road bent round to his cottage. They stepped along the front path, uncoupling when he leant for the door.

'Thank you for escorting an old man home.'

'To see you again, Mr Garver – Jimmy – it's been super.'

He smiled again and brushed her cheek with his hand. When she reached the gate he was still there, raising his stick in farewell, and he stayed there, looking after her, as she made her way back round the bend.

* * *

'Harry asked me to give this to you, dear,' Mops said, once Zara had returned to the table.

'Come on, dear,' said Puss. 'Enjoy the party, and go where your spirit takes you.'

Zara was tucking the note into her waistband,

keen to join Lauren and Lucasz, when the band struck up. A young man from the groom's family, blue-eyed and dapper, bowed before her, side-parting straight as an arrow, and asked if she might accompany him. She allowed him to take her hand, and they foxtrotted proficiently, she thought, quite compact and precise, all neat feathers and turn.

Rey looked from the dance floor to her sisters. 'Now, that was rather a genteel approach,' she said.

'Rather like the manner of the dance,' added Puss, with a slight frown, 'wouldn't you say, dear?'

'I'll hand you that, dear,' said Mops. 'I'll certainly hand you that.'

Chapter 24

'We don't have to marry the whole family,' Harry said with a well-judged sigh. 'And you're so fond of Zaida. You wouldn't want to escape him completely.'

She wouldn't – she knew that. Besides which, her aunts, the ones she knew best, were all… They were on her mother's side. And Lauren had been right about Harry; his invitation to meet by the tennis courts, where they had begun, had proved to be irresistible.

'We could move away, perhaps, by one of the stations further down the line. We'd come home to somewhere…' He sought the words; he would rather not say less Jewish: he liked the feel of these north London districts, where you could ease into a cosmopolitan life without going to the synagogue. He settled for a rough and ready economy. 'We'd come home to somewhere less religious.'

'If we were to have children, I shouldn't want…' She searched for one of her mother's constructions. 'I shouldn't want all that nonsense for them.'

'Nor I, love.'

Something crystallised then, and the balance had shifted by the time another week had passed. She was neither pushed nor pulled by anyone except herself now; Mops had been wise enough not to mention again the note she'd passed on from Harry. Maybe this *was* her chance to build a piece of that world she had imagined. She and he were embarked on a similar journey in their different ways, and to marry for such manifest love as her parents had done... His father had walked from the same place as Zaida; there was a serendipity to that. And while Lauren's success had come from the second generation of the Dodds, she and Harry might emulate that with the next – if thought of the next were admissible.

He knelt again, a year from the Ritz, under the same oak tree by which his unadorned accent had proclaimed he'd seen her on the bus. A soft current stirred the leaf fall, and the ring fitted perfectly.

* * *

At Clapton Synagogue, Harry promised to do everything it 'beseemeth a Jewish husband to do' and Zara 'all of the duties incumbent on a Jewish wife'. It had still taken her an eternity to reach the end of the word. They emerged through the central pair of doors, beneath one of three half-moons, Shields of David set in stained glass. Harry was attired in evening suit, bow tie and top hat, the widest of beams on his face, a beam so wide it was saying without question he was the luckiest man in the world. Zara's fluent white was matched with a bouquet of roses, her gown held by Daphne and by one of their young cousins; she wore a contented, expectant smile.

They had chosen their own venue for the reception, and a church hall was filled with those who had brought Zara to the high point of her life: the Dodds, with children and grandchildren in tow, Lauren and Lucasz among them, Skinners' old girls, and Hilary with a small contingent from Cambridge. Mops was discreetly sharing a torn newspaper clipping, picturing her daughter modelling earrings at an exhibition sponsored by her employers. Isaac had Harry's parents by his side, but conversation was slow. A north Manchester terrace earmarked for clearance and the villa in Woodford spoke of contrasting half centuries.

Hilary was saying, 'But why Poland?'

Zara anticipated the reply. 'For adventure, wasn't it, Lori? To see the post-war world.'

'I didn't want to go back to the village – or even to Cambridge itself – after I graduated. I wanted to keep moving – onwards, outwards.'

'To keep escaping?' asked Hilary.

'If you like, yes. Our schooldays were idyllic. Village life, even in wartime – I know it's strange to say – was so peaceful. Oxford was uplifting. I wanted more. Not money or men, particularly. I wanted more of something, though. I knew that. Look at that table over there – our mothers and their sisters, Za. They settled for good marriages, and we both have one of those now. But to be playing a part in things, that's what I wanted, I think. The law can wait.'

'My parents want me to be an accountant,' Hilary offered, with a vague despondency. Mathematics had become her strong suit after all, and she'd graduated from the University of Durham.

'Remember what our headmistress taught us. It's our world now. Be a great woman accountant. There's nothing wrong with that.'

Zara said, 'Hilary, I wish I had the choices you have.'

'But your children, your children will have those choices.'

'They'll be wonderful children if they're yours and Harry's. They'll have brains; they'll be beautiful too.'

'They'll be good-looking in a very, sort of, Jewish way.' Zara surprised herself: the rehearsal must have helped.

'Here's to that,' replied Hilary. 'Now, one you of you girls, come and dance with me.'

Lauren made to take up the offer, but, before joining her, said to Zara, 'So it's Paris now?'

'My first time abroad, Lori. I've only ever known Stoke Newington and Cambridgeshire.'

'It'll take you to the stars, Za. Drink in every minute.' She left for the dance floor, where Harry was indulging Daphne with a turn, to her obvious delight.

Zara kept the cardboard covenant, though it had been executed according to Israel and was not the marriage she recognised; they proceeded next day to the registry and left it all behind. Yet Zaida remained their guiding star, and he was their Marshall Plan, paying the deposit on a chalet-style end terrace in Bush Hill Park. It would not be the first night they had spent under the same roof. After Lauren had reassured Zara that it was definitely wise to check compatibility, they had booked into a Cambridge hotel one weekend as Mr and Mrs Mikardo, a fine splice of opera and socialism, Harry thought. Nevertheless, the day the boy from Cheetham Hill, who had occupied but a Victorian slum and a succession of London digs, swept Zara Landsman over the threshold at 25 Melbourne Way was the proudest of their lives.

They honeymooned first in Dinard, having walked onto the tarmac at Croydon Airport where Zara posed for a photograph in front of the twin-propelled plane they could board by a few steps at the rear. She wore a pale summer suit, contrasting with the matching handbag and gloves she had received from Lauren. There were those in the cabin that day who mistook them for stars of the screen; Harry could always claim, tongue-in-cheek, that he was a cinematographer, naming the films to boot, and carried that all off rather well. They marvelled at the note the stewardess brought round detailing their height and speed, and found it hard to believe they were travelling at one hundred and seventy miles per hour; upon landing they were excited, less accountably, that Zara's suitcase was among those chosen by customs to inspect. They stayed at the Royal, awakening after a rainy evening to a beautiful blue sky and a breeze sufficient to prevent the weather from overpowering them. Zara was pink by the afternoon, and Harry had acquired the first layer of a tan. They loved the small hills the streets made and sat for much of the day on the terrace overlooking the beach. They patronised the casino in the evening, losing their six-shilling limit, and danced and drank Dubonnet at a café, raising their eyebrows that the coffee cost them twice the price of their digestifs.

Then on to Paris and the Hotel Saint-Petersbourg in the heart of the city. Standing on the *terrasse* of the Arc de Triomphe, they were torn between the competing *arrondissements*, Zara silhouetted in Harry's black-and-white portrait, equal to the Eiffel Tower dominating the background. They raced across the Champs-Élysées, boarded a bus and, hanging from the green livery at the rear, headed out to the Bois de Boulogne, where they sat on wiry public seats in the afternoon haze. Next, the view from Notre Dame with its grim-faced gargoyles, frightening grotesques, which had preserved the Gothic monument from an aeon of evil spirits, defying even the occupiers the Century had sent to waste the city. They peeked at the Mona Lisa, and drank in the last light over the Seine from a bench in the Jardin des Tuileries. Meandering through Montmartre, they smiled at carefree children who colonised the lampposts or carried the bread and milk home, and found themselves alone on a grimy back street below the Sacré-Coeur until a solitary businessman in a mac for all seasons passed carrying a battered briefcase. They embraced in an upstairs restaurant like a tableau framed by Sabine Weiss and were serenaded by a jazz band at a café where the intimate booths were smoky as those of the *Rat Mort*. Close by the hotel, they discovered the Café de la Paix with its gilt-edged grandeur. There, Zara conversed a little in French with three Parisian women, whose double-breasted jackets strained to accommodate them, and who inhaled *Gauloises* with all the passion their animated friendship engendered.

'Les trois grandes dames de la France,' Zara said, as the women stood up to leave.

Their smiles were as wide as Harry's had been at the wedding. 'Au revoir, mes jeunes Anglais.'

'They reminded me of your aunts,' Harry said.

'They'd be pleased at that. How fabulous to be enjoying life so.'

They clinked their glasses, and, a bottle of claret demolished, ordered cognac, before taking the wobbliest of strolls around the marbled exterior of the Opéra Garnier.

Chapter 25

When they were first married, and Harry worked in the East End, they met at Liverpool Street every weekday evening, reaching home by a quarter to seven in time for Zara to hear *The Archers*. She cooked, always, striving to emulate the simpler of the recipes her mother prepared, essaying a nicely browned shepherd's pie or a just-burnt bread and butter putting. They brewed hot chocolate or cocoa, before settling down to the Light or the Third Programme and to the *Manchester Guardian* or the *Daily Herald*. Eden provoked incredulity at number 25, Macmillan sighs of impatience. Grimond against Gaitskell ran and ran.

Zara answered a knock one Sunday afternoon to find the Coes standing arm-in-arm on the doorstep, and called out, 'Harry! Look who's here.'

'Gus, Puss, what can I get you?' Harry enquired as their visitors stepped through to the lounge. He made straight for the understocked drinks bureau. 'Or should I say, can I get you a Campari and soda – or a Whitbread pale ale?'

'First things first, I'm afraid,' said Gus. 'May we sit down?'

It was Zaida, he said. He hadn't risen that morning,

and Estera had gone upstairs to wake him. When she didn't come back down, her daughter-in-law Yetta had followed. Estera was resting her head on Isaac's chest, her arms hung loosely around him. He had often been tired of late, after all, and it had been said that he hadn't been up to his usual mischief.

'Oh, Harry,' Zara said, moving across to grasp his hand. She looked at Puss.

'I'm so sorry, dear. We said we'd come to you. Things are in such a rush, and Mops didn't want you to hear by phone. His church, you know, the religion, dear, they require everything to be done within the day.'

'In twenty-four hours, at any rate,' Gus added.

Zara sank to the couch, while Harry poured the drinks mechanistically. The soda siphon effervesced unaccompanied.

'He just didn't wake up?' Zara asked.

Zaida had been very much alive at their wedding reception, essaying conversation with Harry's father, Zara recalled. Surrounded by her school friends, she had paid him less attention than she might. He'd come up to her before she left.

'These are my friends from Cambridge,' she said.

He looked at each of them in turn, with a nod or a smile or a light shake of the head, and said to Hilary, '*A sheynem dank*. Thank you for looking after Zuzzi.'

'*A sheynem dank* to you, Zaida,' Hilary replied, 'for sending me my friend.'

Zaida took Hilary's hand and squeezed it gently, before turning to envelop Zara.

'A little bit Łódź,' Zara had whispered. 'Always a little bit Łódź.'

'Tell Sol we'll be at the cemetery,' Harry said. He wanted to avoid the service at the synagogue, for Zara's sake at least. The vow that the wedding was to be their final religious obligation was so recent: a burial had the virtue of cloaking the faith in practicality.

They phoned their workplaces on Monday morning, before Gus collected them and headed to meet the hearse at the Edmonton cemetery. Zara saw the rips on the right-hand side of the mourners' clothing, and Harry knew enough of the tradition of *Kriah* to be able to explain the grief and anger that it was intended to symbolise.

He hastened to add, 'I would never have let them cut my suit.'

They followed the mourners to Woodford, to the front room of the Epping Forest villa, where the moggy quickly found a place on Yetta's lap. The concern of the household for the cat would have made Zaida grin, they knew, and the swiftness with which it had nuzzled up to a new favourite would have been of no surprise. What had Zaida said? Woodge to Woodford? No, thought Zara, that had not been so bad at all.

If any *mensch* was destined to chuckle away his mortal coil, it was Zaida; their last loyalty to that which they had escaped passed with him, though Zara never lost the *boychik*, the *zaidalach* and the seven-for-tuppence bagels. She had *Zuzzala*, too, for Harry adopted that. Yet their two empty rooms yawned at them as if to ask quite what it was that they were to do with themselves. Such was the glancing blow the Century landed, for though its provocations receded, it would insist on jogging the memory: the staging of a Dutch girl's diary buttressed the doubts Zara had harboured as to whether to bring children to the world, its Pulitzer Prize scant consolation.

'Is that your old schoolwork?' Harry asked, seeing Zara kneeling at the foot of the wardrobe, stashing away an exercise book in a wickerwork basket.

Harry had his own ephemera, in the creased brown suitcase which had carried his few possessions to London, and on occasion he, too, would dash upstairs to fetch an article of interest. There was a letter from the MP Harold Lever, thanking him for aiding his campaign for the Manchester Exchange seat in 1945, the glowing reports from Mr Whipp, his offer from the grammar school and the rejection on medical grounds of his appeal to the RAF. He'd hung on, too, to his Amalgamated Engineering card, and a wire hammer and sickle he'd bashed out at the factory.

'It's from my time at the old village school,' she replied. 'I had such dreams then you'd never believe.'

One warm summer Sunday, they lay, mirror images, in lengthening shadow on the grass of the grand Jacobean mansion that was Forty Hall, each propped up by an elbow. As the last of their egg bridge rolls lay with mustard and cress on a damask picnic cloth, Harry asked what those dreams had been.

Zara pushed herself up to light a Kensitas. 'Do you remember old Mr Garver from Lori's wedding?'

'Your former headmaster? Walked with a bit of a stoop?'

She nodded to buy time for the smoke to emerge from her nose. 'Something happened one day and, rather than tell us off, he had us write about the future we hoped to see for the world. I don't know why, but I've always kept mine.'

'What did you imagine, Za?'

'Oh, you know, things that could never come about.'

'Was there nothing that might have done?'

'They were achievements, dear, you know, which I hoped humanity might make. Along with a few hopes for myself.'

'And what were they, love?'

'There was university, but I chose not to stay on.' Her emphasis acknowledged that had not been an option for him. 'There was marriage,' she added. 'No regrets there. And...'

He lay back, staring at the patchwork of clouds, and repeated with as soft a touch as he could muster, 'And...?'

'And children.'

His tentative approach became stronger. 'Things *are* beginning to change,' he said. 'Mightn't we try?'

'Should we, Harry?'

While Zara read the classics – often gifts, suitably inscribed on the inside cover – alongside everyday fiction from the library, Harry relied on the recommendations of the *Morning Star*, which he picked up once in a while. He had become enamoured of the London fiction of Alexander Baron. He found himself gripped by *From the City, From the Plough*, which offered insight into the life his brother may have led in the army; on Harry's visits north, which he made mainly to keep in touch with his long-suffering mother, he saw a man reduced to a shrunken version of his pre-war self. *With Hope, Farewell* left him incandescent; the protagonist's despondent observation that 'always the word "Jew" sprang up like barbed wire between himself and the world' transfixed him, synthesising in fourteen words that which about his wife had remained elusive for years. Harry's strong Jewishness and convinced atheism were facts for him, and, while he eschewed religion in every sense, he did not seek assimilation. He was every bit as eager to talk of his father's journey from Poland as he was to decry the absurdities of belief as he saw them; bacon and eggs at a Lyons' Corner House was a matter of affordability and enjoyment rather than a statement that he was no longer what his parents were; he saw no need to disguise that. The option of changing his name had never occurred to him; he would remark when asked that he imagined it had once had a *z* and three *n*'s before an immigration clerk recorded something that made sense to English ears. The complications of life, in his view, were no more convoluted than those faced by members of the Church of England who opted not to send their children to Sunday school.

Whereas Harry had the certainty of where he was from and of how he had changed, in equal measure, Zara knew only the uncertainty brought about by the disclosure she had prompted at the age of fourteen when she held out the newspaper she had lifted from the mat. Harry could see that she did yearn for assimilation or for status deeper even than that: total absorption, the eradication of that strand of her existence. He understood that he was the embodiment of the tensions in her life. She had fallen in love with him but did not welcome what he represented to those who met them or passed them by, by dint of the striking looks he had inherited. She shrank from questions about such matters and, when pressed, preferred her mother's formulation that it was all 'silliness', co-opting Harry with an 'isn't it, dear?'. He would readily agree with that contention, though it had not been evoked by denial.

Harry saw that he was a coil in the barbed wire which stood between Zara and the true envisioning of her world, certainly its realisation, though the bond between them was not in doubt. She had chosen him and adored him; he never thought otherwise; yet, when they were together, she was hand in hand with a man she loved whilst shackled to a world she wanted to escape from. The possibility of children posed new questions. They would be nurtured a long way from Jewish life: there were no Jews in Melbourne Way as far as they could tell; it was a quiet, undemonstrative road. But he, Harry, nobody could take him for 'English' in the sense that most meant it; his ready reply that he was Mancunian raised laughter, though the question never ceased to take Zara by surprise, finding her ill-equipped to prevent the disproportionate letters of that newspaper masthead from flashing before her eyes.

Harry was encouraged by the prospect the picnic had held out. Zara had not dismissed the idea of children. It had been her dream, she said, though a dream shaped by a different life. But their children, he said, would be the product of that dream, of their love, of their hopes for the world. And when, the next August, Zara gave birth to a girl they named Jennifer, she could scarcely believe what she had been thinking. This was her destiny: it was not hers to become an accountant or to join the British Council; unencumbered by war, or by the early travails of the peace, she could now take hold of the Century she'd been so daring as to adopt.

* * *

'Harry,' Zara called, as he left the house one Easter Monday. 'Don't forget your packed lunch, dear.' And now a voice called out among thousands.

''arry! 'arry Landsman!'

Harry turned around. Everywhere he looked, from the National to St Martin-in-the-Fields, from the Column to George IV, from fountain to fountain, and from lion to lion, the heart of London beat with the earnestness of post-war England.

''arry, it's Les. It must be ten years.'

He was shorter than Harry; tight black curls and a straggly, all-enveloping beard combined with some heft, a hammer and sickle lapel badge and a mischievous grin to sculpt an easy combination of the revolutionary and the happy-go-lucky.

'Les Gold! Who would've thought it?'

'You still in schmutter, 'arry?'

'Thread?'

'Fred? Schmutter?' He shrugged. 'The one leads to the other. You were down Clerkenwell way, weren't you?'

Harry nodded. 'Until a couple of years ago. I've a shop now. Neville's Do-it-Yourself Limited – Collier Row.'

'You changed your name to Neville, 'arry?'

'No, no. The business had a good name – I kept it.'

'You done well, 'arry. How 'bout this malarkey? What do we want with these weapons, eh? You still Labour?'

'Every time. I'm not a member as such these days, though.'

'Don't tell me, the missus won't have it.'

'How did you guess?'

He tapped his nose. 'Instinct, 'arry. You got a day pass, though.'

'I joined the last leg, marched into the square. You still in the Party?'

'For me sins, 'arry – still red to me bones – but fifty-six was a tester. First, they denounce Stalin, then they invade Hungary 'cause the people got all encouraged by it. Didn't know whether we was coming or going.'

'We needed the USSR in the war, that's for sure.'

'Boy, did we that. Look, do you fancy a pint sometime?'

'I'd love to, Les. But the hours I work… And it's a good way home.'

'Why, where're you livin'?'

'Bush Hill Park.'

'The stop before Enfield. You have gone up in the world. I'm still in Beffnal. Doing all right though. But you know, we're both on the same line. Shouldn't be too hard.'

'My days in the pubs of the East End are behind me, Les, I'm afraid. My Za wouldn't have it.'

Les chuckled. 'You got a Czar, 'arry? I thought Lenin put a stop to all that.'

'My Zara. We're a team these days. A suburban couple – very respectable.'

'I get it. She wants to blend in. That's not so easy for a fine-looking Jewish boy. Explains why you was marching on your own, I guess.'

'Maybe, Les. So, how are things in the old part of town?'

'Same as, 'arry. Good folk. We still get a bit o' trouble though. Mind you, seen them over there?'

Two young demonstrators were snatching leaflets from a faction gathered on the periphery. Harry looked up to see a policeman wielding a truncheon at them.

'White Defence League,' Les explained. 'Good to see they've got protection. Mosley stood again last year, didn't he?'

'The good burghers of Kensington had more sense, I'm pleased to say. What do you reckon? Will Gaitskell disarm when he gets Macmillan out?'

'I dunno. Gaitskell's a multilateralist, I thought.'

Harry took out his lunch and began to unfold the greaseproof paper.

'What you got there, 'arry – smoked roe sandwiches? You still got a bit of the old East End.'

Harry laughed. 'The Mancunian version anyway.' He offered him one.

'You're the candidate all right. Good book that. I wouldn't say no. Look, 'arry, I'm gonna join me mates again. You coming? I won't tell the wife.'

'I'm glad to see you back in one piece, dear,' Zara said, when he came home. 'I looked for you on the news.'

'It was wonderful, Za, even if the bishop did side with the government. Banners everywhere – no trouble at all. Michael Foot's speech – people there from all over the world. I even met a pal from the old East End – I used to catch him when the boss sent me round the workshops. We had the odd beer together.'

'That's nice, dear,' said Zara. 'And did you make sure to eat your sandwiches?'

'I did, love,' he said. 'They went down very well indeed.'

* * *

Now Harry left at 7.30, armed with one of the previous day's papers, a vacuum flask and a carefully packed lunch, and arrived home at 7.30. He had ought to think about setting up on his own, Sol had said. Keff Timber supplied places; he might take on one of those, and they could sort out decent terms. So Harry had leased the do-it-yourself shop close to Romford, two trains and a bus journey away, with him and his father-in-law sole directors. He and Zara bought their first television set and became expert at thumping it to achieve the required degree of vertical hold. On Sundays, Harry might catch the train again and bring back reminders of earlier days from a Stamford Hill delicatessen, hoping the salmon would stretch to next week's sandwiches. Or they might go together to Enfield, where they had discovered Gentleman's Row, and take Jennifer to feed the ducks by the New River, which lay algae-bound and stagnant in that part of town.

One November Friday, as Harry let himself in, Zara rose to greet him and said, 'Jack Kennedy's been shot.'

She had been preparing dinner when the Light Programme's half-hour newsreel made the announcement; together, they heard the BBC's deputy Washington correspondent report the death of the president. They tuned the television to see a globe revolving and watched *Dr Finlay's Casebook* in a state of shock.

'How could that happen, Harry?'

Zara was to acknowledge to Jennifer years later that the impact it'd had on them must be difficult to imagine. Those, though, had been their days untrammelled; the birth of a second daughter, Deborah, and a son, Christopher, had made their family complete. It had been a time to hope for the brightest tomorrow, tested to be sure as Kennedy played chess with Khrushchev, but validated by the honourable draw they brokered. He represented so much; he was barely older than they were, the first president they had seen on their television. His reaction to the march on Washington had left them in no doubt he was a force for good.

It pulled them up in their tracks. The election of Kennedy, the advance of civil rights and the diffusion of the Cuban crisis had been the bright stars which illuminated the world set to receive their children. Now the flip side was reasserted – assassination, prejudice, the nuclear age, presenting Harry and Zara with a new challenge, to moderate and mitigate the ferment into which they were bringing them.

Zara saved the next day's front page and clipped out the leader: he had backed equality, it said, and like Lincoln it had cost him his life.

Chapter 26

Bush Hill Park bestrode the railway, unsung suburbia between Enfield and Edmonton, enfolding the half-hourly disgorge of those not bound for the end of the line, its eponymous greenery a way down toward the town. It had its genteel quarter on one side of the humpback bridge, graced by a Victorian detached or two of great distinction, while, on the other, Harry and Zara's chalet was itself one up from the dwellings on the numbered terraces by the station, which had evaded all attempts by the planners to give them more imaginative names. The shops mirrored each other either side of the bridge: the greengrocers – more likely the 'and sons' by now, bakers with bread produced, white and sliced, on the premises, butchers whose speared carcasses swayed on hooks, and fishmongers displaying grey backs and stripped flesh on counters strewn with ice. One parade reserved a fine family grocer for itself, while the other boasted an establishment which still called itself a café, but which now served up liquorice pipes and jamboree bags to children clutching pennies and thruppenny bits. The juniors walked to the same school from their different directions, as they did to the café, from terraced or detached, via streets of inter-war semis. But then those from the one side were generally selected, and those from the other merely allocated, and they began to make ready for the different paths along which the sifters-that-be would divert their lives.

Zara had left Goldsmiths; she toiled over the housework, polished the red-tiled step, and pushed her pram to the shops, where kindred mothers passed the time of day without consequence. She watched the trains pick up speed – or slow for the station – in the gap between the gable ends on the other side of the way, the same steam-pulled trains which had trundled by Zaida's place before the war. She discovered the new goalkeeper Spurs had brought in from Dundee had taken one of the houses opposite, and spoke to him by his front garden, thrilled to tell him she had seen the team promoted those many years ago. They outgrew their place and swapped its neatness for a run-down detached over the hill; it offered potential it was said, and was on the better side of the district. Here, the children had rooms of their own and could race each other on the lawned and crazy-paved gardens that surrounded the house.

Jennifer had her friend Georgina over during the holidays.

'Twenty Kensitas tipped,' she confirmed, handing the packet to her mother on their return from the newsagents. 'And the change from two florins.'

The children chased past the rose bushes at the front, and by the rockery in the corner, and were jumping to pick unripe apples from the line of trees they called the orchard, which formed the boundary with their neighbours.

'Look how tall we are,' said Jennifer. Her dark-brown hair had something of her grandmother's mop; though, waved rather than curly, it flowed more easily, and the exertion had freed it from its earlier grooming.

'I think eight is the best age you can be,' said Georgina, who had reached that landmark a few days previously. Her wispy hair was tied up in a bun, and a pale complexion played host to the barest traces of perspiration.

A truck groaned to a halt at the front gate.

'Mummy, the coalmen are here!' Jennifer quickly uncovered the aperture in the wall and ran inside to fetch her.

Zara greeted the pair, uniform in leather caps and donkey jackets, their eye sockets visible only because sufficient soot had been rubbed from around them. Jennifer, unintimidated by the apparitions, watched, compelled, as they hauled the black sacks onto their shoulders and emptied them down the shaft, listening for the sound of the avalanche as the fuel cascaded into the repository off the kitchen.

'Can I give them the tips, please, Mummy?' Jennifer asked, before pressing the coins into their huge, blackened hands.

'Daddy, can I put the coal in?' she begged, when her father came home.

'Och, away wi' you, lassie,' Harry said, dipping at random into Dr Finlay, before lifting Jennifer above the bunker's stable door so that she could half fill the shovel.

'Georgina said the coalmen look like...'

There are words, Zara said, sitting her daughter down, which can have the gravest of consequences, and she was never, ever, to use that one again.

'But in the playground, Mummy, they sing 'eeny, meeny, miny, moe...'

Zara coached her to substitute 'beggar', though in years to come she was to think better of that version too.

The children went first to the nursery school at St Stephen's Church, nearby, competing to play in its canvas-flapped Wendy house, then on to the red bricks and slam-top desks of Raglan Infant School. Zara deepened her acquaintance with the local mums and was often to be seen, Lowry-like, chewing the fat with women who were to become lifelong friends. Their husbands, with professional lives in teaching, banking or medicine, became friends of the couple too; these were Harry's sole friends, now that neither his home nor his place of work were to be found in the inner part of the city. His old mate Les had twigged as much in Trafalgar Square.

'Are we going to Five, Park Drive today?' Jennifer asked one Saturday.

Sol had retired; he and Mops had moved outward, too, to a semi-detached in Winchmore Hill, which Sol remarked with a chuckle had been named after a packet of cigarettes. Not that you can buy them in fives anymore, he would add.

The house was full of life when they arrived, Zara's aunts having descended upon Sol and Mops. Widowed,

Puss and Rey bore their status with the forbearance previous loss had lent them; they knocked back the sherry and smoked with abandon.

'Jennifer, dear, come to your Aunt Puss. How's school?'

'She's doing well, aren't you, darling. They streamed them at Christmas, and Jennifer's in the top class. She's the tallest too.'

'I don't like Mrs Bush, though. She's too strict.'

'It shan't do you any harm, dear,' Rey assured her, looking up from her glass. 'Your cousin was in the first stream, and she went to Oxford.'

Lauren had stayed in touch with Zara, by letter from Warsaw, where she and Lucasz were raising a son. Miss Battensby must have succeeded with the post-war generation, she wrote, because the Old Girls' Association had celebrated her CBE in the birthday honours.

Mops pushed a trolley through from the kitchen, trailing her right leg. She wore her middle age well, her cheeks still full, the grey in the mop accompanied yet by some auburn. 'There's plenty of time for all that, dear,' she said, commencing the serving of fruit cake and tea.

They heard the strains of a Cockney '*Alouette*', and Sol came through the front door bearing a confectioner's-size jar of barley sugars.

'Sweeties, anybody?'

'Sol!' The admonition emerged like a fish possessed of a grand 'O'.

Sol wheezed and put the jar down. A heart diagnosis meant he had been instructed with such urgency to 'pack in the fags' that he'd done so overnight. Mops was not entirely convinced by the substitute.

'Zuzzala!' he said and threw his arms out to embrace her.

'Oh, Pops, really!'

Sol turned on the television and was seized by opposing teams caked in mud – in the opinion of the commentator, sorely in need of an early bath.

Jennifer was intrigued by the various nicknames her mother had acquired. Her grandfather's welcome jogged her memory.

'Do you know Mummy has a radio programme just for her,' she said.

'Oh, which one's that, darling?' Rey asked.

'Woman Za, of course.'

Jennifer could not see why they had laughed so much. But it was certainly the way they would have wanted her to say it.

'Received pronunciation coming along nicely, dear,' Puss said to Zara, to the further enjoyment of Mops and Rey. 'Now that's the way to make a match!'

After she had taken the children home, Zara brought the scene to her mind: her aunts from Tottenham, making enormous fuss over Deborah and Christopher too; her valiant mother, forestalling reliance on a stick; her mischievous, chuckling father, the boy from Łódź who'd found love with one Dodd and looked after them all, settling down to watch the Rugby League, East Ender though he was; all of them a-natter in the front room of the semi, high on sherry and cigarettes, or else fruit cake and tea, or perhaps good fortune and barley sugars. And here, Zara watches her own three children, ignorant of a past sequestered away up the line, set off to play on their quiet suburban road.

Chapter 27

In the photograph taken of their family at Sol's and Mops' fortieth wedding anniversary, Harry, distinguished, in his mid-forties, is standing in dinner suit and bow tie to the right. Zara wears a sleeveless, deep-blue, high-necked dress that stops short of the knees, but, accompanied by a pair of thick stockings, is modest, nonetheless. Set off by a purple brooch, matching earrings and a regulation necklace, she stands to the left-hand side of her children, confident in them, relaxed as the picture is framed, secure in what she and Harry have accomplished in the fifteen years of their marriage. Yet, when she unwrapped the photograph, Zara looked closely at the image of her older daughter and saw an unsmiling acquiescence.

* * *

Jennifer had been granted leave by her school to attend the anniversary and was driven to the hall in Palmers Green by the black Daimler which the local cab outfit retained for hire by special request. She had read the *Malory Towers* books a few years earlier and become intent upon boarding. The persistent expression of this aspiration, surprising though it had been to her parents, had enabled her to pursue entrance to a secondary school that none of her current classmates would be attending, an ambition exponentially nursed by the events of her tenth year.

Jennifer had been riding her bicycle when a boy who lived on the adjoining street smirked and said, 'You're Jewish!' More exclamation than accusation, but said the way it had been still called for rebuttal.

'No, I'm not,' she replied.

'Yes, you are, you're Jewish,' came the emphatic riposte.

Jennifer ran inside and demanded the truth. 'Victor Keeler says I'm Jewish, but I'm not. Am I?'

Zara found herself momentarily taken aback. Jennifer sensed confirmation in her mother's hesitation and cried out, 'No! What does it mean, Mummy, what does it mean?'

Zara, now floundering, fell back on her own mother's inadequate phrasebook: 'Oh, don't take any notice, darling, he's just being silly.'

The children attended the wedding of one of their many cousins once removed later that year. Zara had proudly pointed out their many relatives, reputations she had spoken of made flesh.

'Jennifer, take the others, and introduce yourselves to Ian and Stephen,' she said, as they were gathering for the reception.

Two immense young men looked down upon them. 'Are these our cousins?' one of them said, leaving a subtly loaded gap between each word.

The second laughed and added with feigned discretion as he turned away, 'I'm rather afraid they are.' The remark was for the other's benefit, but Jennifer took the glancing blow.

One afternoon, Zara had met Jennifer at the school gate to find her, head down, clasping a bundle enclosed in a brown paper bag. She'd had to seek permission to go to the lavatory, and to ask for paper, which the headmistress had insisted be rationed. Jennifer joined the queue at the teacher's desk, trying with increasing desperation to attract her attention. She was second in line by the time she had to run from the room. The school secretary rescued her and provided a change of clothing. Jennifer listened to her mother retch for the minutes it took to deal with the offending articles in the bathroom.

Jennifer made no explicit connection between these events, but they coalesced in the crucible of her subconscious and reappeared at will when new devastation sought catalysis. She was not strictly speaking diminished by them, being determined to draw upon her resourcefulness to find a way through. She returned, though, after the incident at school, to find the number of children she could count upon as friends had considerably shrunk, and at Christmas one of the boys announced that he was presenting a card to everybody but her. Jennifer held close at least to Georgina: being in the second stream, she had not witnessed her distress; and she began to strive to put the past behind her.

Zara did have the sense that her daughter had changed. She knew little of the short exchange at the wedding, beyond the look of disappointment on Jennifer's face, and made the natural assumption that the circumstances in which she had fled the queue for Mrs Bush would soon be forgotten by a child of ten. She was fretful about the boy though. Zara had hoped that they could protect their children from the kind of discovery she had made on the day she'd last rushed to the mat; she sought the assimilation for them that she'd been resolved upon gaining for herself.

Harry, on the other hand, rather hoped that his children would attain his own twin certainties: to know their roots but to be secure in disdaining the religious aspect of them. Their children acquired the characteristic of chameleons. Harry, notwithstanding he had lost something of the exoticism of appearance he had possessed at their marriage, was nonetheless visibly of foreign extract. When his children walked with him, his otherness was reflected in them; with Zara, whose dark film star looks had softened into a gentle, greying motherhood, they could pass for an ordinary north London family. The tension she had felt when deciding whether to marry – or to have children – persisted. They were met differently when with Harry, more warmly or with greater distance, depending on the standpoint of their interlocuter.

Zara was delighted that Jennifer had developed an affinity with Darrell Rivers. Daphne had been just the right age when *First Term at Malory Towers* was published, and Zara had sneaked the occasional read, seeing her younger self in its dauntless protagonist.

Though boarding was not a prospect for which she and Harry had bargained, she could see the advantage: a place at a fair-to-middling public school, she imagined, would give Jennifer a head start.

* * *

The pendulum swung with a vengeance: Harry and Zara read of apartheid and Vietnam – and watched the suppression of the Prague Spring. Those neighbouring Israel combined to threaten it, repulsed, a generation on from Belsen. Harry brandished no torch for the state, but had read Harold Pinter's warning that a new Holocaust might be at hand. Meanwhile, a narcissistic classicist prophesied rivers of blood; and a Welsh village mourned the submergence of its children. The times swung upward, too: circumnavigation for one, the long-nosed profile of the supersonic for the few – how they now flew the earth in a jiffy! – and a leap to the moon for the whole of mankind. In Paris, the young staked out hopes of their own.

As the Century swayed, so did Zara Landsman, now swimming with the tide, now forced to the struggle as the wind changed. Her second and third children carried the weight on their shoulders rather more easily than Jennifer. Deborah was often to be found playing football with the boys down the road. She demanded that her hair be chopped and, being the first in the family to bring home a swear word, earned herself a lengthy conversation with her father. Nine at the time of her grandparents' fortieth, she had approached the taking of the photograph with a huge smile, arms folded, a lead leg relaxed at the knee. Christopher, at seven, short back and sides, is bolt upright in the picture, arms stiffly held, paying heed to the cameraman's instructions.

* * *

Harry Landsman had been stacking rods of dowelling in the storeroom when a shout came from the front that his daughter was on the phone.

'Daddy, I've got in!'

'What? Tell me.'

'I've got in, Daddy. I passed the exam. It's a scholarship. They only have five and I've got one.'

'Oh, Jennifer.'

'Daddy?'

Harry closed five minutes before six; by that time Zara had demolished several cups of tea and Kensitas and dashed off a letter to Lauren. Meanwhile, Jennifer had picked up the phone to call Mops and her Auntie Daphne.

She ran to her father; he had his arms out at the ready. This was news to come home to on a Friday!

'The only thing is, Daddy.' She paused. She knew, even at ten, that they were not a wealthy family. They had this big old house, but their much twanged furnishings were expected to last longer than those at Georgina's, and children at school talked of holidays further afield than their own annual week at Westgate.

'The thing is, Daddy. There's a huge uniform list. Blazer, kilt, boater, all kinds of sports gear. Seven blouses!'

He hugged her close, his eyes caught Zara's, and they were back at Forty Hall, inching their way; back, too, at Springfield Park, holding their breath, not daring to imagine that this sort of thing might be possible.

'Jennifer. We'll buy you seventy blouses if we have to.'

Her brother and sister could not contain their excitement.

'Jennifer's going to Malory Towers,' chanted Deborah.

'But that means you'll be leaving home,' said Christopher.

'Yes, but they have weekend passes. Visiting days too – and longer vacations.'

That satisfied Christopher, and he went back to his book.

Harry said, 'I've something to show you, Jennifer, something I received when I was your age.' He produced a letter carrying the crest of the Manchester Grammar School. 'You have the chance that I might have had. Nothing will be too much for us.'

There was an interview to come for Harry and Zara, a formality, they were assured, though the school was keen to stress the importance of good relationships with their parents. They reached the neo-Gothic frontage, with tower and portcullis, an hour away by train and taxi, where the porter made a note of their name and led them to the end of a long cloister. Harry was dressed in his suit, Zara in a conservative, patterned dress that fell to the middle of her calves; she wore her make-up with discretion. Relieved to see an ashtray, she accepted a light from the husband of the other couple in the waiting room.

'It's reasonable, isn't it?' he said, by way of an opener, 'what they charge here?'

'Yes, yes,' said Harry, careful not to risk whatever it was that Jennifer's scholarship might communicate.

'I do love the uniform,' said Zara. 'It reminds me of the one I used to wear in Cambridge.'

The first couple went through, and they were left with photographs of previous headmistresses dating back to the late nineteenth century. Harry felt something of what could have been for him.

'You do realise, dear, that if you'd gone to your school, we'd never have met. There'd be no Jennifer, you know.'

He smiled. The logic was inescapable.

Their turn came, and they were greeted by a formidable-looking woman in her late fifties, with grey hair pulled back tightly behind the ears. She tapped the backs of two chairs facing her desk and it was plain they were to occupy them. She had warmth, though, to go with her brisk manner, and served them tea from a delicate pot, before resuming her own place. She asked about the appeal boarding school held for Jennifer.

'So, it came from her? That's unusual. She's an independent young woman. Now, there's one thing I must ask. We have a daily chapel service; would you want Jennifer to opt out? There are girls who come in solely for the notices.'

Zara was quick to respond. 'We'd like her to join in with all the other girls, Miss Nicholson.'

'You are Jewish, though, Mr and Mrs Landsman?'

Zara swallowed, and concentrated on maintaining her composure; the presumption had struck hard.

'We're Humanists, Miss Nicholson,' said Harry. 'Our upbringing was Jewish, but it's not part of our lives now.'

'We'd like Jennifer to blend in.'

'I think we can help with that. Now, that means she'll go to chapel, she'll say the prayers, sing all the hymns. She'll take scripture lessons?'

Zara swiftly gave her assent lest Harry's likely doubts about the package surface.

'And Jewish holidays?'

'We don't celebrate those,' replied Harry.

'Turkey and Easter egg hunts, though,' added Zara brightly.

'I've got the picture.'

Harry put an arm around her; it had been their most difficult moment as parents. He had confronted the barbed wire and, though they'd seldom discussed Humanism, he'd dispatched it to cut the coil. It meant a stage negotiated for Zara; with luck no female manifestation of Victor Keeler had been granted a place at the school, and the staff would not blink at her name.

Harry said, 'We must talk to Jennifer.'

'Not today, dear.'

'But before she comes here.'

'I think she'll be jolly fine with Margaret Rutherford, dear, don't you?'

The fourth year of the juniors had settled Jennifer, and she had gained respect from the boys with whom she was placed, in order of merit, in the back row. They devised a game whereby they induced their teacher to say their names as often as possible; they tallied the scores weekly and kept a league table. They outgrew the place, and Jennifer was not sorry when the end of term came, and it was time to strip their exercise books for the stock of rough paper and to pack the few items from their desks. She went to the Royal Tournament with Georgina for her birthday treat, and shopped for her new school uniform, which she modelled on a catwalk for Deborah and Christopher.

'They have a chapel at your new school, Jennifer,' Zara said, when she and Harry sat her down for the talk they had to have. 'We told Miss Nicholson you'd probably want to attend.'

'I imagine so. Why wouldn't I?'

'You know that you have classmates who go to Sunday school?'

'Yes, but we don't really go to church, do we?' The 'really' was justified by the annual carol service the school held at a local place of worship.

'No, dear, we don't. And nor did your grandparents.'

'What are you saying, Mummy?'

'Your grandma came from an ordinary London family, but she fell in love with your grandpa, and his family had a different religion.' She paused to give her time to take this in.

Harry said, 'Jennifer, your grandpa is Jewish; your

grandparents on my side are too. Mummy and I aren't religious, but it makes us a bit different from your friends' families.'

'How? How does it make us different?' She knew he didn't look like most of the other fathers.

'Well, it doesn't, not greatly, not in everyday life. We don't go to the synagogue – that's the place where Jewish people pray. You might say that our history is Jewish. It means that we don't go to church. But we thought at your new school…'

Zara moved to the practical choice ahead. 'At your school, you could opt out of the chapel services and go in at the end for the notices, but we thought you'd want to be treated the same as everybody else.'

'Obviously. Everybody would turn to look at me!'

Zara thought back to the Cambridge and County. 'When I was at school, I went to all the assemblies. I bowed my head for the prayers, I sang the hymns – I loved the hymns.'

'But can you remember when Victor told me I was…'

'I know, dear. I said he was being silly, didn't I? I think it *is* silly to call somebody by a religion just because of their grandparents. It's all a bit silly, darling, to be honest. We're all the same in nature.'

'But the way he said it, it sounded…' She couldn't finish.

'It isn't, dear. It's the past for us now.'

Harry sought confirmation. 'Would you like to go to the chapel? We'll be okay, whatever you decide,' he said, adding with a wag of his finger, 'so long as you don't go believing those Grimms' fairy tales.'

'I want to be like all the others. Do you think they're going to know, though, like Victor did?'

'They shouldn't do, dear,' her mother said. 'People will assume you're just like them.' Zara's heart was racing; she hoped against hope that they would.

* * *

The doorman announced: 'Mr and Mrs Landsman, their daughters Jennifer and Deborah, and their son, Christopher.'

Covered with crisp white cloths, some twenty tables lay before them, seating six, eight or a dozen people. Elaborate bowls laden with fruit or flowers lay beside bone china patterned in intricate detail, along with silver cutlery and condiment pots and cocktail sticks topped with the Star of David. A Dixieland band had struck up; Harry recognised them from their formative days in the old East End.

Jennifer scanned the throng of dinner jackets and silken dresses, milling around in the meet-and-greet, the suits on her grandfather's side crowned with *yarmulkes*. She noticed the headwear and nudged Harry, who explained quietly, 'Jewish men wear those on special occasions.' She reddened, but felt relief that her father was not wearing one; it was at least of a piece with what he had said. It dawned on her, though, that this was who they were, not in their headgear maybe, not topped by the *koppel*, but in their bodies, in their looks even, and – surely it followed? – within. She had received her share of bullying at school, none of it for being Jewish: that subterfuge had held. But there were Jewish girls at the school who copped it for being so; she was but a hair's breadth from the same. She tried to put her finger on the quality that made the guests so distinctive. The surroundings were staid, but there was an extraordinary excitability: women gabbled earnestly in cahoots; men rocked back on a leg, clasped their hands behind their backs and raised their heads in laughter at whatever tales were being told. As the direct family of Sol and Mops, their table was at the front of the arrangement, and a steady stream of relatives came to pay their respects. Many remembered Zara, and Harry, too, if they had been at the wedding. They ran their hands under the children's chins, and Jennifer took them in without smiling, trying to work out of exactly what it was that she was part.

Zara drew comfort from the rarity of such events; the connections with the Dodd sisters and their families were matched by no similar bond with her father's relatives. During the recent half term, they had been walking to Sol's and Mops' in Winchmore Hill. Zara had been enthusing to her children about their great aunts, passing on an oral version of the extensive tree on that side of the family, when Christopher had asked about his grandfather: did he have brothers and sisters? Zara had answered sharply, had closed it down; she saw that Jennifer had noticed; also that she had kept quiet. Happy as she was for her parents on their anniversary, this had been a step to be negotiated, where the protection of her children was paramount, an event where not everything was to be explained, the abundance of six-point stars unremarked upon, the words from an alien language simply smiled at, in the hope that the symmetrical caps and distinguished beards would be swiftly forgotten and that the history they might disinter would stay safely buried.

Chapter 28

At the end of a long day in late April, Zara answered the phone to Jennifer.

'Mum? I've got the job.'

'Oh my goodness, Jen. Well done! Where are you?'

'I'm still at the school. They've only just informed us. The head of department's taking me back to the hotel. I should make the last train.'

Harry put the champagne on ice.

In tailored trouser suit, hair mid-length, the figure Jennifer cut when she burst in triumphantly from her interview could not have contrasted more greatly with the one she presented after her first year at university. Then, the first time she had come home since Christmas, Deborah had gone with a hired car to meet her at Paddington, while Zara kept an excited look-out from an upstairs window. She had only half a minute to compose herself: the time the girls took to carry Jennifer's trunk to the front door. She opened it to an older daughter changed beyond recognition.

Jennifer had not checked her appearance, nor looked to disguise what it represented. She embraced her mother and joined her in the kitchen, a ritual enshrined over eight years of such homecomings. She had grown her hair, as far down her back as it would go; waves of curls ran across her, forming a veil in front of her face. Her jeans were ripped and patched; the legs bottomed out in flares that enveloped the flimsiest of plimsolls. In the warmth of a summer's day, she wore a thick, shapeless jumper under an Afghan coat. Except for the last, the whole had struck Zara as a form of conscious dowdiness, an absence of conviction, a statement of indifference to the impression that might be created by how one dressed. She found it hard to imagine her nineteen-year-old daughter meeting a young man, falling in love, walking hand in hand through a park.

* * *

One Saturday, the year after the anniversary dinner, Jennifer had met her mother, as arranged, at Liverpool Street. She had obtained a weekend pass, and the family had planned to visit the Tower of London together. Zara had some news for her, though. A few days before, Mops had awoken to find Sol collapsed in the hall. They had spent their last years at a bungalow on Green Dragon Lane, which, stubborn as she had been to stay on her feet, she could navigate with the help of her serving trolley. The flame ignited in the kitchen on West Bank more than four decades earlier still burned; the sunshine, which on a late winter's day warmed them through the windscreen as they took a drive through the Hertfordshire countryside, gifted them, unheralded, their final hours of companionship.

Jennifer accepted the news, and the change of plan, with equanimity. The train, crowded with Tottenham Hotspur and Chelsea supporters, swept through Bethnal Green, Stoke Newington and Stamford Hill, stations that mapped the generations of the Keffs. The fans serenaded them to White Hart Lane, shining an aural spotlight on the silence of mother and daughter as they willed the train home. Then to Bush Hill Park and Jennifer had felt nothing, not yet in shock at her mother's news; she had felt distant from her grandfather since the conversation with her parents prior to going up to school, a detachment the anniversary dinner had reinforced. Her mother had said not to be afraid to cry, but Zara could only admire her daughter for a certain hardiness in the face of adversity.

Deborah had discovered for herself that she was Jewish. Zara kept a weather-eye out for possible contacts, once advising without compelling argument that she ought to keep her distance from a girl called Diane Rosenthal. Even so, Deborah struck up with a fair-haired girl whose surname provided no direct warning. When, to her surprise, she was served lemon tea at her friend's house, she was quickly informed of her friend's religion and of the assumption the girl's mother had made about her own. This news had been in no way unwelcome, and the next afternoon Deborah had asked for lemon tea at home. 'Because we're Jewish, right?' she said. 'I like lemon tea! What other drinks do Jewish people have, Mummy?' Zara, irritated, had a flashback to the raffle at school and said they could talk about it later. When

Harry came home, Deborah bounded up to him and said, 'We're Jewish, aren't we, Daddy?'

Harry brought Christopher into his confidence in a more deliberate way. He took him to Stamford Hill one Sunday, to what he, too, called the smelly shop. Christopher was enchanted from the moment he entered the half-lit delicatessen, all manner of foodstuffs protected by the deep, dark waters of their ancient barrels, its owner rueful, ever fatalistic, as he wiped his hands on a perma-stained apron and weighed out the orders with half an ounce of generosity. They returned with pickled cucumbers and challah bread, which the family devoured, the context unreferenced, with fried fish and smoked salmon. It became a regular outing, and Harry often made oblique remarks about the Hassidic Jews they passed. He sat with Christopher on a bench one day to share something of the family's background, beginning with the yarmulkes from the anniversary dinner.

* * *

Zara took up work again, part-time, at the secondary school Deborah and Christopher went up to, another with the 'County' suffix, and soon found herself secretary to the headmaster. The family began to frequent the Norfolk restaurant, where the children usually behaved themselves and spotted the odd footballer. They afforded more adventurous holidays, too, flying to the Channel Islands and taking long train journeys to the West

Country, walking proudly to the tables of medium-to-high-class hotels, threading their way between the accountants, the public servants and the small business owners. Zara might catch an angled glance or a whispered conjecture, but they endured no mortifying enquiries, and their teenagers made friends by the pool.

Zara kept her Century in sight as it threw down its challenges. Why have you caused turmoil again, she demanded, as a priest's flag sought passage amongst a murdered thirteen. She read by candlelight during the three-day week and watched on aghast as the country's youth dissolved into vast swathes of material in time to welcome her own. The Peace Prize for Amnesty, though, brought hope, of the kind of world she had envisaged while Mr Garver surveyed his class so expectantly.

Her younger children stood up to it all. Deborah was rebellious at school, which embarrassed her mother at work but rather amused her at home; she protested at the requirement to take at least one 'O' level in the sciences and was permitted to be the sole exception. She was loudly Jewish when it served a purpose, generous with her friendship, played hockey and rounders for the school and wrote the sports up for its newspaper. She kept her hair short, slung a discreet Star of David around her neck, wore dungarees about the house and travelled to watch the Spurs, three stops up the line.

One evening, Christopher slipped into the spare room, which housed the battered old 'upstairs' television, to watch Jack Rosenthal's *Bar Mitzvah Boy*. His father looked in part-way through.

'I had to prepare for bar mitzvah myself,' Harry said, the next Sunday, as the two sat back in deckchairs, basking in early September sunshine, 'thanks to my father.'

'You mean, reading all that Hebrew?'

'I learned it off pat, but my heart wasn't in it.'

'Dad – what made you turn against it?'

'When I was at school, the headmaster thought it would help the Jewish boys if he brought in a rabbi every now and again. It was kind of him, I suppose, but most of us weren't keen: we were Manchester lads, you know, if you get my drift. This rabbi spoke to us about all sorts of things, which we half listened to, and one day he told us there was a Jewish way to get yourself ready in the morning: the order you put your clothes on, how you tuck your shirt in – that sort of thing. My mates and I, we talked afterwards, and we said: if there's a God, would he care about how you got dressed? I think in the end it was that that did it for us.'

'You do talk about being Jewish, Dad.'

'Do I? I imagine I do sometimes. We are Jewish, but we're not religious, Christopher. I don't know if you can understand that. It's rather like in country villages, where most people go to church. They mightn't all believe in God, but they think themselves Christian. It's their history.'

'But you don't even go to a synagogue.'

'Do you know something, love: I don't know where the nearest one is. But you're right: I don't. The one time I went into a synagogue after I reached thirteen was to get married to your mother – and that was a last favour to her grandfather.'

'I still don't get it – what does that make me?'

'Well, if you want to, you can say you're Jewish by descent. People realise that means you don't believe. Or say that you have no religion. You could even say you're C of E: no one's going to mind. I like to say I'm a Humanist. Humanists believe what's important is how you live your one life.'

'I think I'm going to be a Humanist, Dad.'

Zara had brought tea to the patio door. Everything was so complicated. They were, but they weren't – or they aren't. Why could it not be forgotten? Here they were, twenty years or more from their first walk in Springfield Park, and still it mattered. The talk with Jennifer had upset her, not to the extent that Zara's own discovery had, but her unhappiness was evident, caught on a photograph, nonetheless. Then there was feisty Deborah who wore being Jewish as a badge of honour. Perhaps that was the way to do it, always assuming you can pronounce it. And Christopher: there he was, trying to make sense of all the contradictions. He took to staying up with his father on Saturdays to watch late-night films and, side by side with him, learned about the ancestry of many of the stars and the politics of the great Hollywood eras. He came out of his shell and proved to be a fine school cricketer.

Away at her own school, Jennifer put herself forward for netball trials and was nominated as reserve on occasions. She auditioned for school plays, thrilled to be cast as Moth in *A Midsummer Night's Dream*, among a succession of minor roles she was offered. With her friends she found adventure, discovering illicit entrances to the tower, climbing to the top where they scratched their initials alongside those of their forebears; they made a den, too, in the sound gantry above the Great Hall stage, occupying themselves for hours on end. Such interludes were the closest they came to *Malory Towers*.

Jennifer carried with her, though, the remarks of her cousins and the sneer of Victor Keeler, and saw enough to discern that she 'looked' Jewish. Her curls, her light-olive complexion, the incline of her nose: it was difficult to put a finger on it. She tugged her hair straight while drying it in the morning, and declined to raise her hand in the lesson following gym, after the shower had reinvested it with frizz. Gangly in her school kilt, she attracted the soubriquet 'lanky Landsman', which she did little to discourage, finding it preferable to alliteration that might attach to her forename. She had become a regular in the Second VII by the time she left the sixth form.

* * *

University freed Jennifer from the constraints of uniform, and she buried herself in the anti-mode soon to give way to punk.

'You're such a beautiful girl,' Zara said to her in the kitchen one day, during that first summer vacation. 'You ought to come out from beneath all that hair, dear.'

'Mum,' she began, with exasperation, 'I have the hair so I can hide the face.'

'But why would you want to do that?'

'You wouldn't understand, Mum.'

'Jen, don't say that. Try me.'

'Mum,' she began again, the concealment of her rage diminishing with every word, 'I have all the hair so I can hide all the Jewish. There, I've said it now. Are you happy?'

She abandoned the rest of her lunch and ran upstairs.

Zara made first to go after her, but checked herself: there was nothing she could say, no formulation that might work. A despairing sigh hung in the air, unabsorbed. She departed the kitchen, grabbed her coat and handbag, and stumbled through the streets of Bush Hill Park, stopping only to catch her breath. By then on the main road at St Stephen's Church, she hailed a bus, heaved herself upstairs and pulled out a cigarette. She looked down on English suburbia, those semi-detached houses serviceable, but not a patch on the home she and Harry had provided for their children. Why was it always in the way? Why was her daughter more distressed now than she had ever been, in this age where it was more possible to be different than ever before? And yet she, Zara Landsman, had wanted her children to blend in. Was that her mistake? Had she bequeathed Jennifer more shame than she herself had felt, leaving it unassuaged even by the arguments her own mother had been able to marshal? She fled the bus and found a bench by the local library. What she would have given to turn to find Lauren there, as she had on that day at Clissold Park when her cousin had caught her and done her best to put her straight. But she was alone now, and there was nothing for it but to pull herself up, and to go inside, and to choose some books.

* * *

Harry said, 'Can I come in, love?' and there was silence, and so he knocked again.

'What do you want?' There was a distant hurt in her voice.

'To see how you are, dear.'

A quarter-truth reached him. 'I'm okay, Dad.'

He nudged the door open. 'Can I come in?'

'All right, then.'

Jennifer was lying down, staring at the ceiling, while a Fairport Convention track played quietly on the cassette deck beside her.

'I'm sorry, Dad.'

'We're worried about you, love.'

'You don't need to be.'

'To say you want to hide your beautiful face.'

Harry shook his head, and sat down on the end of the bed, resting his hand lightly on the lower stretch of Jennifer's leg.

'Beautiful to you, maybe,' she said.

He paused, knowing what had brought them to this point. 'It isn't something to be ashamed of, love.'

'But why do we hide it then?'

'What do you see when you look at me, Jennifer?'

'I don't know, Dad.'

'Growing up, you'd rather your mother went up to the school?'

She looked up at him.

'Am I right, love?'

'I guess so. But you look great. You could be a film star.'

'In a different life, perhaps. But can you hear what you're saying? I don't think I look all that bad. I'm proud enough when I comb my hair in the morning.'

'You should be, Dad.'

'But if people assume I have religion – or associate me with the deeds carried out in its name – that's when I'm ashamed. Not because of how I look.'

'I don't understand it all, Dad, honestly I don't. But Jewish… it's a religion, isn't it? And if that's as bad as you say, why would somebody want to look it?'

Harry himself saw no such contradiction. His difficulty lay in the certainties he had grown up with. He had lived on a street with so many Jews that a *goy* could make a handy living lighting fires on the Sabbath. There was no embarrassment in your flesh and blood, no thought that you didn't like the look of the boys you played with, no sense either that you were part of a fortunate stratum in society that might invite envy: your poverty was a fact as much as your Jewishness, and both remained facts long after the religion was lost. These certainties, those recollections, of darting below the window line when the rent collector came, of watching his mother boiling up chicken bones to make the scantiest of soups, of seeing his brother become the most handsome of men: these remained intact, as fixed points, incapable of dilution, memories that existed of poverty, yes, of a tough upbringing, and of Jewishness, too. They were inseparable, they had made him what he was; he stood by them. The rejection of religion was part of it all, as he had told Christopher, but that did not undo the rest. It did not negate the poverty or a pride in that, and of having wrested yourself out of it, of being working class, even as a comfortable shopkeeper; nor the resilience of his mother, who had never learned to read and write English, and who had toiled to raise her children, despite her husband's lack of ambition and the Sabbath-day calls he made on the bookmaker once done at the synagogue. And it did not negate his Jewishness: it was of a piece with the rest. He had discarded the belief – that was all.

Zara, he knew, had not the benefit of those certainties. Hers were the English countryside, the Cambridge and County school and the Village Institute; until she returned to Stoke Newington, that is; until she returned, had she but known, to that which she had always been.

'Jennifer, your mother was keen to escape it. You've studied history. Imagine this: Mum heard about the fate of the Jews before she knew that she was Jewish herself. She felt for them, she was angry, and when she was brought back to London...'

'What are you saying, Dad?'

'I grew up in Cheetham Hill: most of the children at my school were Jewish. I came south, to the East End, lived in terrible digs at first. The people I got to know – they weren't believers, but they were Jewish. That's how it was. It's how I was – how I am. Perhaps if we'd...' he searched his childhood, '...lit the candles or spun the dreidel...'

'No, no, Dad.' She couldn't help but laugh. 'I wouldn't have wanted that.'

'Ah, you're a girl after ma own heart, wee lassie.'

She laughed again – 'Oh, don't go all Scottish on me, Dad!' – and he smiled.

'Do you remember that day when you rang me at work?'

'How could I forget, Dad?'

'Me showing you my letter from the Manchester Grammar School?'

She nodded. He inched along the bed and brushed her hair to one side.

'Jennifer, you're intelligent, you're beautiful and you're at university. Don't hang your head, love. Come down when you're ready.'

Her brother and sister were settled at the dining table, giggling at some joke or other, while Harry fetched the plates in. She turned to the kitchen, saw her mother's tired eyes, and put her arms around her.

'I've made your favourite casserole, dear,' Zara said. 'Shall we go through?'

* * *

Zara was delighted that, after taking an upper second in history, Jennifer had opted to take a post-graduate certificate in education. Young women flourished at the school where Zara worked, and she wondered whether she might have done the same herself, had she stayed on. So when Jennifer announced she'd been offered an interview in Sheffield, she set about booking a room for her, at the grand old Victoria, close to the station, and supplied the wherewithal to buy a suit for the occasion.

The Century threw everything at Zara as its penultimate decade dawned. It brought the rule of the cleric to an ancient land, banged Hayek on a table and sank the Belgrano. It fostered pitched battles where coal was dug, and turned the dark over – to tourism, to regale the curious with tales of soot-covered men. In Sheffield itself, forge masters fought for survival, while *Threads* depicted a nuclear aftermath which enthralled and alarmed its citizens in equal measure.

Yet how her children came into their own! Christopher graduated and took up work in foreign aid, a Humanist indeed; posted to famine-torn parts of the world, he met Eloise of *Médicins Sans Frontières*. Deborah, restless, had left school at seventeen and, armed with her cuttings and a pair of top-notch boots, had landed the chance to train on the local newspaper. Her Enfield flat hosted a mean sort of cooking, a capacious drinks cabinet and a steady rotation of boyfriends.

Jennifer still came home for the holidays but never brought the kind of stark change to her exterior that she had presented after her first year at university. They conversed in the kitchen, always: Zara sipped Earl Grey, while Jennifer popped open a can of Tetley's or Theakston's, watching with sullen disapproval her mother stub cigarette butts into an old tobacco tin by the sink.

Jennifer spoke of her election as secretary to the city's anti-apartheid branch. With her denim jacket's 'Coal Not

Dole' badge, she had waved banners by the roadside, urging motorists to honk their support. Armed with a thermos flask, she had joined the Sheffield Forgemasters picket line, one dark morning during their long dispute, and dropped a pound note into their tin on Fargate every Saturday morning.

'The world goes through these phases, Jen, but it does come out again.'

'We can't just stand by, though.'

'But we mustn't despair either. Things *will* improve again.'

'History shows that can take a long time, Mum.'

'I know, darling, but perhaps you can have an influence in other ways. Have you thought about promotion recently?'

'Oh, not that again. How often do you hear somebody on the radio talk about a great teacher they once had. They don't talk about great administrators.'

'No, dear, but I've seen what happens when a member of our staff obtains their first scale point. It spurs them on. The ones who don't manage that: they find it hard to maintain their optimism.'

'That won't happen to me, Mum.'

Then, when appointed to a post to develop multicultural education, Jennifer could assure her mother this didn't amount to hierarchical promotion, but rather fitted with everything she believed. Her success came as something of a tonic. Harry and Zara had made room for Mops in their home. The onset had been gradual, but she had begun to find it difficult to recognise her grandchildren. The send-off accorded with her wishes: dawn had been hers, and the sunset; no single thing abided; no God intruded. Zara herself read from Bertrand Russell, content in the thought that what was possible had been done. In the heart of the crematorium, the organ's Jupiter swept her to her rest.

Chapter 29

Its predecessor had hung on, bequeathing the rush to war, requiring a single shot at a car-bound dignitary to trigger its deadly legacy. 'Don't die! Stay alive for our children!' he'd exclaimed as the world dived to depths theretofore unplumbed. The long nineteenth, born amid fraternity, stalled at the gateway to that perverse measure of equality, carnage unchained. The Century had exceeded even that in its middle age. Now, it brought walls tumbling down, the long walk to freedom, an historic handshake, a new dawn on Good Friday.

Zara wore the grey-white hair and hollower cheeks of her own late middle age with upright accommodation, and, before she and Harry made their first visit to Lyon, she brushed up the French she had learned as a teenager.

'Christopher and Eloise have spoken to us about the nuances of your background, Zara,' Eloise's mother said, in faultless English, having taken her aside. 'Please be assured we understand. We, too, are secular people. And we hold no prejudice.'

Was it that simple, Zara wondered? She imagined Christopher echoing the conversations he had had with

Harry, passing it all off, joking about being Jewish and not Jewish; he had no call upon camouflage.

They dined one evening at a *bouchon* off the Rue Saint-Jean. Zara absorbed every time-honoured detail: the tessellation of black-and-white diamonds on the floor, the rustic artwork, the perfectly rounded wooden chair backs, the small tables they put together to take the six of them, each wedged to its own degree to keep balance across the whole, the scratched chalkboards and fusty wine bottles. The sum of the everyday parts brought a stillness to her, as though the world were pulling neither for nor against. She felt a slow-cooked release and expounded without inhibition, making elegant use of her schoolgirl French when addressing Eloise's father; the topics interesting her became a source of fascination for the hosts, too. They strolled afterwards through Vieux Lyon; Zara took in the admiring glances of the Lyonnaise, sure of them, at home with this family and their city.

'You must come to us in turn,' she said; and they did. A succession of French visitors filled their spare rooms, exchanging conversation over breakfast and, to Zara's delight, accepting the run of the place. Some nights, half a dozen friends of the couple stayed with them, seeing the sights, raiding the wine rack, retiring to sleeping bags all over the house.

* * *

Deborah had stayed with the newspaper, joking that she was a hack now, reporting on significant local stories and the politics of the council. She was dispatched, during the dog days one summer, to a march and rally in the eastern part of the borough, one of the crepuscular zones of the far right, in one of its twilight periods. A disparate collection of a hundred or so, half-matched in number by uniforms, were assembled on a derelict site by Ponders End station. Flags of the union – and the last jacks of the National Front – were borne by ghouls in old-style checks and shirts, by the fatigued and the denimed, the balding and the cropped, and by the rump of the suedeheads and sorts. With the barest of rallying cries, they creaked away, like a slumbering steam engine straining to bring its pistons to bear, loud with bravado, but somehow affected, self-conscious, unused to ploughing the path of the march. They had their slogans, of jobs and houses for their own, for the protection of the old from threats deemed uniquely to emanate from the new, and of rights for the white. They shouted to the wind for a while, up a barren, unpopulated street, but waiting among the tight-knit terraces into which they diverted, were the hackneyed placards of the Socialist Workers, the fresh banners of Red Wedge and the dusted-down arrows of the Anti-Nazi League.

Deborah watched from the outside at first, from beyond the police line, at the ragbag of looks and styles: the flares and the straights, the tattooed scalps and the bombers, the kipper ties and wide-lapelled jackets purloined from C & A before the fashion changed, even a Crombie or Ben Sherman ripped from the modernists. I must get this across, she thought. When, in the old

Victorian streets, the counterblast started and the placards began to see-saw, she made after a group bearing cracked skulls and Germanic fonts on their T-shirts, afficionados of Combat 18, which she took to be a heavy metal band.

A policeman held her back. 'I wouldn't, miss.' Deborah showed him her card. 'Even so. You know who they are?'

'Well, I…'

'First and eighth letters of the alphabet.' He turned away to deal with a remark he had caught.

It clicked, but she pressed on.

'Excuse me,' she said, whipping out a spiral notepad. 'I'm from the *Gazette*. Why the protest?'

'You what, lahve.' He made as though not to hear for the noise and then slapped a placard. 'England fer the English.'

'We want our country back, all right?' said another. 'Not what the fuckin' Zog wants.'

'That's Zionist occupation government to you, love.'

'What?' she said, momentarily forgetting the role in which she was present. The National Front was white versus black, surely? The twist shocked her, the first time she'd picked up anything like it. 'The Tories are Zionists? That's a new one on me.'

'They're all Zionists, love. Some just hide it better.'

Spotting her pad, a third had begun to run from the far side of the group and pointed now to her neck. 'That a fuckin' six-point? You a fuckin' Jew, bitch?'

Deborah stood her ground. A grey-haired counter-protester in cheesecloth and jeans dragged a mate by the denim jacket in a drive to intervene. The assailant's momentum carried him to prod her hard in the middle of the chest, yelling, 'We don't want fuckin' Yids reporting on us.' The force sent her backwards, her new-found protectors too late to catch her. Deborah strove to keep hold of the notebook; her arm buckled in her attempt to break the fall. The officer turned quickly at the fiercer intensity of the noise but could only watch her tumbling to the pavement.

* * *

The caller had said something about her falling – and bumping her head on the kerb. She was alive, but had not regained consciousness: could Zara come straight away? Zara called up to Jennifer, home for the school holiday, and garbled the scant details, saying to wait till her father came in. She ran to the station, caught the train to Enfield and took a taxi, arriving at the hospital, breathless, half an hour later. The doctor could not divulge much, beyond her presence at the march, but was sure the police would come by when Deborah was able to talk. That at least implied odds in her favour. He allowed Zara to see her, briefly, lying motionless, her yellow-stitched boots poking out from under the locker, and then she had to wait.

A friend of Deborah's was pacing up and down when Zara emerged from the smoking room.

'I work with Deb on the paper: the police phoned us. It's an awful shock, isn't it?'

'Do you know what happened?'

'Oh, my goodness, haven't they told you? This thug, this Nazi thug...'

'What do you mean, Nazi?'

'National Front. This brute went for her. She fell.'

'But why, but why?'

'She was asking questions. They saw her...'

She collapsed: she knew.

Deborah's colleague drove Zara home, promising to come and fetch her once there was news.

* * *

Zara put the kettle on. She lit up a cigarette, and said to Jennifer what she could bear to say, in the fits and starts that came.

'You mean she was attacked for being Jewish?'

'Why did she go there wearing that?'

Jennifer was torn. It was the last thing she would have put around her own neck: she still evaded talking about what she was, or what people thought she was, or whatever history said they had been. She could never express even the basic conundrum with simplicity. But when it came down to it, they were a minority of sorts, after all, and why shouldn't her sister front up about it? And why the hell should somebody attack her for it?

'Mum, it's her right,' was all she could find from that.

'But it's asking for trouble, Jennifer.'

She knew that, and she knew too that, in her classroom, she taught passionately about every example of prejudice but this one, approaching even Nazism itself with embarrassed objectivity.

'I know it is, Mum. But she's not the one in the wrong.' Those few words took her to a place she had never occupied.

Zara began to light a new cigarette with the fading glow of the first.

'And how's that going to help? Smoking yourself to death?' She snatched the packet away from her.

'No! No! Give them back. Give them back. Now!'

Jennifer relaxed her hold; her mother grabbed the box. But it was enough for her, and she had her coat again. She reached the front door where she sank to the doormat, one folded leg on the other, propped up on a hand, helpless. A faded newspaper dropped through the mists of time.

She saw Jennifer at the end of the hall.

'My daughter's unconscious in hospital, and you're shouting at *me*? Well, maybe it is my fault. Maybe I *should* be killing myself with this, this poison. What would you care?'

Jennifer remained where she was, the replay of her own words competing with her mother's riposte to numb her. Daughters of those who had kept the past dark, handing the torment on, woman to woman, each now found herself at the other's throat. Consumed by pity, or by anger and exhaustion, the space within their outer shells offered insufficient scope to bond. Zara grieved for the girl who wore her chippy Jewishness on her sleeve; the woman she had raised to reject that tag would deny her the one thing that helped.

'Mum, I'm sorry. I just don't want...' She moved towards her, and her voice weakened. 'Don't go out.'

Jennifer squatted and tried to take her mother in her arms, applying a light touch to her stiffness while she waited for her resistance to subside.

The newspaper allowed Deborah a feature, by common consent the best piece she had written. She was interviewed on a phone-in programme and spoke with gutsy eloquence. Zara, to her shame, though, felt exposed. Each sympathetic remark at work, the calls from friends, the extended sincerity of every thank you Mrs Landsman from the local shopkeepers: all carried unspoken acknowledgement of the cause. And she thought: I brought this girl into the world, and she's suffered more from the Century than ever did I.

* * *

The wedding was to be in England; the night before, the French side were staying in Mayfair, while the Landsmans enjoyed a rare dinner together in Bush Hill Park. The wine flowed, the daughters of the house accounting for much of the intake.

'Mum, I bet you never thought Christopher would be the first.'

'I suppose it has been a surprise, dear, but why shouldn't the youngest lead the way?'

Deborah giggled. 'It'll be your turn next, Jen.'

'I wouldn't bet on it.'

'Why not, love?'

'I don't know, Dad. You and Mum are such a splendid example – I'm not sure I could live up to that.'

Harry smiled. 'There's plenty of time, love, don't you worry. And how about you, dear? Which young man's going to be tamed by you?'

'I think I scare them all off, Dad. They'll have to tame me.'

Christopher said, 'You need guts in your line of work, Deb,' the call he'd received from their mother still fresh in his mind.

'You struck out pretty well yourself, Chris. Look at everything you've done: Africa, France, the world. I've not moved any further away than Enfield. At least you went to Sheffield, Jen.'

'And you've taken on some fine causes there,' Harry added.

'How about your own stand, dear?' Zara said. 'The Aldermaston march.'

'What was that, Dad?'

'The atomic bomb, we called it then. 1960: third of the great marches, Trafalgar Square. Your mother made me rather nice sandwiches, I recall. Michael Foot spoke – now there was a good lad. You should've heard him defend Jim Callaghan in '79.'

'I did,' said Jennifer. 'Didn't stop Thatcher getting in, though. Put me completely off my finals.'

'I don't know,' said Deborah, looking around the table. 'You and your marches, Dad. You working for the good of the world, Chris. Jen with a flask on the picket line. What happened to you and me, Mum?'

'We know what you can do, love,' her father assured her. 'And your mother, she was a mere lass when she took up the cudgels.'

'Harry!' She'd not talked much of the war.

'Dad, tell us!'

'Your mother once earned the admiration of an entire village.'

'Oh, stuff and nonsense,' their mother replied.

'Tell them about the wireless, love.'

'Let's save that for another day, dear. But, do you know, we feared the atom bomb so much in the late fifties that we nearly didn't have children?'

'What changed your mind, Mum? Or was Jennifer an accident?'

'Deborah!' said her father.

'Thank you, Dad,' Jennifer said, laughing.

'We thought,' said Harry, 'that the times were beginning to alter. We thought that children of ours, with your mother's brain and my looks – you'd take on the world.'

We did, thought Zara, or something like that. They're taking on the Century, though, come to think of it. And they're starting to win.

'But can you take on tomorrow, Chris? That's the question,' Deborah asked. 'Have you got your speech ready?'

'I've got a few stories about growing up with you two.'

'Let's drink to that!'

'There'd better not be too much detail,' Jennifer said, with an eye over the top of her glass.

'Now, would I do anything to embarrass my lovely sisters?'

'I don't know about lovely,' she replied.

Zara looked at her older daughter and said to herself: starting to win, yes – of that I can be sure; but it doesn't know when it's beaten, does it? It fires a retort, and leaves scars on the landscape, even in retreat.

There's no doubt about it, she thought, as she began to gather the empty plates: like an aging heavyweight against the ropes, the Century still fought back.

* * *

The reception took place at an old manor house in Hertfordshire. Lucasz and Lauren had flown in from Poland; a group of Zara's old school friends had arrived.

'You must be Jennifer. I haven't seen you since you were knee-high to a grasshopper. Hilary. I knew your mother in Cambridge.'

'She still talks about the place. They go for the weekend every so often.'

'I'm not surprised. She was desperately sad to leave.'

'She was there for the war, though, wasn't she? Evacuated. Away from her parents and everything.'

'I know. But we had this wonderful school. Your mother was so clever. There's nothing she couldn't have done.'

'She might have gone to university, even then?'

'You bet. They'd have put her on the fast track. She'd have gone at seventeen. I did. And look at her cousin: Oxford. They sent their son over to Harrow.'

'Mum went to secretarial college, though, didn't she?'

'Look, I know a tippler when I see one. Let's go grab another.'

They stood with their gins, corresponding elbows on the bar.

'She wasn't the same when she went home to London. It was the practical thing to do. But she met your father, and they were so proud when they had you. I remember their wedding. We all said they'd have such beautiful children.'

'I'm not so sure that bit worked out.'

'Oh, yes it did, Jennifer. Believe you me. Now tell me – what are you doing with your own life?'

'Well, I'm not married if that's what you mean.'

'Nor am I, dear. I've no problem with that. I live with an old friend from my Durham days. She's a headmistress. And if somebody in Harrogate needs a good accountant, they come to me. I'm rather proud of that.'

Jennifer looked up at this smart, silver-grey woman in her late fifties who had such fizz. Hilary offered her business card.

'You're not far from me, are you – if you fancy working through a bottle or two sometime? I'll warn you, though. You may struggle to keep up.'

'I might take you up on that.'

'You're a historian, aren't you?'

Jennifer was sipping the last from her glass; she nodded.

'I'll tell you about Sir Hersch Lauterpacht. Lived on our street in Cambridge. Helped to send the Nazis down.'

'Done! You can show me the keys to success, too. Or perhaps your friend can.'

'You've got the keys, Jen. But can you remember where you've hung them?'

They laughed, and Hilary looked at her with mist in her eyes. 'Another G & T, darling?'

Later, the family waved the couple off as they were driven by limousine from the steps at the entrance. Deborah turned to Jennifer and punched the air. 'One down!' she said.

Hilary moved across to Zara.

'Jen's marvellous, Za. A real credit to you. Do you know something? I think she's going to be all right.'

* * *

Mother and daughter spent their mornings in the kitchen the following summer and, fine afternoons, with the radio playing, outside; while Zara tugged at the weeds, Jennifer looked up from her book, and they talked. It offered distraction, the conversation discontinuous; it did not require that each must always meet the other's eye.

'Mum, I heard you getting up last night.'

'I didn't mean to wake you, dear.'

'It's not that; it was the coughing. Are you all right?'

'I think so.'

'It *is* the smoking, you know.' She breathed a long sigh. 'Have you thought about…? I could find a way to help you.'

'I can't, dear. I can't. And I don't want to finish my life in the way your poor grandmother did. Your father's a good deal older than me.'

'What do you mean, Mum?'

'I wouldn't want to survive him, not for too long.'

'But for us, though? We love you.'

'I know, dear. I love the three of you, too.'

After the conversation with Hilary, Jennifer had given thought to promotion, though she wouldn't contemplate the ultimate step.

'You know, one day that might be the logical thing to do. You may decide you can do better than your boss. Imagine how much you could change from the top slot.'

'It'd be all admin and finance, Mum. That's not for me.'

'Oh, I think you'd be good at that, darling. You're so organised.'

'But you lose the time you spend with the kids.'

'Well, Mr Mulley at my school makes a point of seeing pupils. He interviews every member of the upper sixth and completes all their UCCA references. He says he has "people" to do the admin for him.'

Jennifer did bring welcome news to Bush Hill Park every now and then. With Christopher absorbed abroad and Deborah easing into status at the *Gazette*, she phoned home to say she had become head of department and, three years later, that she was to leave Sheffield for a deputy headship in Leicester. Slowly, her daughter was growing in ambition, Zara saw, convinced that might be harnessed one day to grasp a destiny for which she herself had once reached, under a benevolent eye, with a gas mask next to her, long, long ago, in a schoolbook that a fraying old basket still held.

* * *

More than sixty years had passed since Solomon and Mary Keff had given life to the girl they named Zara. Now that her own children were swimming with the tide, tilting upward with the turn of the times, she and Harry became more adventurous, taking elongated breaks to a plethora of capitals and old towns, to Paris again, by Eurostar, for their anniversary, welcomed with fizz to their first class seats. And then Harry retired, and they swapped the ramshackle old house, which his bent for do-it-yourself had never fully conquered, for a compact detached situated on a close in Winchmore Hill. It was the first time, in London, when either had lived away from the line that chugged on to Liverpool Street. It brought them a mere stroll from the restaurants of the old part of the area and from those of Palmers Green and Southgate. Here, they talked away the evenings, over more wine than each had ever imbibed, and prompted curiosity from the proprietor of the French restaurant on the Green. Noticing their rings, he asked whether he might enquire as to whether they were married. To each other, I mean, he added. Why had he asked, they wondered, and he engaged them for a while. Forty years, he repeated. Forty years. And still to have so much to say.

Song of Songs

1996–1998

Mr Garver is circling the room more frequently now. He taps a book here, to pinpoint a spelling mistake, inclines a questioning glance there, to encourage the writer to expand their thoughts a little. He nods with approval at a pair of folded arms and a neatly completed script. At Zara's desk he stops. She's toying with a fine strand of hair that has poked free of its weave. He sees what she's trying to pull off; he hopes that she can do it. Zara has just five lines left to fill. *I am going to be seventy in the year 2000, if I live to be as old as my headmaster, and the world will be a very peaceful place. I imagine that if my Century could talk, it would say that two world wars were enough for anybody.* Zara looks back over her work and picks up her ruler to underscore the title. I do like the sound of that, she thinks, as Mr Garver calls time on the decades to come.

Chapter 30

One day, late in the century, as a dawn mist began gradually to clear, Zara knelt at the bottom of her wardrobe. She had rifled through the hamper there before, of course, and alighted upon an object of interest. But this was the occasion when the rifling, and the alighting, preceded something, something other, that is, than the bounding down of the stairs to show a particular item to her husband of forty years. For this was the first time, in all that time, that she had said to her cousin Lauren, rather rashly she thought now, that she would come to Poland.

The hamper had been Zara's grandmother's; it had once held flasks and blue-rimmed cups, fruit cake and crackers, potted spreads and jam. Once it had housed a red-checked cloth, and the cloth had been spread out in a copse, as the sunlight and the trees cast a shadow on the times. She had a sense of foreboding about the Polish trip, though counterbalanced by nervous excitement: it was the land of her grandfather, and her father, too, as a child. It was the land of the Jews in her family, the land of a history still largely unexplored, by herself at least. It had sent her to cast her mind back, and she was sifting through her things in the morning, before leaving home for the flight.

She picked out a note, inked in a signature black script, which bobbled in places before regaining its form. 'Go where your spirit takes you,' Puss had said. Like a diorama, the scene came back to her: Gus Coe, Malcolm Imlach and her father, all beers and smiles, Mops and Rey looking towards each other and nodding. Then there was the piece of foolscap card, folded carelessly in half, branded Clapton Synagogue on either side, the one otherwise entirely in Hebrew, bordered by Hellenic columns, the reverse an unembellished translation to English.

There were the pair of yellowed cuttings, which had lain wedged against the basket's side, creased and embrittled, for a long time now. An advert for Peter Scott knitwear poked above the shorter of the two, which lay folded, obscuring the other, attached by a rusty bent paper clip. There have been newspaper front pages I would never have saved, she thought, but could see at once that this was *The Guardian*. She spotted the date below the Manchester-shorn masthead and knew instinctively what lay beneath, though it took a while to intuit why it was that she'd kept it. Then she knew. She recollected her certainty that, as Lincoln's legacy had persisted, so would that of his modern-day counterpart. Had she been foolish to hope for that?

A photograph of the family was next, taken after Jennifer had arrived in the black saloon, and a few of her letters lay alongside. Zara had written weekly, she recalled wistfully, when Jennifer was first away at school, more frequently still when she had exciting news to share, such as when Christopher had topped the Middlesex under-elevens chess league or when Deborah had been chosen as inside left for the borough. The frequency had declined a little by the time Jennifer was in the sixth form, but her rate of reply had remained consistent, even when at university, at roughly one to every three of her mother's. There was the letter she had written at eleven, full of excitement in the dormitory, proud of her hospital corners, the one that clipped to it a cutting from the front page of the *Western Morning News*, picturing her railing at Enoch Powell, and there was the third of those she had kept, written from the occupation of the vice-chancellor's office, on his very own notepaper. They had been protesting against the charging of fees for overseas students, extravagantly altruistic Zara had thought.

Zara dug into the corner of the hamper, where a low-rise stack of notebooks was neatly piled. She knew which was which, by touch, from the skimpy covers of her elementary jotters to the parcel-wrapped quarto of Skinners', her fingers slipping smoothly over history's Gestetner-packed bulge and the crisply folded pages of algebra. *Zara Keff, Form V, Français*, read the legend on the one she pulled out, illustrated on the front by a crayoned *tricolore* and a playfully enlarged cedilla. You did me proud in Lyon, she remembered.

* * *

Lauren had asked, in that late spring of 1996, in the days before Zara stooped to the hamper, how she was, and in reply she could but confirm that, given the circumstances, she felt surprisingly well.

'Right you are, Za,' she said. 'Why don't you come to Poland?'

It was the last thing she had expected to hear. She had written to Lauren with an update on her daughters, news of the latest posting for Christopher and Eloise, and, buried within, an understated assessment of her health, though she had not downplayed it to the extent that she had with Jennifer. With a straightforwardness still characteristic in her late middle age, her cousin had picked up the phone.

'Square it with Harry,' Lauren said. 'I'm coming to fetch you.'

They pulled in at Łódź Fabryczna and took a taxi to the Grand on Piotrkowska, stepping out half an hour later to take in the great street, the longest thoroughfare in the country. Maybe this was the place, Zara thought, where Zaida had gathered with too many of his comrades and had felt the lash of a Cossack sword's reverse. The street was at a crossroads in its life, distressed façades giving way to restoration, degraded roadway to pedestrianisation, cracked pavements to street furniture and faux cobblestones. They had only to walk to parallel streets, close by, to see pinch-front trams creaking in tune to the impoverished legacy of the communist years. Lauren dropped her cousin back at the hotel to give her time to rest, adding that she had some organising to do for the next day.

The following morning they met Gabriel, a professor from the University of Łódź, whom Lucasz had put their way, in one of the hotel's ornate side rooms.

'What you must understand about Łódź is that its dynamism was shattered by the Nazis and was barely understood by the communists. It's only now that it's demonstrating signs of new life. But make no mistake, Łódź was a magnificent industrial city, and the heritage of that period – though not of most of its creators – is still visible. I'm going to show you something of that.'

Gabriel had booked a driver and directed him to the huge complex that had been Izrael Poznański's textile factory. Here they saw, decayed, a grand palace of industry, which dwarfed those such as Robert Owen's New Lanark that Zara had read about back home. Multi-storeyed, with windows eight panels high, set between towers of brickwork topped by cornices, its triumphal entrance arched above them alongside strings of balusters.

'They have plans for this place,' Gabriel told them, 'to make it a huge centre of culture, the arts, leisure, shopping even, if the Poles will come this far out. They've seen Dean Clough in Halifax and Titus Salt's Saltaire – perhaps you know of them. It's long overdue. But Poznański himself – he hasn't had a great press. He was enlightened in many ways – founded a hospital, for instance – but he kept wages low, and he wasn't exactly a byword for workplace safety. But when you look at this complex, his achievements were undeniable, and there is factory upon factory in what was once the old town that testify to the impact of the Jewish industrialists – and to the fortunes of the city itself.'

Zara was pulled in different directions. Here she was, in Zaida's old city. His father's shop must not have been far away. But this barren landscape painted nothing of the picture for her.

'We're at the edge of the ghetto here,' Gabriel continued. 'Everything to the north-east: that's where your grandfather's relatives were herded together, to work without reward, to die as meaningless statistics or to be taken by train to camps serving no other purpose than the same. The Jewish problem resolved by instalment, as one writer had it. Let's move on.'

Thoughts recurred to her. Why had the Germans done this? What was it about the Jews that meant that, even now, in late twentieth century Britain, a thug could push her daughter to the ground because of it? Zaida had said she was a little bit Łódź; so, she reasoned, she was herself part of something which had caused hatred so intense that, wherever you'd lived in the city, you were piled upon each other in this one quarter, expendable, or ripe for planned excision.

They drove to the eastern edge.

'The Jewish cemetery: one hundred and fifty thousand graves. It's been here for a hundred years and extends over forty hectares. Don't get me wrong; they're not all victims – we'll discover those who were later.'

They walked through the entrance, which mocked the great factory in miniature, and took in the city of graves and *matzevahs:* tree-lined thoroughfares and overgrown side streets; tall, proud stones alongside the broad and muscular, others flat or flattened, each adorned with ancient Hebrew; graves here and there tended with pebbles or flowers; the whole a representation of the great community of the diaspora which had found its place in the Manchester of Poland. They walked for half an hour or more absorbing the history of that vanished population, passing the grey-white mausoleum of Poznański, which spoke less well of him than his factory. And then they stepped out to an expanse of more ordinary graves, of which few were marked by a stone.

'These are the graves of the ghetto. There are plans to clean this part up, to create a more fitting memorial.'

They wandered through the vast field, and Zara asked Gabriel the question that forever came to her. In her mind, now, this was about 'us', but she put the questions she had formed at fourteen: why them? what had they done?

'Zara; that factory we saw was once filled with a Jewish workforce. As were scores like it. A quarter of a million Jews lived in the city before the Nazis got hold of it. Good and bad, up and down. Ordinary folk. Not despised, in the main, by their Polish compatriots. Our philology department has for years been recording the memories of older citizens. Regarding the Jews, yes, there is hostility from some, but not from those who knew them best, not from those whom they lived among. I remember one example. An old gentleman remarked, "With Jews we lived very well. We did not beat our carpets on a Saturday, and they did not beat theirs on a Sunday".'

He gestured at the rows of graves. 'What I'm trying to say to you, Zara, is that these people buried here did not in some way ask for what they got. When you come here you're reminded that they occupied all the layers of an expanding city until everything they knew was struck down by philistines hiding beneath a veneer of civilisation.'

'But why? Why, if they hadn't done anything?'

'It's complex, Zara. It goes back to the Middle Ages – or deeper still into the past. Their customs kept them apart, but their bankers could charge interest – which Christianity forbade – so particular Jews became established, initially, at the courts of kings and princes, and then in capitalist society. Jews became scapegoats at times of economic crisis, reinforced by the myth that they had condemned Christ to death. Later, you have Social Darwinism – the idea of the struggle, that one race is bound to survive while the remainder go to the wall – and anti-semitism becomes racial as well as religious; that starts to infect Western society. Add to that the concept of the *Volk,* which played so strongly with the German people, and you have a set of ideas the casual or ruthless can exploit. Throw Hitler, with all his destructive motivations, into the mix, along with the *Führerprinzip* – the notion of the leader of the struggle, and you have Nazism.

'Forgive me; entire volumes drawn from years of research have attempted to offer explanations. As Hannah Arendt said, "Human history has known no more difficult story to tell". I've done the best I can. But hold on to one important fact. Most Germans did not vote for Hitler. He exploited the cracks with cunning, but, while they still had a free choice, the majority didn't vote for him.

'Come now, it's time to drive a little further.'

They came to Radegast station, a broken-down, disused halt on the northernmost edge of the city. The rotten remains of goods trucks hung on to their chassis without resolve. They stood in a vast, cracked, overgrown yard.

'Lucasz has told me something of your family, Zara. This is likely the place to which your great grandfather would have been forced to walk. It's the *Umschlagplatz,* the loading place.' He pointed to the platform. 'Cattle trucks took them from here. The rest you know.'

Zara was back with Zaida after he'd met Harry for the first time. He hadn't heard from his father beyond a certain point. Had he lined up here, where she stood now, on his final day in the city? It was sufficient for her to forget her own struggles for a while.

Gabriel turned to her. 'Imagine this place packed with hundreds and hundreds of the Jews of Łódź, men, women and children, factory owners and their workers alike. Nothing can justify that. Nothing did. It was not their fault, Zara. Their mistake, if they made one, was not to have got away before the war – if they could have done. Even that didn't always work. I read of families who left for the free city of Gdańsk, guaranteed by the League of Nations. That didn't save them.'

'But in the ghetto? Could they not have escaped from there?'

Gabriel did not reply at first, turning away as if to

think, taking in the wasteland around them. Then all he said was, 'We have one more stop to make.'

They drove back in the direction of the factory and reached the Museum of Łódź, hosted by the grand former mansion of the Poznański family. Gabriel took them inside to an exhibition devoted to Jan Karski.

'This man tried almost single-handedly to warn the west about the Holocaust. He was born here in Łódź and was part of the Polish Underground State during the war. Twice he went to the Warsaw ghetto and obtained evidence about the activities of the occupiers. He met directly with Eden, he travelled to see Roosevelt, but their response... it wasn't strong. He's alive and well, thankfully, in the USA. Lech Wałęsa presented him with the Order of the White Eagle, Poland's highest honour.

'My point is: it was exceedingly difficult to do anything, even for somebody with his bravery, his access. No wonder the individual Jews couldn't. Escape was virtually beyond them. And if they did, well, come this way.'

He led them to a small library and picked out a book whose cover carried the stark image of a prison cell.

'The diary of Gusta Dränger, from the dark of the resistance. She escaped the Nazis and fought on before they recaptured and executed her. She wrote in captivity on toilet paper and managed to smuggle most of it out. I think it's published in English now too. Listen to what she wrote:

"It is very easy to say, 'Just run away before they

deport you!' But how do you manage to sneak out of a ring of barbed wire closely guarded by police? How do you take your first step into the outside world? They will see the armband on your sleeve, and you can be certain that a bullet to your head will follow. Should you remove the armband? As soon as someone notices that white symbol sliding down your sleeve, he will betray you and deliver you into the hands of the police. Perhaps you should try to slip into the blackness of the darkest doorway... to remove the ornament adorning your arm. No matter how dark that doorway, there will always be someone who notices that you stepped into it a Jew and stepped out as if you were a human being. Why 'as if you were a human being'? Because to take off the armband successfully, you first have to regain your sense of human dignity. Without that, you are nothing more than a Jew without an armband. You would reveal your Jewishness in a thousand small ways: every anxiety-filled move; every step taken with a back hunched over from the yoke of slavery; every glance that bespoke the terror of a hunted animal; the entire form, the face on which the ghetto had left its indelible mark." [1]

'And that's from somebody who did manage one escape. To say it was just about possible is to acknowledge that it was practically impossible. There was no real escape, merely the remote possibility that you might somehow survive it all.'

Zara thought of Belsen and the survivors who were

---

1   Reprinted from Justyna's Narrative. Copyright © 1996 by The University of Massachusetts Press. Published by the University of Massachusetts Press.

found there; they had not escaped; they had lasted; that was all. And she thought of what Zaida had once said, that you couldn't cast off your shadow.

'There are few episodes in history which are simple matters of right and wrong, Zara. This is one of them. It was menace personified, evil without precedent, and that's why people make the mistake of wanting to push it away. It can't be. Even Jan Karski, who taught Bill Clinton at Georgetown University, kept quiet about his role for decades afterwards.'

They were driven back to the Grand and thanked Gabriel with a beer in the bar.

'Say hello to Lucasz – and ask him when he plans to come down himself. So what's next?'

'Tomorrow,' said Lauren, 'we're heading off to find some living Polish history. But first, to get ready to eat. I've warned Zara to prepare for an experience.'

* * *

The restaurant, two blocks from the hotel, occupied the ground floor of a building the shed-skinned upper floors of which moulted history as the city passed by.

They looked at the menu in the window, and Lauren said, 'I've been to a *kosher* place, and you haven't, Za. We're going to rectify that.'

'No! No, Lori. I don't want to.'

'Zara Landsman.' She didn't often say that. 'I'm your host, I've booked, and you don't want me to have to cancel. We must eat.'

She took her by the arm and coaxed her in. Zara stopped, and gasped, as ancient portraits met her eyes: she'd stepped into another time, another place.

'Ah. Mrs Nowakowska isn't it?' the maître d' said, in an everyday sort of way, which flattened the edge of her brusqueness. 'You dropped by yesterday.'

She led them to one of the two remaining tables, small and circular like the others, and lit the candle. Zara was well-practised in handling new environments, armed with a stock of small talk to suit most occasions, but here she dispensed with the formalities and picked up the menu, holding it rigidly, relieved to find recognisable options. Lauren said they should have the borscht to start with; she chose goose liver for the main and Zara plumped for the Wiener schnitzel; they took a carafe of red. They spoke a little of the day's encounters and their plans for the next. Zara began to relax and, by the time it came to saying how much she had enjoyed the veal, she was back to the usual restaurant version of herself. She caught sight of the bearded old Jews on the walls, and, once the wine had worked its spell, took them in with more deliberation. This was Zaida's town, and here he was, or those like him, everywhere you looked: this one studious or businesslike, quill in hand, that one be-shawled and concerned, crossed hands on staff, eyes gentle in revelation. She could have stood and stroked his beard.

The next morning, they travelled by train to Wrocław. Lauren had booked them in for two nights: she wanted Zara to soak up a city where history was conspicuous, much though the archaeology of Łódź had testified to a truth of its own. She had wondered about Kraków, but the ubiquity of adverts for excursion to Auschwitz might have prompted a prospect too far; Wrocław offered much that Kraków did on a smaller scale.

They arrived at the faded magnificence of Wrocław Główny, a veritable castle of a station, and having checked into mid-range accommodation, orientated themselves in the afternoon before enjoying a meal of wild boar goulash with beetroot in a dimly lit restaurant. They eschewed the hotel breakfast and wandered, before settling on a quirky café, which held an extensive stock of vinyl records, a serviceable turntable and a predilection for jazz and swing. They chose their seats from a collection of cushioned oddities and spent an hour or more over coffee and toasted sandwiches. They took a tram to Cathedral Island and walked across the iron bridge with its thousands of memories padlocked to the girders; they admired ecclesiastical architecture that impressed at every turn and came back via the city's university. Here, they roamed the corridors and stairwells, with their black-and-white tiled floors and oil paintings of past rectors, prior to entering a vast lecture hall with gold-plated furnishings and the most intricate baroque ceiling. For dinner, they decided on borscht and pierogi at a place on the main square, overlooked by magnificent five-storey edifices, each manifest in its own tone, all in sight of the centuries-old town hall with its Renaissance and early Gothic heritage. Zara had not anticipated that Poland could offer so much. They finished off with apple crumble and a glass of mead.

Lauren explained something of the city's history, of a re-established Jewish community vanquished again by the policies of post-war government. Zara looked up from the honied glass and blew smoke into the evening bustle. The remarkable thing about Poland, she thought, is that she was here because it was part of her past; Lauren's purpose had been clear from the start; she had come round to that. What she found compelling, though, was that she had spotted no one redolent of that past. She looked at the sea of Slavic faces before her, and the occasional Teutonic one, and thought: there's nobody living here who could be any sort of distant relative. There are no old men with long beards, save the museum pieces on the restaurant walls, no hunched shoulders, no characteristic hand gestures.

Here, on Wrocław's Rynek, Zara Landsman unravelled a few strands of herself. She was the grandchild of one who had left in time, with time to spare; the presumed fate of his father testified to the wisdom of that decision. The man who walked from this country, upon whose knee she had sat, who had welcomed the man she loved and paid the deposit on their first home, had said he was from Łódź, that nothing could change that, that she was 'a little bit Łódź' herself. Here in this country of which she was palpably no part, in this beautiful country rising again to an independence denied it for so long, Zara asked herself why she kept on burying her head.

Lauren gave her a penny for them.

'Thank you so much for bringing me here, Lori, to this country, to Łódź, to this wonderful city.'

'Gabriel was superb, wasn't he?'

'He was. And it's more than that. I've come to appreciate something. I'm not wholly English, not by descent. I know that. But the part of me that's not English, it isn't anything else either. It's a missing segment I must complete myself. Zaida said there's a part of me that will always be a little bit Łódź. But the Łódź I'm a part of – it no longer exists. That's the gap I must fill – it's the gap my children have to fill. Deborah fills it with her plucky obstinacy – and a pair of Dr Martens. Christopher, bless him, transfers it to the good of the world. Jennifer? I'm not so sure.'

'Do you remember the conversation we had at my wedding?'

Zara nodded. 'And I remember Harry and I at the park afterwards. We wanted our children not to have to put up with any of the nonsense.'

'That's what you've done – you and Harry. Jennifer, Deborah, Christopher: they're the great grandchildren of Łódź, the grandchildren of Stoke Newington and our beautiful wartime village, and they're the sum of everything you two have made – of the home that you brought them up in. They're all fit to fight the nonsense, Za, and, more than that, they're doing it.'

The cousins looked at each other, as they tossed the exchange between them like a ragged tennis ball.

'You've discovered how to stop thunder, Za.'

'Feels like we've known each other for a century, Lori, doesn't it?

'At least, Za, at least. You're ready to go home.'

The next morning they caught the train to Warsaw. After stumbling off the airport bus, Zara asked Lauren to hold her cigarettes while she fumbled in her bag to find the change for two bad coffees in plastic cups. They drank them in silence before Zara gathered up her things and they hugged. She walked toward passport control, turning to wave goodbye.

'For always, Lori.'

'Always.' Then, 'Oh wait. Your Kensitas.'

'I'm leaving those behind,' said Zara. 'Be sure to write.'

'You too, Za! You too.'

Chapter 31

Harry Landsman walked, head down, along the alley by the railway line, the line they lived by now, the one into Alexandra Palace and on to Kings Cross or Moorgate. It lacked the familiarity, for him, of the one through Stamford Hill and Bethnal Green, whose very route maps, encased above the slashed cushions of the old slam-door trains, had been linear representations of the journey his life had taken in London. He turned down Station Road, to take the short walk to Green Lanes, handsome in his early seventies, with rather more weight, a headful of grey hair brushed back to expose a well-tanned forehead. He wore a substantial though well-groomed moustache carrying flecks of ginger, and thick-rimmed glasses in a frame of restrained crocodile. The striking looks of his youth had marked him out as different, exotic, essentially Jewish; now they sculpted a kind of north London everyman. Greeks and Cypriots in the bustle of Palmers Green, Italians in the restaurants he loved to patronise, and even a Pakistani man, taking a breather on a bench, nodded at him, or smiled, taking him for one of their own. He'd had the morning with Zara over percolated coffee and the *Guardian* crossword, before she'd left for the world of school reports and bells. He was on his way to renew the well-tailored prescription for hypertension he had received from an old Jewish doctor, with whom he waxed about the old East End in consultations that paid due heed to back pain and blood pressure but lasted for much longer than their allotted time.

'How are things with the family, Mr Landsman,' Dr Stern had asked, and he was keen to tell him about Christopher's relocation to East Finchley, having been offered a post at the headquarters of his charity, of the birth of their first grandchild, Louis, and of the joy with which Zara greeted every opportunity to babysit. Deborah was happy too, he said, inviting them over to Enfield for Saturday lunch at regular intervals, rarely with the same boyfriend in tow. Jennifer was doing well at work, as was to be expected, and came to visit more often than she used, living as she did that much closer to London, though, despite the spare room being available, she tended to take the last train back to Leicester. Why was that, the doctor wondered, and Harry spoke of her mother's cough, of its amplification at night, of the time he had heard his daughter crying through the modern home's thin stud walls. 'Is this why you've come, Harry?' he asked, placing a soft hand on his knee.

Jennifer took a call from her mother one evening, the call that would never leave her.

'I've been in hospital for a couple of days, dear. They say I've a collapsed lung.' Zara paused to gain strength. 'They've discovered a blockage.'

'A blockage? What kind of a blockage, Mum?'

'It's in the airways, dear. They think… They hope to treat it, with radiation.'

'Radiation?' She felt her pulse racing.

'Yes, dear.'

'You mean it's…' She could hear it emerging as an accusation but managed at least to take an edge off the first syllable. 'You mean it's cancer.'

'Yes, dear; it is.'

'Oh, Mum.'

'I know, dear; I've been so very stupid.'

'No, Mum. I didn't mean… Did they say anything else?'

'The other lung may hold up, they said. We have two of them, after all. It'll give me time to do a few things with Dad.'

'I love you, Mum. I'll see you on Saturday.'

'I love you too, dear.'

Slowly, at each end of the line, the phone went down, and they stood common in self-reproach. Why didn't I stop when she tried to persuade me? Why did I chide her, and fail to do more to encourage her?

Zara brought Jennifer to the Quaker Gardens, which she and Harry had discovered shortly after they moved. The walk past the Green and on to Church Hill, even allowing for the boutique shops and restaurants, reminded her of the days she had spent in a village, which this must once have been, when in the worst of times everything had been possible. They sat on a semicircular bench looked over by a dozen rows of simple round-topped stones that commemorated Quakers gone by.

'Mum, I know you said you'd been stupid, but we all do things we go on to regret.' She had located the tone, but the insufficiency of the words rebounded to scold her. She had assigned them the role of softening despair, but they fell short.

'Cigarettes had been my crutch, dear. And I persuaded myself they would equalise things between your father and me. We assumed he would go first – and I didn't want to live long without him. Do you know the silly thing? When I flew back from Poland, I left my last packet at the airport. I haven't had one since.'

'Oh, Mum.'

'I realised a thing or two in Poland – I realised too late.' She looked at the headstones. 'Jennifer, we must never be ashamed of the piece of us which comes from that country. It's the part of us that makes us search for something. My grandfather said that my children would still be a tiny bit Łódź. I think I know what he meant now.'

'I'm not sure we ever find the things we search for, Mum.' Jennifer stared ahead, willing her to pick up the thread.

'Perhaps it's the search that matters, Jen. Do you know what? If I were to have a religion, this would be it. I love the silence, the reflection, the way people speak when they find it comes to them. If there were a God, that's surely what he would want.'

'Or she, Mum.'

'Or she, dear.'

Zara pulled a small package from inside her coat.

'I made this for you, dear. It's just a little thing.'

Jennifer opened the paper bag to reveal a white cloth base resting inside a circular wooden frame, half a dozen inches in diameter, with a bordered 'J' at the top. A myriad of colourful mini-patterns was crocheted onto it: a neo-Gothic frontage; the red bricks of a university; degree scroll and mortar board; a placard urging unity; a book and a globe; a blackboard bearing the legend '1066 and all that'; a white rose; a beer tankard; a wine bottle and a restaurant menu; a telephone, scripted letter and the British Rail logo. There were a dozen more, too, ending with the flourish, *docendo discimus,* and the year, 1996.

'There's a tiny hook you can hang it with, dear. One for the loo, maybe.'

'I was thinking the kitchen, Mum.'

'I do believe in immortality, Jennifer. I believe we survive in those we have loved and those we've influenced. You'll live on in hundreds of your pupils – and their children.'

'You'll survive in them too, Mum.'

Zara leant across to her daughter and, encouraged by her arm, rested her head on her shoulder, aching with the fortitude of the silence.

* * *

On Sunday afternoon, Zara walked Jennifer to the edge of the Green. They kissed goodbye, and she watched her take the forty or so paces down to Winchmore Hill station. At the entrance, she turned, and they each began to raise a hand, tentative at first. Their eyes met, if two pairs of eyes can meet at that distance, and they stayed rooted for several seconds before, seeing the other begin to reciprocate, both waved, with abandon, like characters in the final scene of a film, holding their position as the camera panned back.

They caught the train to Finsbury Park every weekday for six weeks, Harry and Zara, and picked up the Victoria line, walking on from Warren Street to the Middlesex Hospital, arm-in-arm, or changing for Goodge Street if it felt a bit far. They met with the oncologist: they could avoid chemotherapy, he said, and still hope for a couple more Christmases.

Jennifer often brought work along when she came for the weekend. Zara spotted the school's handbook on the dining table and, turning to the roll of staff, saw Jennifer Landsman listed as deputy headteacher. Her eyes lit up, and she replaced it, open, on the table. She pointed to the second line and said with unselfconscious admiration, 'That's chuffing, dear.'

They might dine in, over chicken piri-piri, which Zara had discovered, boasting of the 'three chillies' it attracted from the manufacturer, and settle in front of the television together. Or they might go to one of the restaurants nearby. When Jennifer joined her parents at the French place on the Green, Zara said to the proprietor, simply, 'Our daughter.'

Chapter 32

John Mulley and his secretarial staff held a drinks party for Zara, and long-standing teachers dropped in. She had known them for twenty-odd years; one had climbed the ladder from probationer to deputy head within that time. She had gone back to work after the weeks of radiation and was retiring ten months on from her diagnosis.

'Zara. Your last day. Who can believe that? How's Jennifer getting on?'

'Oh, very well, thank you, Huw. She's a deputy herself now, you know.'

'She'll beat me to headship. We'll end up on the same shortlists.'

'She insists that's not for her, more's the pity.'

'We'll see. Thanks for everything, Zara – even if you did manage to keep me from the boss most of the time.'

'That's what I'm paid for, Huw. Or was, anyway.'

Zara turned from the school gate to see a crescent of well-wishers waving in unison from the door. It took her a few moments, but she broke into a half-smile, while a barely perceptible shake of the head disputed the fact that they stood there for her. A moment more and the disbelief gave way, and the joy spread to her cheeks. She waved her own farewell and walked home from work for the final time. She passed a boy playing football in the road and advised him to be careful. She laughed at the reply: my first 'old bag', she thought, on my last day at the office. A letter from the chairman of governors had dropped onto the mat wishing her a long and happy retirement.

The family took her to Abetone, on Green Lanes, the kind of suburban Italian place which offered an expertly crumbed *Scaloppine Milanese* and its own unique take on tiramisu. The owner embraced Harry and Zara, for they were regular diners, and pressed them all to have an aperitif on the house. But this was their mother's night, and, keen to have the family's attention before her daughters had demolished most of the wine, she spoke between the starter and the main course.

'Today I left the second of the County schools in my life. I had to leave my first after the war, and it was the hardest thing I ever did. I'd have gone much further in my education there, but I would never have met your father; so enough of that. I believe that whatever one has done in one's life, the fruits of that survive into the future through one's children. And I am proud of you all.'

She was content with her few words and raised her glass. 'My children.'

'Do you think you'll miss it, Mum?' Christopher asked.

'I shall miss feeling the breeze.'

Conversation turned to football. Deborah was the one hardcore fan in the family, but like many in this part of North London they all took an interest in the Spurs.

Zara recalled, 'You know I used to go along when I was a teenager?'

'No, Mum,' said Deborah, 'you never told us that.'

'Oh, it was such a talented team. They were promoted and won the league the next year.'

'The days before consistent mediocrity, eh, Mum?'

'Push and run,' added Harry, his 'run' still manifestly from the north. 'Push and run. It was Arthur Rowe's style.'

'Have you been since, Mum?'

'No, dear. But I made sure you supported them.'

'How? Mum! Tell me!'

'You came in from Raglan one day and said, "Mummy, should I support Leeds or Chelsea?". They were playing in the cup final, and the boys had all been chanting for one side or the other in the playground. So, I said, "Darling, I think you ought to support your local team. You should support the Spurs". And I'm pleased to say that for once you took my advice.'

'Wow, Mum, I hadn't remembered that. And you haven't been to a game since you were a girl?'

'I was probably twenty when I last saw them.'

'Mum, you've got to come to a match. Next season: I'm going to take you.'

'Let's see, dear.'

* * *

Winter approached, and, as the leaves fell, Zara too lost something of her colour. Yet she stuck with her enthusiasms, frequenting the library and settling down to view films with Harry and Jennifer at weekends. The three of them were half-watching a repeat of *Morse* one evening when Zara mentioned a rediscovered interest in Amelita Galli-Curci, a recording of whom she had heard on the radio, explaining to Jennifer that she was an opera singer from before the war.

'A magnificent soprano,' said Harry.

Jennifer made a mental note to track down her work.

On Christmas morning, they exchanged presents; Harry and Jennifer had each given her the same record.

'Oh, how funny,' said Zara. 'You didn't know I'd asked for it from Dad.'

Jennifer unwrapped her Christmas jumper, a lilac turtle-neck from Marks and Spencer. The rest of the party arrived, and they enjoyed a boozy beginning, as always. Then Jennifer saw the table had not been laid and found her mother and father in the kitchen, holding each other; she could see at once how hard this was for them.

'Shall I put everything out?'

'Yes please, dear.'

More than half a century on, Zara drew on the spirit of her village Christmas.

The new year came; her treatment was palliative now, but the good days she enjoyed outnumbered the bad, and the days stretched to months. When Jennifer came next to visit, Zara saw that her hair was cut, and unblown, and that the waves had been scrunched into curls.

Jennifer had presented an assembly on the Holocaust the previous week, she said, on the anniversary of the liberation of Auschwitz, a day that the powers that be were thinking of designating as an annual memorial.

'As they do in Germany, Mum. I told the students I was partly Jewish, that this country had given our family its chance, that we simply must stand up to prejudice – you know the sort of thing.'

'That's lovely, dear.'

'Oh, and that my parents had instilled in me the importance of education.'

Jennifer noticed an old scholars newsletter lying on the dining table.

'Oh wow!' She read from it. '"We send our very best wishes to Mrs Z Landsman, the head's secretary, who is retiring after guiding Mr Mulley for so many years with her wealth of knowledge and wisdom". Finally celebrated in print, Mum. I should hope so.'

Deborah made good on the promise to take her mother to White Hart Lane. She had bagged a couple of passes from the *Gazette*, and they sat at the front of the west stand, behind the club's gesticulating manager. They cheered as a Norwegian and a Frenchman scored for the home team, one late-spring afternoon, and Zara found sufficient courage to chant, 'Come on you Spurs,' in rough unison with the crowd. She wondered how many of those sitting close by lived in the streets she had grown up in, and asked at a certain point what the Tottenham fans were singing.

'Mum, it's slightly embarrassing. They're chanting, "yiddos". They're taking pride in being a little bit Jewish. Getting in before the opposition does.'

'Oh, how priceless.' She could hear the words of Zaida echoing across the decades.

They sat side by side on the train and, for the second time in her life, the supporters with the blue-and-white scarves serenaded Zara part-way home.

Once a week she went over to East Finchley to babysit, where little Louis, encouraged by his mother, called her grand-mère. She and Harry dined out more than ever, and he kept every receipt in his wallet. If they were less chatty on occasion, the usual animation returned before long.

She was taken into hospital for a few days; her skin had become sallow. Jennifer brought a pocket television for the side of her bed, and, as it was Sunday, Harry suggested lunch at a pub. Jennifer had passed through the corner entrance of the Marlborough Head when, turning to hold the inner door open, she saw a hunched, drawn figure framed in the vestibule. It took her a second to realise that this was still her father, taking a short breather, permitting a fleeting relaxation of the resolve he strove to project whenever he could.

Zara went home. She read an article on Martin Luther King and sent it to Jennifer. *For assembly maybe?* she wrote.

She devoured half a dozen library books every week.

And now she glimpsed the book in the basket at the bottom of the wardrobe and thought she had not been so foolish after all.

Chapter 33

By the time Harry came back upstairs, Zara had swung her legs to the side of the bed with moderate ease, though not without aggravation to the pain that days earlier had spread to her back. The hamper was open, and their wedding photograph, top hat and all, was resting on one of the corners. Her husband's confidant, Dr Stern, had arranged a hospital bed; the paramedics, upon attending her bedroom, had recommended a stretcher. But she would not be carried from her home.

She said, between breaths, 'Harry, ask them to go outside. Then walk in front of me, please, love.'

She clutched the top of a chair, steadied herself with the chest of drawers and grasped the door-handle. By placing her right hand against the door-frame she assured herself of balance and, moving her left to the radiator on the landing, was able to lean for the ledge at the top of the stairway. She transferred her weight and gained position at the top of the stairs. She saw Lauren, in her Cambridge and County uniform, floating before her and reached for the banister. She took the first painstaking step, with Harry two or three stairs ahead, watchful, grim with admiration, hand half-extended should it be needed.

With each step of her frail legs, a segment of life dissolved away. St Mary's went first and with it the boy who had called her names; next, the journey to the village, labelled like Paddington; Duck End, and a kind old farmer looking out for her; then, skipping willingly to school; now, the wheelbarrow with which she had masterminded the paper-salvage operation. They were gone; they had had their final remembering. She gripped the rail again and regained her breath.

'Are you all right, Zuzzi?'

Next, the bus to the County; the village Christmas; Belsen; driven home, too soon, to London. Halfway: the ancient masthead in her hand; her first cigarette; Pitman; Eddie Baily; recollections in morass, banished in one.

'Only a few to go, love.'

She swung high and low on her final descent: West Bank and Łódź; Woodford, Wrocław; Stoke Newington and Goldsmiths, modelling jewellery; the Bohemian; Clapton Synagogue; the Café de la Paix.

At the foot of the stairs, the front door open, she could see the ambulance. Unaccountably, Gabriel flashed before her. And then she thought: the loading place, and brushed the image away. On the drive opposite, two youngsters were thrashing a ball against the wall. It bounced towards her, and she ached to pick it up. One of the girls retrieved it, sending it high to her friend, and Zara gazed at the sky on this cold October day, late in the century, searching the clouds for a storytelling of rooks. Autumn blew its leaves at her, and one last time she walked from home.

Harry telephoned. She's doing as well as can be expected; he would keep them informed. Eloise answered for Christopher; he was abroad for work and was due back the next day. Jennifer said to announce himself as Harry if he had to phone her at school.

She was with a fifth-former when the call came; she asked her to step outside.

'Mum's d...' The line went silent. She had heard the initial consonant, no more.

The phone rang again. The receptionist said, 'It's Harry; you must have been cut off.'

'Jennifer, dear, Mum's deteriorating.'

'I'll be there, Dad.'

She apologised to her pupil and told the head's secretary she had to go; it was the first they had known that anything was wrong.

Leicester station was half an hour's walk from her school. She counted on making the next train, just, if she hurried, rather than chancing to call a cab. She dashed through the catchment area, a startling vision in skirt suit and heels, her dark mop tilting like an athlete's, struggling for form, surprising parents of her students to whom she made no gesture to explain. She headed for the platform, reckoning to pay on the train, taking a seat at the front end of the first carriage, thence to spring out to the Underground. She rested her head on the back of the seat; silent drops slid down; there were no outward sobs, simply the quiet, heartbreaking realisation that she may, if she were lucky, be about to witness the last moments of her mother's life. A ticket collector approached, stopped short of her, and turned away.

She was out of the Tube station, along Goodge Street, on to Mortimer, beneath the neo-Doric pediment of the Middlesex. Deborah, in the reception area, was pacing up and down with a roll-up.

'Some days you just have to, Jen.' She pointed to the sign for the ward.

A palliative nurse was stroking her father's arm. Harry stood to intercept her. 'Prepare yourself, love.'

Her mother lay with tubes taped to her arms and an oxygen mask to her face, but her eyes were fierce with life and, fortified by infusion, her complexion glowed with a rosiness unseen for months.

'Oh, Mummy.' She reached out to touch her, squatting on the floor as she did so, one hand on her own knee, while the other stroked her mother's arm.

Christopher came at the last, paged upon landing, bearing an impossibly large rucksack. Deborah followed him up, bashing the straps on his back.

They were to spend the next week enmeshed with each other. Christopher drove across daily. Deborah joined Jennifer to stay with their father; her cooking was so finely judged and so tastefully seasoned that the hunger which accompanied their loss could be assuaged with a kind of pleasure. John Mulley called to pay his respects; Zara, his wife had said, always struck her as the archetypal English gentlewoman. When the whisky ran dry, Jennifer discovered that the local Oddbins was holding a tasting session for its twenty-three-year-old

Speyside. Its audacious bourbon touch appealed, and she brought it home for her father to try. She was investing in a second bottle three days later, and they would share many more in the months to come.

The Landsman children were to spend the years building family – or else satisfied independence; they were to find their challenges, their triumphs, their downtimes and their happiness, whether through children, fresh relationships or the burgeoning corridors that nurtured the next generation. Jennifer was to pay regular visits to Harrogate where Hilary remained a source of inspiration and her friend a purveyor of the most practical advice; she journeyed to Winchmore Hill station now and again where she would turn, with admiration, to see her mother waving.

Harry was to relocate as soon as he could, to a flat in a small block in Southgate where, following grief's dolorous cycle, he settled into comfortable widowerhood. He noted with wry amusement the mezuzahs fixed by the neighbouring doors on his landing, and marvelled at the access afforded by the Piccadilly Line for the theatre, the Curzon Cinema, Shepherd Market and Green Park. He was to change for Liverpool Street, on odd days, and wander the back streets of Shoreditch, eyes peeled for some Les Gold or other, though few worked on cotton thread now. For two decades Harry was to bring his family together, for quarterly brunches in the West End, calling his children to agree the dates, travelling to book the tables in person and recognised by front of house for his discreet requests that a cushion be supplied for his chair.

Lauren was to live long into the next century, returning after Lucasz died to live in a small town in Cambridgeshire, where she threw herself into the activities of the book club, the Women's Institute and the amateur dramatic society, looking to the heavens from time to time and saying, 'You'd be proud of me, Za.' Łódź was to be rejuvenated, Piotrkowska to become a vertiginous mall of modernity, designer shops competing with restaurants and cafés in renovated courtyards. A heritage trail was to guide tourists through Bałucki Rynek, close to Abraham Kevlov's shop; his country would shake off client status and leap to the aid of those whom the Czar's successors would reabsorb. The Manufaktura complex would bring renewed vision to Posnański's vast industrial shell. Radegast station would become a memorial to the deported, and a long, carefully lit tunnel displayed the lists that ruthlessly efficient brutality had published for each transportation, in the hope that never again may youth pore over a newspaper with photographs so impossible to contemplate as to make one ask why them, or why me. Jan Karski, commemorated as *Righteous Among the Nations*, was to live beyond the close of the century he had graced with such selfless distinction. Stoke Newington would become sought after; the Bohemian had successors by the score. And children were to cycle the loop in a still-preserved village that had proved the making of a pigtailed evacuated girl.

All of that was for the long twenty-first. The Century had eked things out as far as it could, but, shorn of its eponym, it would struggle to fulfil the hopes held out for the vast dome it had prepared for its wake. The short twentieth, its lights had been deemed extinguished when the walls tumbled down, its successor springboarded nine years early by revolution as powerful as that which had launched the long nineteenth.

Here, in a ward off Goodge Street, Zara Keff took the final breaths of her own short century, her husband and children rotating through the curtain surrounding her bed. Each searched for the right words, but they did not know, in truth, whether she could hear them. Then tears began to roll down her cheeks, and they thought, she must, she must be aware, she must be able to hear us, and they commenced their exhortations anew. Her eyes closed, and they were thrown back to uncertainty, but still she was breathing, battling now, harder and harder, to take in the oxygen. It was Jennifer's turn; she had decided what to say, and in doing so confirmed a determination in herself. 'Mummy, I'm going to be the best headmistress you can ever be.' Now she knew her mother had heard, for her switch was flipped, her grey eyes alight with green once more, eyes opened, opened as wide as eyes can ever be open, in unaffected joy, such that Jennifer wondered later whether she had conveyed mistakenly that she had already secured such a position. Zara strained to speak, a distant croak emanating from a parched throat as she lifted her head from the pillow to force the words out, and Jennifer whispered, 'I know what you're trying to say, Mummy,' and repeated it every time she tried, alternating that gentle reassurance with words of love.

Her family faded from view. She saw it, the glory of her life now: Zaida in his wooden chair, stroking his beard; Lauren at the bedroom door, helping to pack her things away; Mr Garver inviting her to unwrap the wireless; Harry on the number 73, stepping out from an oak in Springfield Park, carrying her over the threshold in Melbourne Way. She saw her children at the Italian restaurant and, in the last, a vision of a Landsman on a school hall stage welcoming new children and telling them tomorrow would be their world. She felt the swish of the curtain; but oblivion's crevice offered one last glimpse of the sun, and she reached for the light, exalted.

Jennifer parted the screen and looked towards Harry; the nurse slipped by – to lift the oxygen mask from her serenity.

The Professor IV

Camden, 1999

'I'd have thought,' the emeritus professor had said, giving her that look over his glass of fine old malt, 'that there were regulations against this sort of thing now.'

She'd lifted her eyes from the decanter. 'There probably are,' she replied, 'but I don't go looking for the rules I don't want to keep. Besides, if my dad dropped by, I'd never live it down if I couldn't offer him a Scotch.'

'He sounds like my kind of chap.'

'Oh, he is, Professor. You should meet him. He read a publication of yours recently. He doesn't often reach the end of a book.' She hesitated. 'He dug out something which surprised me: something my mother wrote when she was a girl.'

Jennifer pulled the dog-eared notebook out of her desk drawer. 'From the birth of my grandfather to her three score years and ten. She wasn't so far short. I took it into assembly last month – and set the year sevens the challenge of emulating it.'

He'd looked at Zara's double-page spread. 'You've given me an idea for my lecture,' he said, asking if he might borrow the book for a few days. 'Why don't you come along? They won't all be students; for some reason I attract an eclectic crowd.'

* * *

And now, in the lecture hall, as he reaches the peroration, she is jotting down a note or two in a hardback diary.

'I have lived myself through a number of the events of which I've spoken – by no means all of them here in this country, as you might have guessed from the crusty old accent I've had difficulty shaking off.'

Jennifer looks up quizzically at that. She'd caught the occasional inflection, it was true, a dwelling on the end of a word here or there, the light trill of a rolled 'r', but you'd have to know he'd spent his adolescence in *Mitteleuropa* even to begin to notice.

'I was that boy from Berlin. I walked home from school on the January day when nemesis took the reins: a visceral experience that has stayed with me to this day. So, you see, I've been conscious of living in history for a very long time.

'And last week I met the daughter of the little girl I spoke to you about, her mother's life moulded by events every bit as much as mine. Which of us, do you think, has bent the arc of history? I, who have sought to record and interpret, or she, who so inspired her daughter that she heads up a huge comprehensive a stone's throw from here and shapes the future of a great metropolis, which the worst that history has fashioned could not destroy? Who breathed life into the Century? I, who look down the tunnel and fix the points of departure, or she, who looked to the sky and scoped out what is to be? And who faced the greater challenge? I, to explain the catastrophe to the world, or she to make sense of it for herself?'

He steps from the rostrum and walks toward the student with the glossy folder, inclining his head that he might feign to catch her notes; he smiles and nods, and makes for the centre of the floor. And then the lightest of shakes of the head.

'Neither one of us, though, bears true witness to the Century's defining malevolence. As Primo Levi wrote, we are those who never touched rock bottom: those who did, and who saw the face of the Gorgon, did not come back. David Beigelman is one such, who bent the arc for a few precious years, who gave the Century the fight of its life and bore witness to the last. As did Anne Frank.'

He pauses, turning his back to the audience, and begins to gather his papers from the stand. Jennifer wonders whether he has chosen to end on that minor chord, but he has no need of the manuscript for his closing bars, and he turns to them again, brandishing the rolled-up text like an old-fashioned football rattle.

'You're embarking upon the study of what Isaiah Berlin called "the most terrible century in Western history". Never has a century brought more trouble to the world. Solzhenitsyn longed for it to serve as healing inoculation. Perhaps, indeed, the heights scaled by science as opposed to the depths plumbed by humanity will serve as legacy, though the mushrooming of the modes of destruction may yet have something to say.

'Let me leave you with hope and the sentiment of Leo Valiani, an historian of my long acquaintance, who died last month, that while the victory of justice and equality can be ephemeral, the message of the epoch of which I have spoken is that, if we preserve liberty, we can always start over, that we can turn the leaf at the end of the darkness, even in the most desperate of ages. Is *this* what the Century is saying, if only – *if only* – the Century could talk?'

The applause is replaced by the babble of conversation as his audience turn to leave. Some crane their necks toward him, thinking to catch his eye, while those passing close by the dais see a more distant look. Jennifer stays until the professor alone remains.

He delves for her mother's book among his bundle of texts. 'Here. I'm so pleased you came, dear.'

'You've rather made me wish I were still teaching my subject!'

'Well, how about dinner with an old historian? There's a good Italian around the corner.'

They step into the crisp October evening.

'She did, you know – your mother – she did bend the arc.'

'That was such a wonderful thing to say.'

'And here you are, two generations from Łódź, taking on the world, three months from the end of the Century she'd given her name.'

She takes him lightly by the arm.

'I'll always be a little bit Łódź, professor.'

They disappear into Bloomsbury, and the youngsters of the long twenty-first weave their way around them, starting over, headed for the best of times.

Acknowledgements

Zara's village was inspired by Girton in Cambridgeshire, though it's by no means an exact replica. I'm indebted to *Girton's War: The Village 1939–1945,* by D R de Lacey, and *Keeping in Touch: News to Girton Servicemen and Women from the Home Front 1943–1945,* by F C Barrett, edited by D R de Lacey and M Parnwell, for immersing me in the life of such a locality in wartime. Zara's friend Hilary lives on Cranmer Road in Cambridge, and her neighbour, named late in the novel, is one of the principal subjects of Philippe Sands' *East West Street.*

Zara's grandfather came from Łódź, and the city is seen at contrasting moments during the course of the Century. *Jews in Łódź, 1820–1939,* volume six of *Polin: Studies in Polish Jewry,* edited by Antony Polonsky, taught me much about the development of the city and its Jewish community. *The Missing District: People and Places of Jewish Łódź,* by Pawel Spodenkiewicz, provided insight into street life and culture. The compendium, *Łódź Ghetto: Inside a Community Under Siege,* compiled and edited by Alan Adelson and Robert Lapides, brings together a vast range of primary sources. Quoted therein, but extraordinary in its own right, is *The Diary of Dawid Sierakowiak: Five Notebooks from the Łódź Ghetto,* edited by Alan Adelson and translated by Kamil Turowski. *Ghetto Kingdom: Tales of the Łódź Ghetto,* by Isiah Spiegel added useful detail. I found *The Holocaust,* by Laurence Rees, to be an excellent recent work. London's East End, where Isaac first settled in Britain, is evoked in *I remember, I remember, Chaplin in Brick Lane,* by Michael Chapman.

My professor is inspired by Eric Hobsbawm (1917–2012). The publication, which Jennifer is proud that her father has read, may have been *The Age of Extremes,* his seminal study of the twentieth century, published in 1994. The references to Berlin, Levi, Solzhenitsyn and Valiani, which appear in the novel's final section, are to be found therein. I have drawn also from Eric's autobiography, *Interesting Times,* and from a 1994 televised interview with Michael Ignatieff. Professor Hobsbawm was indeed known for his naming of centuries, and had indeed been conscious of living in history for a very long time.

Finally, on a personal note, I owe a debt of thanks to my first reader, Nils Battye, for his constant encouragement, and to Vee Walker, author of *Major Tom's War,* whose challenge, support and belief in my work enabled me to develop it considerably.

About the Author

Jeremy Waxman came to the writing of fiction after a career in education. Initially a teacher of history, he was subsequently headteacher of schools in Yorkshire and London. Jeremy now pursues enthusiasms for literature, travel, film, jazz, cricket and Tottenham Hotspur. He was made OBE for services to education in 2006.